THE COMPLETE CASES
OF DRAGO

THE COMPLETE CASES OF

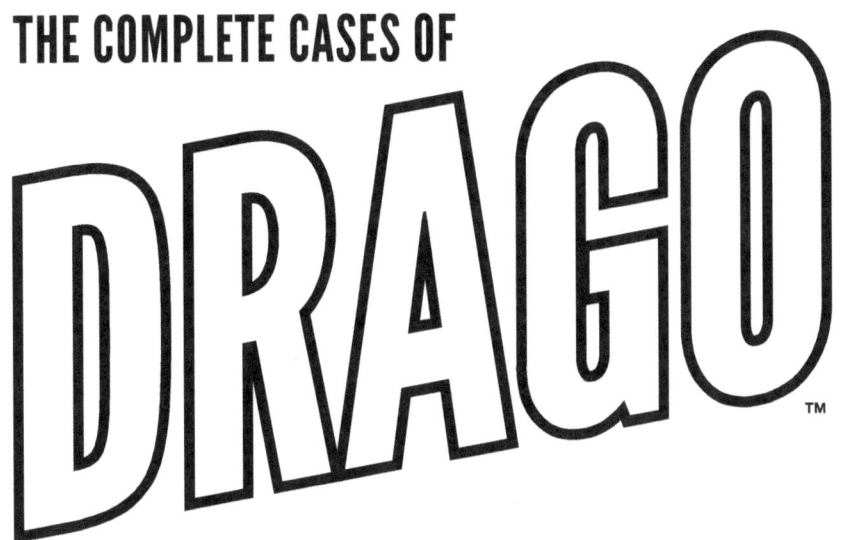

DRAGO™

JOHN LAWRENCE

ILLUSTRATIONS BY
JOHN FLEMING GOULD

POPULAR PUBLICATIONS • 2025

TABLE OF CONTENTS

MURDER BY MAGIC

"AND SO YOU WILL BE STRANGLED—AT 2 P.M. TODAY." THAT WAS THE MESSAGE STUART TEMPLE FOUND WITH HIS BREAKFAST MAIL. WHAT HIDEOUS MANIFESTATION OF THE BLACK ART MADE THE PROPHECY COME TRUE— EVEN WITHIN THE WALLS OF HEADQUARTERS WHERE SCORES OF COPPERS ROAMED THE CORRIDORS AT THE MURDER HOUR, AND THE CHIEF OF THE H.Q. SQUAD HIMSELF GUARDED THE DOOMED MAN?

CHAPTER ONE
DEATH ON THE DOT

IT WAS a strange note—and certainly a threatening one. It would have bothered anybody. It not only
bothered Stuart Temple, it threw terror into his meager
soul—almost to the point of panic—according to three of
Bryson Temple's servants.

The first of these was the butler. He had been serving
Stuart Temple's one-o'clock breakfast in the small wing of
the Fifth Avenue house—the wing Bryson Temple had set
aside for his brother.

The butler said that Stuart Temple had been breakfast-
ing alone. Bryson Temple, by one o'clock, of course, had
gone to his office; Mrs. Temple to shop. The note was the
first in the small pile beside Stuart Temple's plate. He had
opened and read it through—at the beginning, startled.
Before he was halfway through, the fright in him was a
visible thing. His courage—he had never had much—
seemed to run out his toes.

A spoiled, wan boy, Stuart Temple had spent the first
eighteen years of his life in unhappy dread of having to
coarsen his pale, thin hands with work. A doctor with
an eye to business had treated a chest cold for him; to
indulgent parents hopefully hinted at a threat of consti-
tutional weakness. The doctor passed on, but the hint
remained—a clean-cut escape from sordid toil for, as far

as Stuart Temple was concerned, the rest of his life. When the *Titanic* disaster removed the indulgent parents, who, in the end, left nothing, he found it no great trouble to ease his weight onto his brother. Bryson Temple, by that time, had been considerate enough to make his first Wall Street fortune, and was far too engrossed in his business to take time to decide if he should demur at supporting Stuart.

Twenty-odd years of this leeching, of indolent, luxurious living, complete spoiling by women—he was the pale, interesting type, who "understood"—utter lack of exercise, rich foods, good wines and no stint of them, had

He flung the briefcase into the cockpit.

sapped him, physically, to a shell. At forty-one, he was a thin, brittle, aging man, with a hectic, permanent flush and rum-tinted eyes. Bud-like lips were almost purple, and he had internal troubles. His moral stamina was like that of a child.

When he had finished the note he stumbled to his feet, his chair tipping over, his face sick yellow. He backed away from the note, stood as though transfixed, shrunken. His fumbling hand went to his necktie and the butler saw sweat shine on his forehead.

THE HOUSEMAN was cleaning old toys from the hall cupboard, when Stuart Temple burst out into the hall, white-faced and jittery. The houseman had called Bryson Temple's office for him, and stood by while the other blurted everything hoarsely to his brother. The houseman got the impression that the stockbroker was not much impressed, though he finally told Stuart Temple to go to police headquarters. At Stuart Temple's order, the houseman ordered the car.

Riding downtown, the chauffeur could see him in the mirror, in a huddled crouch in one corner, his pinched face white under the brim of his hard hat, the note on his lap, his hands grinding together.

The day helped. The latest Florida hurricane was having its New York showing—a storm so leaden that the city was darkened. Street lights—necessary for the first time in years that early in the afternoon—gleamed through the slick wet. Sheets of straight rain came down like thunder on the roof of the car.

When they reached headquarters he would not get out till the chauffeur had carefully surveyed the street and assured him that the rain had driven everyone indoors— that no one was lurking on either pavement, or on the steps of the headquarters building. When he did slide from the tonneau, he fairly scuttled up the steps, his frightened face swinging jerkily from side to side over his shoulder, till the plate-glass doors swallowed him.

He braced, momentarily, when he was shown in to the large, modern, comfortable office of the chief of the headquarters squad. Inspector McTigue's grizzled, long face, china-blue eyes, and gleaming bald head, radiated reassurance as he rose from behind the green-shaded desk lamp.

"Your brother phoned us you were coming, Mr. Temple. Poison-pen, eh?"

Stuart Temple's hand was clammy as it touched the inspector's big one. He dropped the note on the desk, sat down, taking off his hard hat, and mopped his face and neck. His attempt at a smile was a terrible grimace. "I—of course I pay little attention to the—to the thing, but—"

"Of course," McTigue boomed politely, and sat down, squinted at the envelope. It was postmarked Brooklyn, the previous night. The address was typewritten, but it was typewritten in italics.

McTigue's eyebrows went up. "Not many machines with type like that. This looks interesting." He opened the note. It was in the same italic script.

Mr. Stuart Temple,

This is to inform you, in order to give you time to arrange any necessary affairs, that your present span of living, if it may be so called, ends at or about 2 P.M. today, Friday. I warn you against ignoring the courtesy of these few hours of warning, which cannot be extended further for any reason whatever. This is not a question of personal animus against you, but we are bound by rules over which we have no control.

I warn you against confusing this with a "crank" letter—for your own good. I also warn you against seeking the protection of any police officer, or hired protector of any sort. Not that it will make the slightest difference to us, except that we do not wish to have such men, as innocent human beings, drawn into the vibration with you. Should any person of this sort attempt, even mentally, to interfere, he, or they, inevitably fall into very real danger of sharing your fate. You will be strangled.

I need hardly add that I am not referring to a gross physical attack by another human body. Inasmuch as you are, however extraneously, a member of the outer order of the Sons of Light, it may suffice to state that you die by the noose, or cable tau.

There was no signature.

McTigue laid it down. His bottled breath blew out in a gusty: "By God! And he has the nerve to call the time!"

Stuart Temple blurted: "I—it's five minutes to two already, almost. You'll—"

McTigue nodded understandingly. "I've already fixed things." He indicated the only two windows of the office, behind him. They were of clouded glass, woven with fine-mesh wire. "Those face a brick wall across the alley. A couple of the boys are keeping an eye on 'em from below. Those two doors—the one you came through, and the one in the end wall—each have a man on duty outside. You can consider it settled that your magician-strangler won't crash this office—at two, or any other time. Now tell me about this *Sons of Light* business."

Temple's voice shook. "I swear to God I haven't the faintest idea what that means. I belong to no such society! I never even heard of it!"

McTigue's bony forehead lined. "Then—this *cable-tau* stuff—this noose—"

Stuart Temple squirmed. "Are—are you a Mason, Inspector?"

"What...! No! No!"

"It—there are symbols like that in Masonry. They—they don't mean anything. *Cable tau* may be a corruption of *cabletoe*—and the noose—in initiation, it—I—but there's no sense to it—none at all—on my word!"

MCTIGUE LOOKED muddled, sour. He leaned back and there was silence. Finally he said: "I'm going to get a certain member of my staff in here. His name's Drago. You've got to kind of know him to—well, he acts funny sometimes. He calls himself my—my mascot, and he won't take on a thing he doesn't like. All the same, he's razor-keen, and he's had plenty of book-learning. Maybe he can make sense of this." He got up and started toward the door in the end wall.

Stuart Temple gulped, "No! No! Please!" and scrambled to his feet, grabbed the inspector's arm. He licked his lips, burning eyes on the clock. "We—let's—can't we just wait here till—till after—there's only five minutes now."

McTigue's eyes took on an irritated glint. "Hell, I've told you nothing can—" Then he recalled that he was facing the brother of the dynamic and powerful Bryson Temple. He said stonily, "All right," and rolled back, thumped into his chair, veiling his eyes from the yellow-faced, trembling sybarite, who, all pretense gone, was pulling at his turkey-neck, staring desperately at the clock.

It seemed an eternity, before the minute hand on the clock ticked once. Stuart Temple was bottling his breath. McTigue claimed later that the violence of the other's terror was such that it spread through the office like a dank smell.

He wanted to sneer, yet somehow, he didn't sneer. He felt color creep into his weathered face, straightened in his chair, sent angry eyes around the room. There were two armchairs, back against the wall, plus the one that held Stuart Temple. A filing-cabinet in the corner and his own desk and chair completed the furniture in the cork-floored office. There was no cupboard, no place for a cat to hide, much less a strangler. He cleared his throat.

"We might as well get on with this thing, while we're— waiting. Have you any enemies—anyone that might, by any wild chance, be responsible for this?"

Stuart Temple croaked: "What? No, no. I—I can't think of any."

McTigue drummed on the desk, tight-lipped. "You've had no requests for money—no notes before this one?"

Temple's eyes flickered between the inspector and the clock. "No. No." He hesitated. "I—I'm probably mad to mention it, but last night, around dinner time—I came home. A man in a turned-down black hat and a long black overcoat—was on the sidewalk, waiting. He came up as I got out of the car and said, 'Mr. Temple?' but when I—" He lost the thread of what he was saying, let it dwindle off, ran his handkerchief inside his collar, gulped: "Two minutes more. God, if—"

McTigue said grimly: "This bird called your name. And then what?"

Fog obscured Temple's eyes. He blinked it away. "What? Oh, yes! Yes! Nothing. When I turned to him, he said, 'Hell,' and walked away."

"What'd he look like?"

"He—well, he was tall—his coat and hat muffled him pretty well. His face—he had kind of a doughy face—dark eyes. That's all I saw. I never saw him before. He—" He shook physically, as the minute hand ticked again.

MCTIGUE'S FACE was beet-red as, in spite of all he could do, he felt his own eyes drawn furtively to the clock. Without realizing it, he came silently to his feet, one hand touching the gun through his pocket, his eyes driving around the room—for what? He wanted to kick himself—

Then it was two o'clock.

The minute hand ticked again—and the clock's mellow chime tolled softly, twice.

Stuart Temple dropped into a chair, mopping his forehead with a shaking hand. "Thank God! Thank God! I—"

McTigue was ready to explode; his forehead was crimson with disgust. He kicked his chair away, plowed for the door and—Stuart Temple screamed.

McTigue whirled back to see him, alone in the middle of the bare room, jerked to his feet, as though by a giant hand. His face, saffron-yellow a second before, went purple, flooded with congested blood. He was lifted to his toes, shaken like a puppy. He screamed again—and the scream was cut in the middle—bottled to a frantic, horrible gagging. His hands clawed at his throat and he flung himself backward. His eyes seemed to swell—larger and larger—till they appeared about to swallow his face. His feet threshed. His mouth opened and closed as he staggered, stumbled wildly around the room, falling. Jerking, choked sound shrilled from his throat again and again.

McTigue gasped, "Wait—God's sake!" jumped, grabbed him. Every vein on Stuart Temple's face was bent out like a whipcord. McTigue cursed crazily, fought to rip the man's own small fingers from his throat. Temple's face was blackening.

McTigue yelled: "Wait! You won't help—"

Stuart Temple collapsed in McTigue's hands like a sack of meal. His face went from black to muddy white, and his eyes set. He slid from McTigue's clutching grasp, spun over once like a flipped coin, then settled back and lay still.

McTigue dropped to his knees beside him, grabbed frantically for pulse. He sprang to his feet, his china-blue eyes bulging. "Mother of God!"

For a split second, he was shocked beyond sense. Then he dived to the phone, yelled hoarsely for a doctor, slammed down the receiver and ran to the door at the end of his office, ripped it open. "Drago—for God's sake—there's a dead man in here! He's just been murdered! Murdered by—by Heaven knows what—by magic!"

Drago ran in.

Before he could reach the body, a doctor from the M.E.'s office—Goetz—burst in the other door.

McTigue, toweling face and neck desperately with a handkerchief, poured out what had happened, shoveling one big palm from Goetz to Drago to the body, as Goetz ripped open the dead man's clothes.

After a bit, the doctor got up, a bleak look in his eyes. "He's good and dead. He didn't die naturally. What killed him, I dunno."

"You don't know?"

"No. Ring the autopsy-room."

CHAPTER TWO
THE ROD IN RUSH ALLEY

DRAGO GOT the case at that stage. He was not in charge of it—he was never in charge of a case. He was ineffectual at formal police work, but he had created his own unique place on the force. He was, officially, secretary to Inspector McTigue. No one was quite clear what that covered but, because the full weight of McTigue was solidly behind him, his irregular methods were tolerated.

He was a little under six feet, built like a fullback, but his darkness, smooth tailoring, and cat-footed, silent poise made him look smaller, even dumpy. He had curling black hair like shining wax, and his clear, deep-sunk brown eyes were luminous, knowing. His chin was short, square, hard, his mouth carefully molded and red-lipped. He kept himself swarthy, winter and summer—in the winter by lamp treatment. A neat, compact, polite, silent man, with more than a touch of Asiatic blandness. He looked forty, and was thirty, had an outside income and no relatives.

Since his name never went on a report—his work being credited to McTigue—only McTigue knew his quality. He had a wide mind, unerring observation, and a cold, brilliant logic—without being a theorist.

Within fifty minutes he was in the offices of Bryson Temple and Company—an immense square suite, comprising the entire eighteenth floor of a skyscraper deep in Wall Street. There the din was terrific—staccato chatter of telegraph wires, tickers by dozens, subdued quick voices murmuring like a huge wave from every direction, muted continuous phone-bells, boys running like mad through doorways with papers—a modern, prosperous commission house, in full blast.

A neat girl in blue took him around an L-shaped corridor, skirting two sides of the plant. He brought up at the end. There was a closed door on his left, an open one at his right. The open one showed a long, oblong room with floodlighted quotation board of red, green, gold and white, dazzling in its brilliance, at the far end. The room swarmed with men, noise, smoke, high-pitched sound.

The girl, after knocking, opened the high, arched, walnut door at the left and showed him into an immense, luxurious, walnut-and-blue private office, and into the presence of Bryson Temple.

He was a gray man. His eyes piercing gray, in a well bred face as sharply etched as a corpse's, his hair a peruque of powder-gray, his small, pointed moustache the same color, over thin, well shaped lips. His nose was a straight, smooth line. He was perfectly turned out—gray trousers, short black coat, black Ascot tie in a winged collar. He radiated power—controlled, fierce power—and drive. He stood behind a vast flat walnut desk, a spurting ticker at his left, a half dozen sheaves of papers on the blue blotting pad in front of him. Only his gray eyes moved to follow Drago's progress into the room. His voice was clipped, level, vicious, yet somehow as dry and soft as chalk.

"I told your homicide squad I would be over immediately after three."

"They are expecting you. I am headquarters squad. I thought you'd be anxious enough to clear your brother's death, to see me, also."

The gray eyes shone steadily. Emotion was not visible in them. "I won't refute that, of course. And I'll provide you with no excuse for failure. This hellish thing is beyond human belief—that a man can be killed in police head-quarters itself. I am going to give you twenty-four hours to produce—"

"We know exactly what you will do," Drago said. "When you said you couldn't come to identify the body till the market closed—a half hour from now—I thought the few minutes spread worth the effort of coming here. Please don't waste it with threats."

For thirty seconds, Bryson Temple's gray face was a mask. "What are your questions?"

Drago took a cylinder from his pocket, unrolled it and laid the photostat of the death note on the desk. "You are an intelligent man. You know what I want. Who could have—or might have—written that note? What is the situation—your brother's background?"

Bryson Temple studied the note. He sat down without ceasing reading, opened a drawer by his knee and brought out a folded sheet of blue notepaper, laid it to one side. Drago sat sideways on a leather chair.

BRYSON TEMPLE'S voice was acid when he had finished the note. "This note threatens danger to any police officer who interferes. That means nothing to you, of course?"

"Sarcasm is something we can dispense with, too."

Temple leaned back and made a steeple of his fingers. "Very well. I do not know who wrote this note. I do not know the names of any people who might have written it. I was not over-fond of, nor very intimate with my brother. He was a worthless soak, and he sponged on me for fifteen years. He was a rotter with women. He had something that appealed to them. Don't ask me what. It was always a mystery to me, but he seemed irresistible to a certain type. He was exceedingly cautious, and secretive about such affairs."

"If you felt that way toward him, why did you support him?"

"I was too busy to do anything else. It is more than likely that I would have cast him adrift before very long. I have had it in mind for some years. His pretense of lung trouble never impressed me much."

"Did he know this?"

"I don't make a display of my thoughts—unless I'm ready to do something about them."

"You think then that this murder can be traced to one of your brother's affairs? A husband—or something?"

"I do not. I have said nothing to indicate that I thought that. I am simply giving you the information you ask for. He had no other life—or background—save that of entertaining himself."

"Can you give me any names?"

"I told you I wasn't a confidant of his rotten affairs. My information as to the type of life he was living was relayed to me by men at my clubs—men who are above mentioning names, of course."

Drago indicated the photostat. "Do you know what kind of typewriter writes like that?"

"No."

"Do you understand the wording of the note?"

"Some of it. There is a sort of pseudo-occultism implied. In nearly all systems of symbology, the noose represents the creative principle—either physical or mental. I am not a Mason, but I believe the *cabletoe* in that system, is derived from the Egyptian *cable tau*, which is a cross surmounted by a circle, representing, usually— But that is of no interest to you. This *Sons of Light*, I do not understand."

"You are interested in symbology—occultism?"

"I was at one time."

"Do you see any possibility of a secret society being behind this thing?"

"Absurd. There is no sincerity in that note. I think it a concoction to divert suspicion from the real truth. *Sons of Light* is hardly a name for a secret society."

"There is a sect—various sects—in this country that call themselves Rosicrucians. They claim some connection with the Order of Freemasons. They claim the ancient Hebrew words, *phree messen*, mean Sons of Light, and are the root of the word Freemason. This is all adding up to the same thing—your brother's love life. You know nothing about it that would help me, eh?"

"Not about that."

"You do about something else?"

Temple's long gray hand tossed the blue letterhead over. "I also got a note this morning."

Mr. Bryson Temple:

The writer is in possession of certain private, and, I may say, ominous, information that has a vital bearing on your life—extremely vital. The information is for sale. The writer will phone your office at two thirty today, and if you wish to make a reasonable proposition, believes you will get full satisfaction. This is positively the one and only time of asking. After today, I give you my word, it will be too late.

A Friend

This, too, was typewritten, though not in italics.

DRAGO QUICKLY turned up his wrist watch. It showed a quarter to three. "He didn't call, unfortunately," Bryson Temple's incisive voice said. "If he had, I'd have made short work of this so-called mystery."

"You think this was written by the same man?"

"I fail to see where the doubt arises. Someone is attempting to threaten my life. They killed my brother to show that they could, and would. This note, presumably, is only a prelude to a demand upon me for money—or something else."

Drago's eyes sharpened. "Something else? You've something in mind? Something specific?"

"I have not—most emphatically not. Except that I think it is my affairs that should concern you, rather than my brother's. And on that angle I'll answer your question before you ask it. I have a hundred—a thousand enemies—some of them ruined, some of them powerful. In my business one does not always know even the names of the men he bests. There are lots of white chips in the game, you understand, but only a limited number of blue ones. I play for blue ones. When I win, someone else loses—a lot.

"I have made so many enemies that I think it futile even to try and tabulate them. If—"

The phone rang. Temple excused himself and answered. The instrument was equipped with a Hush-A-Phone and he spoke well inside it. No word of the ten-second conversation was audible to Drago. Bryson Temple stood up, replaced the receiver. "That was a call I was waiting for—no, not the extortionist's call—a business one. I shall have to ask you to excuse me. I have given you all the information I have. I'll be at headquarters within a half hour."

"Was there an envelope with this note?" Drago asked.

Temple said, "Probably, I believe it came by messenger," and touched a button on the desk.

"It should be easy to trace that," Drago said.

In a second, the slim girl in blue appeared in the doorway. "I will see him now," Temple told her. "And please see if there was an envelope to this blue letter, this morning. Quickly, please."

When the girl hesitated, he added "Give it to Mr. Drago if you find it."

Drago blinked slowly, got up, tapped his brown hat against the knee of his trench coat. "Your business seems to be very demanding, Mr. Temple."

There was not the slightest change in the expression or tone of the spare, gray man. "It is."

There was nothing for Drago to do, but follow the girl into the hall.

A fat, greasy-looking, swart man, covered with diamonds, brushed past him and closed the door of Temple's office in his face, from the inside.

The girl in blue said nervously, "Just a minute, Mr. Drago," and vanished into an office adjoining Temple's.

He had about a minute's wait before the girl reappeared at his shoulder with a crumpled blue envelope in her fingers.

"It came by messenger. I'm sure this is it," she said.

He noted the telegraph company's stamp—midnight, the night before, New York—and put it in the glassine envelope that already contained the blue letterhead, restored it to his slash pocket "Could you please tell me how to reach the nearest branch office of that messenger service?"

"It's just a short walk. Rush Lane is the first corner east of here. A narrow little street, it's almost an alley. Turn north a block and a quarter. The office is right there, on the ground level."

THE BLACK storm still whipped and flooded Wall Street as Drago emerged from the building. He buttoned his trench coat to the throat, bent into the wind. Street lamps along the rolling, wide pavement gave the scene the impression of early evening.

There were no street lamps in Rush Lane. It was a thin, cobblestoned alley—a chasm, cut through the middle of a large block. One truck might possibly get through it. Water poured down like cataracts from the roofs, high overhead on either side, to splatter loudly, monotonously on the cobbles below.

Hugging the wall to escape the cascade, Drago nearly fell into a cross-alley that cut across Rush Lane—a delivery alley for the building that faced behind him, on Wall Street. The curb broke here and he went up to his ankles in water, but he was absorbed in his thoughts.

He made a momentary effort to line up what few scraps of knowledge he had, but it was too early. Stuart Temple was dead—that was a fact, and everything else a question. And that was all, so far.

Then he realized with a start that it wasn't all. There was the matter of the dough-faced man in black coat and hat—the man who had spoken Stuart Temple's name the night before, looked at him, then walked away.

Drago stopped short, cursing softly. His abrupt dismissal from Bryson Temple's office had cut off his intended mention of the queer man to the stockbroker. Meager as it was, he might have been able to recognize the description, name the man.

He stood in quiet indecision—in the very middle of the inky little block. If Bryson Temple's life were indeed in danger—and Drago was becoming willing to believe it might be—certainly the broker was entitled to warning of this unexplained stranger.

A clock striking three—market-closing hour—decided him not to go back, or phone back. Bryson Temple would be on his way to headquarters now—or within minutes anyway. Drago trudged on, bent against the wind-whipped sheets of rain that came fitfully down the black alley.

He reached the second cross-alley—the one that was delivery alley for the buildings facing on the street above—and checked himself on the miniature curb, but the alley was on a sharp slope and this part had drained. There was no pool of water to ford. He stepped across on slick, gleaming cobbles.

A hand seemed to poke out of the dark mouth of the cross-alley—a hand with a gun that jabbed into his ribs. A vicious voice clipped in his ear: "Freeze, copper!"

Drago froze, thunderstruck.

A second went by and the savage undertone said distinctly: "I'd kill you as soon as look at you, Drago. I probably will before we're through. When you want it—make just one wrong move. Take your hands out—slowly."

Drago's hands came from his slash pockets, slowly, raised to the level of his shoulders. For all its darkness, he realized that Rush Lane had a faint luminosity from the lighted street sixty yards ahead, but that the cross-alley where the gunman stood was pure black.

"Back in here—not too far. That'll do." There was another second of silence.

Drago could hear tight, compressed breathing behind him.

THE MAN said deliberately: "Get this, copper. There's no reason why I shouldn't drop you where you stand. I'm a desperate man. You're stepping into a deal where you've got no chance. This deal has got to go through. Understand— *got to go through!* If you—or anybody else—gets in my way, I'll pump lead down your throat so fast you won't know what hit you. I've got nothing to lose now. And don't get me wrong. You—or anybody else—can't stop me. All you can do is delay me—but I don't want delay. You hear me?"

"Sure," Drago said, "I hear you."

"Then get this—and if you don't want your brains blown out, get it right. You pull in your horns—between now and tomorrow morning. After tomorrow morning you can investigate till you're blue in the face—nobody cares. Until tomorrow morning—just get in front of me once, and I'll shoot you in the back—on sight. I won't give you a chance. That goes for all of you. You can't stop this deal— it's a natural—and you go down like a tenpin if you try."

In all this, the faint sibilant accent was clear. The gunman seemed waiting for an answer.

"All right," Drago said slowly, "I see your point."

The gun was pressing against the tip of his shoulder blade. He had heard that bluff—the threat of death—a hundred times—yet something cold inside him cried warning that this was not a bluff. There was sweat on his dark face, as well as rain. He swayed a half-inch away from the gun, let his knees sag a little, got the gun back quickly against his shoulder, an inch or two higher.

"You want a clear field till tomorrow morning. That all?"

"Not quite." The other's body crowded close behind Drago's. Swiftly, his hand poked into Drago's left-hand slash pocket, and the glassine envelope crackled. "I'll take this."

Drago whipped his shoulder back, ducked down—and grabbed. The gun's nose jabbed over his right shoulder and his hands flashed to it, clamped the gunman's hand to his shoulder.

The gunman's savage curse was lost in the thunder as the gun went off. Drago was stone-deaf in one ear. He dived forward, throwing bone-crushing leverage on the gunman's wrist across his shoulder. He went to his knees and the gunman, far lighter than Drago had expected, whipped over in a complete somersault, his soles whacking the pavement. Drago yanked at the gun—and got it unexpectedly. The gunman spinning over, could not check himself, was flung across the alley, crashing head-on into the wall, while Drago, late in releasing his tug on the gun, bellyflopped on the wet muck.

Drago grunted warningly: "Stand still, or..."

The gunman bounced back from the wall and, like a shadow, dived into the alley-mouth opposite. Drago, still sprawled, fired hastily. Glass crashed far down the alley. He clawed himself up, swearing, raced into the alley, his hand ripping down the top button of his coat, diving for a flashlight.

Down the alley's blackness there was a sudden short glow of light and he fired again. The light was gone before he realized that he had seen the radiation from a basement door opening below ground level. He skidded, staggered, found the cement balustrade of the steps leading downward and swung round, plunged down slimy wooden stairs and drove open the door at the bottom.

He was vomited into a tan-tiled corridor of a long office building—one of those opening on Wall Street that ran all the way back. Being a few minutes past three, the corridor was packed and jammed with hurrying people leaving broker's offices.

Drago's lips set in a straight line. He retreated, went slowly out the back door again, and was halfway up the steps before he suddenly turned the flash-beam on the gun in his hand. It was an old Savage automatic. He dropped it quickly in his pocket, safe from the rain. Then, with his own gun in his other pocket sweating his palm, he went up and back to the alley.

As he turned into it his foot kicked something soft. He whipped the flashbeam downwards. He had toed a soft black hat, its brim turned down all round!

CHAPTER THREE
HEADQUARTERS VS.
HOMICIDE

WHEN HE slipped into his own cubby-hole office ten minutes later—it had been useless to pursue the messenger-lead—McTigue was pacing the little room, his big Irish face drawn, his china-blue eyes bloodshot. He blurted, even before Drago had closed the door: "Have you got anything?"

"I think so. I saw Bryson Temple—the world's hardest guy. I was jumped, on my way from his office to a branch of a messenger service—he'd got a threatening note, too, this morning. But things don't jibe. Temple and his secretary were the only ones who could have known just where I was go—" He broke off suddenly and lines came into his dark forehead. "Unless unless somebody was listening in—right at the door of the boardroom—when the girl told me how to—hell and damnation, that's it!"

McTigue looked blank. "What?"

Drago hung up hat and coat, scraped mud from his trousers with a towel at the corner basin. "It doesn't matter. I was jumped in an alley. I got the guy's gun and his hat. It was a turned-down, black hat.... Sure, probably the guy that Stuart Temple mentioned. I just now left both hat and gun down at the identification bureau. I don't expect anything from the hat, but they think they can bring out a print on the gun. Have they come through on the autopsy yet?"

McTigue shook his head, looked pained. "No. I suppose you know we'll both get kicked out of here if we miss on this job?"

"Temple told me. Here's another headache to add to it. Bryson Temple may be in danger, too. If it was the killer that jumped me—believe me, he isn't fooling. He offered to cut me down on sight if I didn't lay off till morning."

McTigue gasped. "Then you think they may try to get Bryson Temple—tonight?"

"God knows."

The door burst open and a tall man with an oversize head came in. He wore immaculately pressed blue clothes, a blue tie. His hair was red, his face was red, his eyes were red. He slammed the door behind him, roared at Drago, "Who the hell do you think you are, any—" and stopped as he saw McTigue in the corner.

Drago's eyes were dull, his dark face smooth. "My name's Drago. The gentleman in the corner is Inspector McTigue. Inspector—this is Lieutenant Craven of Homicide, with whom we've had trouble before." He looked at the red-faced man brightly. "Surely you remember us?"

Craven's teeth bit shut. He looked over at McTigue, and his eyes were still nasty. "All right, smart guy. Inspector, I've always tried to cooperate with your department. I'm even willing to play games with the Chink here, most of the time. But this isn't one of them—I'm talking about the Temple case. I want cooperation—and I'm going to get it. Damn it all, I stand in danger of losing my shield...."

Drago said dryly: "Ah! Bryson Temple has reached your office. All right, Craven—listen to me. I knew you when you were a precinct dick and the storekeepers in the district called you Come-Across Craven. How you got on the homicide squad is one of those things, but you're a goniff at heart. You've tried to cut our throats too often. If I *have* dug up something, you can hold your hand on your neck this time—and that's final!"

CRAVEN'S FACE purpled. His hands clenched at his sides. "See?" he urged McTigue. "That's cooperation? He admits he's got something—by sneaking in ahead of us? This is a hell of a police force! I thought there was supposed to be some team work around here? Drago—don't be a heel! Let bygones be bygones! This case'll shake the town—and it'll shake us all right out the window if we—"

"Nuts, Craven." Drago spread his hands. "Nuts. Absolutely nuts."

Craven's hands clenched and unclenched. His eyes went from McTigue to Drago. His upper lip curled to show his teeth. "O.K.," he snarled finally. "O.K. If that's the way you feel about it—if you want to play it dirty, maybe I can think of a trick or two. I was in police work when you were rah-rahing in college, Drago. I'll show you who's going to make monkeys of who. Meanwhile—kick in with the evidence you snaked out of Bryson Temple's office—that blue note."

"It'd be a pleasure," Drago said sadly, "but I seem to have lost it."

There was a second's silence. Then Craven's breath blew out. "Lost it!" he bawled. "Lost it! Nice, good evidence—and he loses it! Oh, ah! Excuse me, gents—excuse me just a minute! I got to see the commissioner a minute! I'll be right back! Loses the evidence! A multimillionaire gets a poison-pen, and he loses it! With a murder behind it!"

He made no effort whatever to move toward the door. His eyes, foxy now, swung from McTigue to Drago, back again. "I guess—I guess I'll let you break the news to Bryson Temple, yourself, Monsoor Drago."

McTigue blurted: "What are you talking about? You can't tell an outsider about this!"

Craven's eyes narrowed. "I never seen anything in the manual says I can't."

"It—hell—that's not police ethics!"

Craven said, "Oh-h-h-h!" nastily.

Drago's eyes turned glumly up to McTigue's.

Craven put his red hands on his hips. "All right, Drago," he snapped grimly, "come across with what you've got—or I belch."

Drago sat down slowly, tilted back in his chair, and his expressionless eyes looked up. "I'll give you my word," he said slowly, "to tell you everything I've turned up—if you'll give me yours to play the blue envelope thing to your chest—and answer me one or two questions."

Craven said, "O.K." quickly.

"First off," Drago asked, "did the writer of that blue note call, as he promised?"

"No. And I've got the place staked out, if he does."

Drago was silent a minute, looking at his short, brown hands. "All right," he said, "and if you don't like it—it's your funeral. I don't know how Stuart Temple was killed. As far as I've gone, there're three possible angles. First, someone popping up out of the pup's love life. Second, someone trying to shake down Bryson Temple for money, by killing his brother and then threatening him. This blue-note writer may be behind that—the blue note may be a prelude to the shake. Third, it may be a shake-down on some business matter—the same set-up, but planned to force Bryson Temple to make some move in Wall Street. I don't know.

"I left Bryson Temple's office to start tracing that blue note. I was jumped in an alley. I think somebody at Temple's office overheard me being told where to go. The gent that jumped me was a tall man, slight, and he wore a turned-down black hat. It may be the one that braced Stuart Temple last night. Anyway, he got away from me—with the blue letter and note, while I was getting his gun. His hat and gun are down in the "I" bureau now...."

THE PHONE on the desk rang. Drago blinked, answered, and a self-satisfied voice said: "This is downstairs. On that Savage automatic you left us—we found a beautiful thumbprint. And it's in classification—and how! A guy named Savard—a killer, wanted on the other side. I've sent a man up with what we've got on him. He's big."

"Nice work," Drago said, and hung up. He looked up at Craven. "They got a print off the gun. An international killer named Savard."

McTigue started. "Leo Savard? My God! I—"

Knuckles rapped on the door of the office and a uniformed man from the "I" bureau came in with papers. "We haven't a picture, seems like, on this Savard, Mr. Drago. He's wanted in Germany for murder, and in France—and in Maine; they've got two extortion indictments on him in Frisco. He's a blackmailer, an extortionist and a killer, and according to this, he's got T.B." The man was reading now. "He's supposed to be a poison murderer. He did one rap in England for robbery, but he's never been inside a can since. I—"

McTigue said, "All right, Feathers. We know," and the man went out.

McTigue looked at Drago with uneasiness in his eyes. "We're up against it, if we're up against Savard. He's—"

"You know what he looks like?"

"Hell, yes. And I'll swear it was he Stuart Temple saw—"

"Put the alarm on the short-wave. Have a half-hour repeat."

In one long smooth movement Drago caught up his hat and coat. He looked the red-faced Craven squarely in the eye, said, "You've got it all now—one way or another, Lieutenant. You'll excuse me? It's been a pleasure—" and barged out before the homicide man could begin to sputter a reply.

THERE WAS a squad car parked before the Temple house when Drago left his cab within a few yards of it. Rain still poured down viciously, as he mounted the one-step porch, but the sky had developed a light streak in the west.

The house was white—immaculate white sandstone—set back ten feet from Fifth Avenue, facing Central Park in the Seventies. The second and third floors had bowed-glass windows. Light shone from behind drawn blinds of nearly every window in the house.

He was admitted by Fred Barry, an Italian detective under Lieutenant Craven, who looked like a gigolo and was a smart youngster. The high-ceilinged, polished-dark-wood hall was somberly lighted. A pile of toys was still on the floor, directly before the hall cupboard. Drago beat water from his hat and asked Barry: "Anything turn up? I'm working with Craven on this."

Barry shrugged. "I bet you are!" he said goodnaturedly. "I haven't anything to hold out, however. None of the servants know anything. Oh, wait a minute—there was something, too. There's a kid's nursery on the third floor. They're redecorating it while the kid's away at school. They were plastering today. There were supposed to be two plasterers at work, and they used the back door, naturally. Only, at about eight this morning, Mrs. Temple let one of them—or a guy supposed to be one of them—in the front door. It didn't strike her as funny—she was thinking of something else. We reached the contractor and he swears none of his men pulled the front-door trick. So there you are. Nobody saw him go out again. Nobody saw him around the house. It looks like somebody worked his way in here—you master minds can figure what for—and copped a sneak when he was through. Or else one of the plasterers is lying."

Drago looked at him narrowly. Barry grinned. "Thanks," Drago said. "I won't forget to cut you in, if anything breaks. You know damn well Craven would skin you for cracking that to me. He'll never know. How's chances for seeing Mrs. Temple?"

Barry went over and stood with a finger on the bell-button by a closed door near the front, till a butler in livery appeared from the rear of the hall. "Ask Mrs. Temple if she will see Mr. Drago, from headquarters."

"I'll just keep her a minute," Drago added. The butler came back almost immediately to say Mrs. Temple would see him and Drago left hat and coat in the hall to follow him into a small Louis XIV drawing-room at the rear.

Francine Temple was standing with her back to a grate-fire, smoking a cigarette inexpertly. She was a small woman, ash-blond, her deep-blue eyes strained. She was poised, intelligent, nonetheless; her shapely, thirty-odd-year-old figure smart and young in tailored black suit, a powder-blue waist with thin white stripes buttoning to her throat under the jacket. Her features were small, little-girl features. Her hands and ankles were exquisitely dainty, and she was made up to exactly the right degree. There was an air of experience about her. She searched his dark, somber eyes almost pleadingly.

Drago bowed faintly. "Excuse me if I seem abrupt, Mrs. Temple. It is only because I know you must be upset enough by now—and I want to make this very short. I am working on your brother-in-law's murder. There is a possibility that it might have arisen out of your husband's affairs—business affairs. Can you suggest anything?"

She shook her head, wondering. "I know nothing"—her voice was a little-girl voice, too—"absolutely nothing of my husband's business affairs."

"Another angle, as you probably know, concerns Mr. Stuart Temple's—well, private life. Your husband couldn't give me any names of—well, ladies who had been close friends. I am hoping for better luck from you."

She shuddered. "The other officers asked me that. I don't understand why you should think I would know anything—about his wretched affairs."

"You disliked him?"

"He was too vulgar to either like or dislike. He sponged on my husband, all these years. He was utterly stupid, and spoiled, and indigent. I don't think even my husband knew how much of our money he was spending."

"Not enough to cause Mr. Temple any embarrassment, I hope?"

"No, nothing like that. It was simply such a terrible waste. I—but it's not my affair, of course."

Drago nodded as if in polite agreement. "This painter— or plasterer you saw this morning. Could you describe him?"

"I—really, I didn't even look at his face. He—I think he was rather dark. He didn't seem like a large man, but—well, I really didn't notice."

Drago bowed. "Thank you very much. That's all, Mrs. Temple."

IN THE hall outside, Drago asked the youthful Barry: "Can you leave the door long enough to show me through Stuart Temple's rooms?"

"Why not?"

The homicide man led him through the suite in the small wing—living-room, dining-room, small library on the ground level; on the second floor, two master bedrooms, each with bath.

In the medicine chest of the bathroom which the dead man had used, were mute evidence of his many debilities. There were bromides, cathartics, purgatives, antacids, a box of stomach capsules for morning use, kidney pills— all these prescribed by a doctor named Anton LaPlace, with offices only two blocks away. Too, there were patent medicines by the score, as well as proprietary remedies for restoring hair, and preparations for cleaning false teeth. At forty-one, Stuart Temple had been falling to pieces, judging by this display.

There was nothing else in the suite that could be imagined to have any bearing on the murder.

When nothing turned up, the name of the doctor— Anton LaPlace—played through Drago's mind. He took another careful look at a label before he followed Barry downstairs again.

In the hall, the youngster grinned. "All right. Who did it? And how?"

Drago nodded gravely. "Elementary. A band of Tibetan conjure priests put him out by thought control."

"My theory exactly," Barry affirmed, as Drago again donned his trench coat. "No kidding, though. Catch anything?"

"Sure," Drago said. "The doctor's name. Doctors know things."

He stepped casually to the refectory table, to retrieve his hat from where he had tossed it—and suddenly became motionless, staring.

A tray of letters, evidently fresh from the mail-box, and as yet unopened, were stacked within an inch of his hat.

The top envelope was typewritten. It was addressed to Mrs. Francine Temple. And it was typewritten in the same italicized script that had formed the death note received by Stuart Temple.

Drago's face went copper-colored.

Without taking his eyes from the letter, he threw over his shoulder at Barry: "Get Mrs. Temple—quick!"

"What is it?"

"A bad dream. Never mind Mrs. Temple. Somebody's gone crazy. It may be me. Where is a phone?"

CHAPTER FOUR
SUICIDE OF AN M.D.

Mrs. Francine Temple:

For unavoidable reasons, it has been found necessary that you depart this life, tonight, Friday night, at midnight. We assure you that we regret this necessity, and especially the short notice, but the choice is not ours. We promise you a painless taking-off, or as nearly so as your own actions permit. Please do not make the task harder for either ourselves, or yourself, by futile efforts at resistance. The means which we employ—as you must realize by now—have nothing in common with the gross physical forms of lifetaking usual on your plane. I assure you sincerely, though I suppose you will doubt me—your police officers are completely powerless to thwart this. This is no reflection on them as a body, but rather, on the stupid state of your civilization, which calls our use of natural powers "magic."

Inspector McTigue's big Irish face—even his bald head—was flushed and crimson, as he finished reading the note aloud. There were more than a dozen grim-faced men in the hall of the Temple home.

The place was in a state of siege from the newspapers. Doorbells had been disconnected. There was a cordon of uniformed men outside, with the cruel assignment of clubbing, if necessary, the swarming hordes of reporters drawn by the sudden influx of headquarters men.

It was just an hour, to the minute, since Drago had found the note and thrown the telephonic bombshell to McTigue and Craven. Centre Street had already gone taut, fuming under a newspaper lashing. The incredible details of Stuart Temple's killing, as given out, had been choice prey for early editions. Even the headlines screamed derision. In three short hours, it had become a cause *cèlébre*—the policeman's nightmare.

McTigue's voice was grim, savage, as he ran his eye down the line of men—the cream of the headquarters and homicide squads. "We are here," he told them abruptly, "to prevent a murder. We don't know exactly what we're dealing with. We don't know what to expect—so we'll expect everything. You men know your assignments. We have no doubt that the threat received here, is from the same killer that was behind the death of Stuart Temple this morning. It looks like the work of some sort of homicidal maniac. Maybe it looks *too* much like it. You know what I mean.

"The death of Temple this morning has not been solved yet by the M.E.'s office. We are expecting a report any minute, but as yet we don't know how he was killed. All I can tell you is that it was damnably clever. Two matrons are upstairs now with Mrs. Temple—a fine, pluckily little woman. They are responsible for her person. They are going over her with a magnifying glass. You men are responsible for this house. The threat is timed for midnight. We have over six hours. There is no excuse whatever for not stopping this proposed killing. You men are seasoned and intelligent. You know what to look for—trick weapons of any kind, infernal machines, death traps of any sort. Over and above that, I want you to use your imaginations. You've got lots of time to work in. There will be another detail here presently, accompanying Mr. Bryson Temple when he comes home.

He has not been threatened but we are taking no chances. We will guard both of them during the hours the threat might cover. Lieutenant Craven will select the rooms in the house in which the watch will take place.

"All right—go ahead. If you men do your work properly, no one but a magician—" He stumbled over the unfortunately chosen word, flushed purple, went on loudly, "I don't have to go into that. That's all."

The hall emptied save for McTigue and Drago, hunched on a wooden bench in the darkest corner, staring at a cigarette in his cupped hand. He got up as McTigue came over, asking anxiously: "Do you think of anything else?"

Drago nodded. "Yes. A doctor."

"A doctor!"

"There seems no other logical answer than that Stuart Temple was poisoned—some way. There may be another poison attempt here. My advice is to get a doctor—somebody who knows—to clean Mrs. Temple out. I know enough about poison myself to state that, with six hours to work in, a competent doctor can almost guarantee results. By results, I mean that he won't leave any poison in her system that might cause death at midnight. Naturally, you'll see that she doesn't get any from now on."

McTigue ran a finger inside his collar, went over and called up the stairs, "Mrs. Pratt!" When a police matron came in view above, he said: "Ask Mrs. Temple the name of her doctor."

The matron went away, came back to say: "Doctor Zimmerman, on the other side of the Park."

Drago's eyes lit up. He said quietly, "Thanks, that's all," up to the matron, and turned to McTigue. "I'd get him—if she has confidence in him—and just to be absolutely safe, get two surgeons from the M.E.'s office to check every move he makes—every drug he uses, and every instrument."

HE ARRIVED at six. He was a tall, distinguished-looking man of forty-five or fifty, with a fine, wide forehead and brown kindly eyes. His curling brown hair was only slightly grayed. If running the gauntlet of the mob outside, on an errand of which he had been told nothing, disturbed him, he did not show it. He asked quietly, as the door closed behind him: "What's wrong with Mrs. Temple?"

McTigue said: "Nothing, Doc—and we want you here to keep it that way." He introduced him to the two men from the M.E.'s office, who had already arrived, and led the three of them upstairs.

When McTigue came down again, Drago asked: "You told the matron to dress her from the skin out in clothes that no one could have foreseen that she would wear?"

McTigue nodded. "And she won't have so much as a hair-pin made of metal. Even rubber-soled shoes. That's in case there's any funny business about electricity."

"They're bearing down on the broadcast for Leo Savard?"

McTigue nodded again. There were pools of dark worry in his eyes. "You think he killed Temple?"

"He's mixed in it, somehow. Whether he's the brains—I don't know. I—" He stopped short, a sudden jumping light in his eyes, was silent.

"What the hell?"

"I just thought of a question," Drago half turned toward the stairs. His eyes were thinner, as he checked himself. "But I can't do anything about it till the doctors are through up there. Incidentally, you'll keep them around—till after the deadline?"

"Yeah. That's a good idea."

At eight, Bryson Temple came home. When he was told what the plans were, he expressed more silent, cutting contempt with his gray eyes than a book of words could have. He neither assented nor dissented but marched ominously upstairs.

Not till ten did one of the M.E.'s doctors, standing outside the closed door of Francine Temple's room, tell Drago and McTigue, in a half-whisper: "She's clean. There's no poison in her. I'll swear to that. Zimmerman is a fine medical man. I watched him like a hawk, as you told me to. It's absurd to suspect him of attempting to introduce any poison—"

"We didn't say we suspected him," Drago said quietly. "We're simply not overlooking anything. Can we go in?"

They got in and Drago finally got his chance to propound his question. If he could have foreseen the answer, he would have broken down the door, hours earlier, to hear it.

Bryson Temple was in the room, his mask-like face seeming grayer, grimmer than ever. He stood by the head of his wife's bed, his hands behind him, unmoving, agate-like gray eyes following their entrance. Zimmerman was closing his bag on the bureau, the other M.E.'s man watching him.

FRANCINE TEMPLE lay on the bed, white, weak-looking, but game. She managed a ghost of a smile for them, and her little-girl's voice wavered. "I—I hope you're not going to do anything else to me?"

She wore a white linen peasant dress, with a few red decorations around the neck where a red pucker string drew it in. The dress was badly crumpled. She wore no stockings, and buckskin, rubber-soled shoes.

Drago said; "No—except to take good care of you, Mrs. Temple…. Mac—now would be a good time to take Doctor Zimmerman down and have one of the men show him the billiard-room that Craven picked for the watch. I'll see you downstairs."

McTigue blinked, mumbled something, but went over and held the door open for the physician.

Bryson Temple said coldly and contemptuously: "If this furor is an attempt to distract attention from my brother's death, Mr. Drago, I may say that I am not impressed."

Drago eyed him stonily. "You rarely are, are you?" He looked down at Francine Temple. "I was wondering who Anton LaPlace was."

She looked up at Bryson Temple, and there was sudden darkness in her blue eyes. She seemed to expect her husband to answer, but when he did not, she said thinly: "He was our family doctor for years, until last week, when he—he died."

Something sprang to attention in Drago. "Doctor Zimmerman has only been attending you for a week?"

Her "Yes" was lost in the louder tones of Bryson Temple's, "Now are we to see the spectacle of a leading physician suspected of murder because—"

Drago stepped to the door, whipped it open. Down the hall three homicide men were emerging from a room. He beckoned one of them in and indicated Bryson Temple. "Take Mr. Temple outside. Let him go anywhere he wants, but keep him in sight."

Bryson Temple did not move. Staring steadily at Drago, he said to the homicide man: "You can go on about your business. I prefer to stay with my wife."

Drago's hands were flat in his pockets, his dark face muddy. "Your house is in the hands of the police, Mr. Temple. I'm not asking—I'm ordering you out."

"You—damned—puppy." Bryson Temple's only sign of emotion was in his gray lips. They seemed to curl around each word as though reluctant to let it out. "I promise that you will be broken for this. I do not leave this room—unless, of course, I am under formal arrest."

"All right. You're under formal arrest—suspicion of murder."

Bryson Temple did not move. Drago went on: "I haven't really got round to suspecting you, but I'm human enough to think anything I don't understand is queer. I don't understand you. You're harder than anyone in my experience, so you may not think the way we do. You may have a hundred queer motives that we never dream of. Out, Jeffers."

Another man would have exploded. Bryson Temple breathed slowly, adjusted his cravat and walked unhurriedly out.

Drago turned and asked the woman on the bed: "Tell me what is queer about the recent death of your former doctor, Mrs. Temple. Obviously, there is something."

"He—he committed suicide, last week. He—he shot himself."

For a second it was just a plain surprise to Drago, like an unexpected knock on the door of his mind. Then a shoot of excitement swirled through him. He could not rationalize it as he hurried from the room, and down the stairs, made for the phone. He called headquarters.

When he hung up, McTigue was at his shoulder. Drago told him grimly: "Doctor Anton LaPlace, long-time doctor for this family, shot and killed himself in his office last week. He was broke. He burned all his papers before doing it. McManus, who handled the case, is an ace, and he says there's no mistake—it was clear suicide. This is queer—damn queer. I'm going to look over his house."

"Good God! You're not going out now! It's—it's eleven, nearly!"

"He lived just around the corner—it shouldn't take me but a few minutes. Keep a watch on that Zimmerman, and check up on the Savard broadcast!"

McTigue mopped his head and said hoarsely: "I'm going crazy. If you must go—go out the back way—we've fixed it with the people who live behind here—arranged a bolt-hole to duck the reporters out front. There're men there to get you through."

He was out within two minutes, alone, seemingly, on the black stretch of wind-and-rain-whipped street, hurrying, almost running toward the cross-street above.

THE HOUSE was one of the few single houses left in that exclusive section. It was white sandstone, too, but it was dirty, somber. It was a narrow little crushed-in build-ing, with less than three feet between its sides and those of the two towering apartment houses that hemmed it in. No spark of light showed in its three stories, and the blinds were drawn. Apparently, no one had yet moved into the place.

Drago climbed the flight of stone steps, stooped, played his flash over the doorlock. It was a simple one. His pick-lock made short work of it, and he stepped into a musty, antiseptic-smelling, black hall. There was a carpet under his feet, and his darting flash-beam picked out various pieces of hall furniture.

Halfway down the hall, on the right, the edge of a partly opened steel door protruded out into the hall. It was chocolate brown, but the inside face of it was pure, gleaming white—the dispensary.

He stepped down the hall and pulled the door open.

Flame and roar thundered from the darkness in front of him. The bullet hit his flashlight, exploded it in his hand. Fire seared his forearm.

There was no question of trying to reach his own gun. His wildest imaginings had not included finding anybody here, and he was trapped cold. He tried to fling himself to the ground. The gun in the darkness vomited again. The second bullet hit him high in the right shoulder, whacked him over backwards. He hit spread-eagled, his feet flying up, then flopping down, with the edge of the open door between his ankles.

The lights flared on and Leo Savard stood across the room from him by the light-switch, a gun in his hand, his doughy face contorted, teeth bared.

He yelled: "Don't move! Damn you! You rat—I told you what would happen to you if you got in my way again!"

He stepped away from the white wall inside, strode grimly toward the fallen detective, the gun in his fist unwavering, dilating pupils telling his purpose as plainly as his words.

Drago eased up to his elbows. "Take it easy, Leo. Wait a—"

Savard's teeth showed as he threw the gun-muzzle down, straight at Drago's face. "Wait hell! You're gone...."

Drago spun. Every ounce of his strength went into his ankles as he whirled over onto his stomach. The door, as though shot from a catapult from between his whipping ankles, slammed shut—smashed squarely into the dark-coated killer. The gun roared as the startled gunman jumped backwards and Drago twisted, dived.

He crashed the door home, grabbed for the key, as thunder came again from inside the room. The whole of Drago's left arm went numb from the transmitted impact. A ragged hole of light appeared in the steel door, a foot over his head. He whirled himself backwards and away from the door as the man inside blasted again—and again.

Then, on his feet with his own gun in his hand, he backed a few feet down the hall, drew a sleeve over his dripping forehead. When there was no further sound from within the dispensary, he called: "Savard—can you hear me?"

There was no answer.

He called sourly: "Don't sulk. You're through. You'd better make the best terms you can."

THERE WAS still no answer. A faint whine came from within the room. Drago's eyes screwed up in quick question. Then he said, "Hell and damnation!" and raced for the front door. He dived out onto the steps, crouched over, half slid to the bottom, whirled to cover the aperture between the right side of the house and the apartment adjoining. No one emerged.

Then—even above the soft hissing of the rain—he heard a *crack* and a scrabbling sound, far in the back yard of the house. He cursed, shot up the steps again and through the house, banged out into the back yard.

There was no one there. Lights from the adjoining apartment house made the back yard clearly visible in detail—and something sparkled, near the high board fence that closed the yard in. He ran for the object, snatched it up. It was a silvered flashlight, flattened on one side.

Drago groaned, threw himself back into the house again, on through. When he hit the sidewalk in front again, the crouched, racing figure of a man was just vanishing around a corner, a long block crosstown, moving like lightning.

Drago's teeth clicked and he threw himself in pursuit, tried one snap shot. Behind him, pounding feet were suddenly audible and a hoarse voice boomed: "Stop—you! Drop that gun, or I'll...!"

Drago threw a glance over his shoulder to see the shining slicker and visored cap of the cop on the beat, pounding up.

Then the street started tilting, spinning. He stopped, turned round, raised his hands. The cop ran up, threw light in his face. "Drago? Hell, what—"

Drago said: "Don't talk. I'm bleeding, I guess. Get me to the house behind Bryson Temple's place. I've got a slug in my shoulder. Get me there fast!"

How they escaped the notice of the prowling newshounds was a miracle—a uniformed man, half supporting a stumbling detective, both running—but they did.

As the plainclothesman on post by the areaway entrance to the house behind Temple's came out of his shadow with a startled exclamation, Drago said stiffly, hastily: "Tell the guy who owns this place he's got to let me sit in his basement a while. Get a doctor, a quart of whisky, and McTigue."

When McTigue ran into the laundryroom, a doctor on his heels, Drago, holding his shoulder, said through stiff lips: "I just had a fight with Leo Savard. He's evidently been hiding out in LaPlace's house. Put it on the radio that he was in this district."

McTigue ran off, and the doctor stepped closer. He had the bottle of liquor in his hand. Drago took it gently. "Take the slug out, Doc, fast—and button me up." He tilted the bottle to his lips.

It was three quarters empty when the doctor put his clothes back on him and eyed Drago in awed wonder. "What are you made of—rawhide?"

"Yeah," Drago said, and rolled off the table. His knees wobbled, so he took another drink, stood swaying, and then said: "O.K. Let's go. What's the time?"

"Nine minutes to twelve."

CHAPTER FIVE
MURDER BY MAGIC

THE SILENCE in the Temple house was like something physical. Sulphurous, pulsing, it struck Drago like a wave as he entered the basement door. Everywhere, he could see silent, waiting men.

The passage from the back door only extended one third the depth of the cellar. Furnace and storerooms were all segregated in the rear. The front two thirds of the cellar blossomed into one enormous, high-ceilinged room—the billiard-room that Craven had chosen for the death-watch.

Men were scattered about in a rough circle. Against the right-hand wall of the cellar, at the foot of the plank stairs, was a telephone, a man beside it. There was a group of three detectives crowded about the open door of the billiard-room. Stronger light shone out from within.

Drago told McTigue, as they hurried toward it: "I don't know what I accomplished. It may be that I threw his plans all off—or maybe this is a bluff. God knows. I'm at my wits' end."

The men at the billiard-room door fell back to let them stand in the entrance.

The room was cream-plastered—walls and ceiling. It was like the inside of a box, unbroken by windows. A wire mesh guarded the ventilator in the wall. The room had never been fitted up with billiard equipment. Five armchairs, without upholstery, had been carried in and set on the bare floor—one in each corner, and one squarely in the center.

On those in the corners, detectives sat rigid, alert. One man stood by the ventilator with a large, thick, white cloth over his arm to guard against pollution of the air supply.

Francine Temple, in her white clothes, sat in the chair in the center of the room, under the globed light that was the only illumination. Her little-girl's face and eyes were sick and drawn, and she worried a balled handkerchief between her palms.

Drago looked at his watch, said cheerfully in his soft voice: "All over in a minute now, Mrs. Temple. Kind of silly, all this, isn't it?"

She tried to smile. She couldn't—nor could she speak. She made her head shake up and down.

Drago stepped away from the doorway, taking McTigue with him. His eyes were live coals. "The kid! They have a kid named Peter at boarding-school. Could this be an attempt to divert attention and kidnap him when—"

"Craven thought of that. We got word twenty minutes ago that the police up at Haverstown had reached the school and that the kid was safe. They're bringing him home under armed guard."

They were silent a second. "You've done everything?" Drago said.

"Everything. If she is killed now—I'll believe in magic. Nothing but magic can get to her."

IT STUNNED the city. War-scare headlines were jerked into use by the papers. Blase editors refused to believe the first reports of her death. Police headquarters rocked, strangely enough with laughter, at first. Every move of the men in charge of the Temple house had been relayed through the nerve centers of headquarters, and every officer who was interested—and that meant all of them—*knew* that Francine Temple could not be killed. The first flash that she had been, simply made no impression. When the mad, incredible truth finally was pounded home to them, a thousand men were dumbfounded.

The men in the house itself were not dumbfounded—they were paralyzed with terror.

At a half-minute to twelve, there had been a sudden, velvet silence in the basement. Drago and McTigue stood outside the billiard-room, not quite on a line with the two M.E.'s doctors and young Barry, the homicide detective. Those three filled the doorway of the room.

At a quarter-minute to twelve, fascination urged Drago a few feet to the right, where he could look over their shoulders into the brilliant room. McTigue followed him.

Francine Temple sat in the exact center of the room. The four detectives in the corners were strung taut as bowstrings, hands on guns, though no weapons were in sight, on Drago's orders.

No one was less than twenty feet away from the woman in white.

And then something came into that room! Something invisible—something horrible! Every man in the place felt it and their scalps crawled.

Francine Temple suddenly cried out—a pitiful little-girl cry. She sprang to her feet. Her eyes circled the room—wide, terrified. Her hands pressed to her heaving breast.

They all saw what happened—yet it happened so fast that no one could move.

They saw her suddenly look up—look up at absolutely nothing—at the empty air above her head. They saw her suddenly stagger—saw the frantic, crazy fear come into her eyes, saw her mouth open to scream—but no scream came.

Her knees suddenly buckled. Her face went red, then white, then red again. She threw frantic, pleading glances around—and was suddenly flung to the floor, as though by a giant hand.

Every man in the room dived for her.

Drago's hoarse voice roared, "Back! Back!" as he flung himself in.

The woman on the floor was arced in an impossible position, her heels and head only touching the floor, her face contorted, bursting with congested blood.

Drago yelled: "What is it? Where is it…."

She suddenly slumped. Her body whipped, writhed, her heels beating a devil's tattoo. Her hands crawled up her body to her throat like she was in some awful nightmare—and then suddenly she arced again, slumped once more, shuddered once—and lay in a heap.

Drago sprang to his feet, his dark eyes mad. He croaked: "Doctor—fast!"

The two M.E.'s men kneeled beside her together. Drago saw their faces go white, in the one-second examination that they gave her.

Donnelly, the senior, staggered up as though he had seen a ghost.

"She—she's dead!"

In the second's stunned silence, the phone outside in the cellar rang wildly.

THERE WAS panic in the basement—in every corner of it—stunned, numbed panic. No one dared to think ahead—there was no ahead—and no before—nothing but the slain woman lying in the room, the feverish doctors ripping her clothes open.

Donnelly exclaimed sharply, and the two bent together over her right breast. Donnelly whirled to look up at Drago, jerked: "Here it is—a glass dart!"

"What!"

The other doctor, bent close to her skin, mumbled up: "It's hollow! There's a yellow liquid inside it! It must be poison—shot into her with that glass dart!"

Drago stood in the middle of the room, swaying, his palms wet, fists in his pockets, dark face livid. He stammered under his breath—and didn't know he was doing it—"A glass dart! A glass dart! A glass dart...."

A man put his hand to his mouth at Drago's ear and shouted: "The phone—headquarters wants you on the phone! For God's sake—can't you hear me?"

Drago jerked. "What?"

The jittery detective blurted: "I've been shouting...."

Drago raced out to the phone.

The voice that answered him said: "Hey—where have you been? I've got two ripe items for you. This is the 'I' bureau."

Drago stiffened. "Go on!"

"One—the M.E.'s department has finished the autopsy on Stuart Temple. He was killed with a dose of atropine—enough to drop ten men like him in their tracks. They found it in his stomach. They swear he couldn't have carried it in his stomach two seconds and lived. Pass that to Craven of hom—"

"All right! What's the second?"

"Right. Two—with our customary *savoir faire*, we did some more work on the Savage automatic you sent us—the one you took from Leo Savard—and did nothing else in the world but trace the sale of the gun and its ownership. It was not Leo Savard's."

"What! Whose was it?"

"A gent named Guillaume LaPlace, who lives in Marlborough, up in Westchester—"

"Wait a minute," Drago said hoarsely, "You mean Anton LaPlace—the doctor!"

"We do not. We mean Guillaume LaPlace. He was an aviator during the war, and seems to have dough, from the remarks on the permit. He had—has—a private hangar up there, and—"

Something like an explosion took place in Drago's stomach. He whipped down the receiver, yelled: "Barry!"

McTigue and Barry spun toward him. To Barry he snapped: "Go out front and grab a squad car. Get round and pick me up at the back in two seconds flat!"

The young homicide man ran off, raced up the stairs. Drago threw at McTigue: "Don't ask me what's happened. I'm sick. The information came too late—I think. We've got a million-to-one chance of blocking the getaway, if I'm right. Though I can't believe it myself yet. Carry on—let no one leave the house—or that room!"

As he ran out through the cellar, mad, lightning-like jabs of thought were threshing, igniting in the chambers of his brain. For the first time he saw into the inferno of death and murder. Saw—not fully, but almost so—the terrible thing behind it all. Saw, in his mind's eye, the killer of Stuart and Francine Temple—yet he could not quite make himself believe. It was too horrible....

CHAPTER SIX
THE EASIEST WAY

THE RIDE was a nightmare. Barry sent the squad car careening through the night like a blazing, sirening comet. They hit Marlborough in less than an hour, with only one stop, while a local cop gave them directions.

Guillaume LaPlace had a wide estate, not in very good repair, five miles from the center of the town. He had a private hangar and a small, red monoplane....

They flew along farm-bordered roads. When they were within a mile of their destination, Barry yelled suddenly: "There it is! The field's all lighted up! It's equipped for night fly—Look, there's a plane standing in it, prop turning over. See! In the floodlights, you can...."

He jammed down the accelerator. The orange hangar shone through the pelting rain, larger and larger—and then warning signs popped up along the roadside, and they found their own road was at an end. They had to take a right-angled turn, two hundred yards short of the field. They almost went over, as Barry caught it a second too late, skidded wildly to make the turn, went down into the ditch and up again, fighting the bucking wheel.

Drago ripped suddenly: "Look—along there—there's a road leading in to the field—a private road."

They shot ahead, whirled, crashed through a flimsy, white painted gate with a Private sign—and were rushing up the road. In the second that the gate went down before them they saw the hangar door burst open. A man's figure shot out, paused only a second, his face flashing toward the thundering squad car—then he sprinted wildly toward the plane.

Drago cursed hoarsely, flung his hand back over the seat and whipped the automatic rifle from the clamps over the back seat, drove out the side curtains of the touring car with his elbow.

They were jolting, bumping. He laid his cheek alongside the stock of the gun, sighted. He paid no attention to the man, now halfway to the plane. He squeezed the rifle—and lead thundered—eating into the fabric of the plane—white-hot lead pellets.

On the sixth shot it happened. The running man was less than twenty yards from the plane, when the first lick of flame shot from its side. He did not see it but ran on.

There was something in his hand—a briefcase, it looked like. A dozen feet from the plane, he flung it ahead of him into the cockpit, took a running jump, and dived.

The gas tank went and the plane blew just as the squad car shot onto the field.

Drago roared at Barry, "Not too close!" dropped the rifle and whipped out his pistol. Even as he yelled, he saw a blackened figure stagger away from the plane, weaving drunkenly, turn and start to run. Drago whipped up the pistol, fired once—twice—and the figure fell down. It crawled, struggled desperately to rise—and Barry threw on the brakes, brought the squad car to a long, side-slipping stop.

Drago flung out. Far to the right, on the side slope of a hill, he saw a house ablaze with lights. He ripped at Barry: "Go up to that house and grab anybody that's there! I can handle it here! Move!"

The mystified Barry hesitated, his face pained, bewildered, but at last he jumped out and raced up the hill.

Drago took one look at the plane as he ran past it. There had been a vague hope in his mind of rescuing the briefcase—but the hope died. The plane was a blazing furnace.

He ran for the crawling man, his pistol ready in his hand, and called warningly: "Don't move, you! Stretch your hands out, or I'll plug you again!"

The figure slowly rolled back to a sitting position, and the hands went up.

Drago slid to a stop, five yards from the man. "I thought so. Get up, Savard."

"I can't copper. You broke my leg."

DRAGO FLUNG a look up the hill. Barry had vanished into the dark. He looked back at the open door of the lighted hangar-shack. "All right," he said. "Stretch out on your belly."

He went through the international killer's pockets, reaped two automatic pistols—Colts, this time—a number of inconsequential odds and ends, and a wallet of black sealskin, bulging.

The wallet contained seven hundred and eighty dollars, and two worn and creased documents, encased in the same glassine envelope that had been taken from him earlier. Drago almost held his breath as he fingered out the documents.

The first was the final message of a dead man.

To whom it may concern:

I am taking the coward's way out. Once, during the war, I committed a crime. The crime was discovered by a bloodsucking blackmailer. He has recently located me, here in America and bled me dry—more than dry. When my money was gone, he still threatened me with exposure, and I—God help me—to save myself, delivered another soul into his bloody hands. I cannot stop him now—it is too late, and I can no longer face myself.

Anton LaPlace, M.D.

Drago snatched open the second document. It was on the letterhead of Dr. Anton LaPlace, and consisted of three short paragraphs of pen-and-ink writing, under the heading—

Test results show:

Sample (1) (Marked P.T.)—

Serum agglutinates no corpuscles. Corpuscles agglutinated by sera of Groups 1, 2, and 3.

Sample (2) (Marked S.T.)—

Do.

Sample (3) (Marked B.T.)—

Serum agglutinates corpuscles of Groups 1 and 2. Corpuscles agglutinated by sera of groups 2, and 4.

Remarks: There is no relationship between Sample 1 and Sample 3. Possible relationship Samples 1 and 2.

Mendelian Equations, with Sample 4 (Marked F.T.) shown in detail, second page this report.

There was no second page—there didn't have to be.

Drago stared, aghast. And in the second that he stood with chills running up and down his spine, every crazy detail of the whole mess of double killing, of cruelty and foulness, fell into line in his logical mind. He saw everything, crystal clear—incredible and mad as it was—and realized that the murderer behind it all was the one person absolutely unsuspected—and his soul was sick.

He came to with a jerk, stuffed the glassine envelope and its contents into his pocket. His gun was on the prone figure on the ground. His lips were like paper as he said in a grinding voice: "Get up, you filthy rat—and get into that office!"

It was a second before he realized that the man had fainted. And when he did realize it, a fresh idea burst into his head. Something in his bland, shining round face went stiff and hard, and his now coal-black eyes sunk almost out of sight in his head. Swiftly, almost furtively, he looked from the man on the ground, up the hill toward where Barry had disappeared. The young homicide man was not in sight.

Drago stooped quickly, threw the stringy body of the extortionist-killer over his shoulder, trotted to the hangar shack.

THE PLACE was bare, save for a desk, chair, washbasin and wall mirror. Drago's eyes darted round the room, and his teeth showed. He dumped the unconscious man on the floor, propped him upright against the wall.

He had to draw two glasses of cold water and dash them in Savard's face before he brought consciousness back.

The man started. His eyes—glassy—opened, and he winced. Then his eyes cleared, and he looked up.

"And they told me you had brains," Drago said.

The other's eyes dropped. They were dull, hopeless, licked. "Brains don't help much when you're desperate for money, copper—and the heat's on you."

"You know you're through, don't you?"

"Yes, I guess I am. It doesn't matter much. The doctors only gave me another year anyhow. Just so I'm caught in this country, it's O.K. by me."

"Why the preference?"

"Just a complex. I can stand the chair, I guess—but I'd hate to die by any of the tricks they give you in Germany—or France either, for that matter."

"What you ought to get, is to die in that fire out there. I don't care much whether I drag you out and toss you in, or not. You'd better talk—from start to finish. I got the two papers from your pocket, and I know most of it. I want confirmation from you—fast."

Savard stared up with crawling eyes. "You—" He swallowed, licked his lips. "I'll talk. God, you wouldn't—"

"Go on—talk."

"Yeah. Well, I had something on these LaPlaces—something I picked up on the other side. They—"

"I don't care what they'd done. Where is the evidence on it? And where is Guillaume LaPlace now?"

"The evidence was in that brief case. I guess it's ashes by now. LaPlace is all right. He'd tied up in his cellar."

"All right. Go on. You came over here to blackmail Doctor LaPlace. You blackmailed him till he had no more money, and then he turned this other paper I've got over to you—and then what?"

Savard nodded slowly. "I called Mrs. Temple on the phone and tried to sell it to her. As I say, the heat was on me. I'm sick—and broke. The last two years, they've been catching up. I had to have money—a flock of it—to get myself in the clear. You know how that is.

"I offered it to Mrs. Temple for fifty grand. She never saw that much in her life. She didn't have anything—to speak of. I had no choice then—I had to try and sell it to her husband. I inquired around, found he was a hard guy—the kind who'd pay through the nose for dope on his wife. I tried to get him to make the offer. By God, I couldn't contact him. I tried last night in front of his house when his car came home, but he wasn't in it. I wrote that note you had. I was in his office, sizing up the lay, when you came in. I saw you come out with the letter in your hands, and heard the girl tell you directions how to go. I beat it out, cut you off and got the letter.

"I knew the heat would be on then, for fair. I knew, since the doctor—LaPlace—bumped himself off, nobody was in his house, and I figured it a good place to lay low in. I was planning to make another stab at seeing Temple tonight.

"While I was in LaPlace's I tuned in on the radio, and I saw what a mess I'd gotten into. I didn't kill those people, whatever you think. When I was talking about the chair, I meant the Maine rap that's—"

"I know you didn't kill them, you rat. Go on."

"Well, I knew the game was all over, as far as getting to Temple. And when the broadcast went out for me I knew the only thing I could do was lam—money or no money. I knew I could make LaPlace here lend me his plane for a getaway. And here I am—"

Drago's face was a livid mask. "Why do vermin like you get born? Well, you're going to die the hard way, Savard."

Savard's eyes jerked to Drago's nervously. "How's that?"

"You're going back to Germany. They have ideas for rats like you."

Savard's face went sickly green. "You—you're crazy! Maine'll never give me up. They—"

"Maine isn't going to get you. From here we go straight to the German consul's office and turn you in. Then you're on German ground and you go straight back to Berlin. I hope they put you through hell."

Savard's throat contracted. He cried wildly, desperately: "Oh, God, Drago—no. They hack your head off with an ax...."

DRAGO, LOOKING through the desk drawers hastily, found some sheets of white paper. He whipped out his fountain pen, went over and put paper and pen down beside the almost sobbing killer. He slipped the clip from one of the Colts, dropped it on the floor.

Drago's eyes were hot coals in a sallow face. "I'll give you the *easiest* way—if you do what I say."

"You—you mean..." Savard's eyes flew to the clip of bullets. His voice was a croaking whisper. "You—all right. What—do—I..."

"Write what I tell you."

Savard's hand was shaking, as he reached in fascinated dread for the pen. Drago spoke through tight jaws. "And hurry up. My partner will be back soon. It's got to be done before that. Ready? Write this—

"I, Leo Savard, hereby confess to the following—"

The killer's hand went to the paper.

Drago's voice was like slate. "I conceived the plan of terrorizing Bryson Temple, and extorting money from him. I knew he was a hard man, and I would have to do something drastic to make him listen to me. I decided to kill his brother by mysterious means.

"I discovered, through careful surveillance, that his brother used gelatine capsules containing a stomach remedy, every morning. I bided my time, till there were workmen in the house, then prepared a gelatine capsule, identical with the ones he used, and filled it with atropine.

I estimated the amount of gelatine necessary to prevent its being discharged into his stomach for three hours, and I wrote a note telling him of his approaching death. Because of my timing of the capsule's coating, I could name almost the very hour when it would take effect.

"I wrote Bryson Temple a note, preparatory to demanding money. He did not react. He called in the police, and I determined to add weight to my demands by killing his wife as well. This, also, I had planned, and foreseen.

"I had written her a note also, and at the time when I made my way into their house, disguised as a plasterer, I concealed a hollow needle filled with poison, in the hem of the dress that seemed next in line to be worn in her cupboard. The hollow needle had a very long, sharp point, and I knew that sooner or later it would prick her. A minute speck of the pure poison would be enough, injected in a wound. I had to hope for luck to help me here, as I knew no way to be certain of her death. However, I wrote the note, timing it for midnight. The effect would be just as strong on Bryson Temple, even if the time were wrong.

"I intended making my demand on Bryson Temple early tomorrow morning, but I was overtaken by Detectives Drago and Barry and captured. I am writing this of my own free will and accord, knowing that I am dying from gunshot wounds received in this capture. No coercion has been used, or promises of any kind made me."

Drago's face was shiny with sweat as he came to the end. "Now sign it."

Savard signed it, looked up crazily. "God, Drago—you don't believe that!"

"I'm not a fool," Drago said, and took the paper and read it. Then he stood with the clipless gun balanced on his hand. The killer looked at it, his beady eyes crawling.

"I'm going outside a minute," Drago said, "to look for my friend. When I come back—you are going to be taken to the German consul."

Savard's eyes were fixed in dreadful, almost prayerful wildness on the gun in Drago's hand.

Drago walked to the door, turned, tossed back the clipless gun and stepped out into the darkness. Far up on the hill he saw Barry's flashlight, threshing, as the young homicide man came running back toward the hangar-shack.

Drago shielding the confession under the skirt of his trench coat, said over his shoulder: "Hurry up! My partner's coming."

The gun boomed once, inside the shack.

Drago spun and dived in the door. Savard was dead, half his head blown away. His hand, with the gun in it, was sinking slowly to the floor. Drago threw up his hands dramatically, jumped further into the room.

When Barry came running in, he was leaning over the gunman, feeling for his heart.

He straightened. "God, I thought I had him clean. I took one gun from him, but he had another. He confessed—and then did it. Here's his confession. You won't mind witnessing it? I just turned out to take a look for you, and he— here, just stick your name there, anywhere."

"He—he confessed?" Barry said eagerly, and started to read the paper. Drago jabbed a finger on the lower margin.

"Please—for God's sake—we've got to get back to the house. This is only half of it—just sign. Read it later!"

CHAPTER SEVEN
BLOOD WILL TELL

THE MINUTE they were inside the basement of the house back of Temple's, Drago said to Barry: "Run ahead and get Bryson Temple into the little drawing-room on the ground floor. Tell McTigue and your boss not to ask me any questions yet—you can tell them the case is cracked but don't say how. Got it? Then run!"

He smoked half a cigarette, before he, in turn, pounded into the back door of the Temple house, through stunned, gasping men. Every eye in the cellar followed him breathlessly as he strode across it. From the corner of his eye he caught McTigue's pleading, desperate glance. He shook his head, went up to the main hall.

Bryson Temple stood in the open door of the drawing-room, Barry beside him. There was a queer purple band across the lower half of Bryson Temple's gray forehead, as though blood were suffused there. His eyes were silver nails. There was no other sign of emotion.

Drago halted in front of him, stared solidly into his gray eyes. "It's all over, practically. It will be when I've had three minutes with you—alone."

Bryson Temple's lips curled inward. "If..." He checked himself, turned and stepped back into the drawing-room.

Drago closed the door behind him. Temple stood with one hand on the table by the window, straight, erect, rigid. His eyes had gone hollow, but his mouth was a grim, cruel slash.

Drago deliberately took off his hat, slapped it against his knee, and skimmed it across the room, hard. His brown eyes bored into Temple's gray ones. He said slowly: "It's been an experience knowing you, Mr. Temple. It's going to be even more fascinating—I think—before we're through. I've met grim guys in my time, but nothing like you. You are physically unable to understand such a thing as a mistake, aren't you?"

Bryson Temple's voice ground. "There is no such thing as a mistake. There is selfishness, stupidity, unfitness. If this is a plea for mercy—"

"No," Drago said.

HE TOOK the papers from his pocket. They faced each other—the brown man and the gray man. "I have just come from seeing a murderer die. Before he died, he signed a confession. Here it is."

Temple's eyes flickered, as the paper was slapped down by his hand. He snatched it up, raced his eyes over it—and his chin jerked in. Red flooded slowly into his face—then it became livid.

He finished it, and his little white teeth were visible between his lips as he lifted furious eyes to Drago. "You criminal fool! This is the most preposterous, foul lie I have ever seen! The needle with the curare wasn't in her clothes! The killer couldn't have known in advance which dress she was going to wear! You took care of that yourself! Every inch of her was searched. Do you think anybody is going to credit this blundering, criminal attempt to cover up your own ghastly inefficiency?"

"The newspapers will," Drago said, "if you come out flat-footed and say it is true. They might dare doubt us, in print, but not *you*."

"Doubt *me*—I have no time to waste on this mad, childish—"

"Wait a minute," Drago said quietly. "I have to ask you one question—and then I'll tell you the truth. I never said this confession was the truth. I only said I could make the papers swallow it. And—mark this in your memory—burn it in! I am the only one living that knows the real truth. When I tell you—that will be two of us. And I'll have to tell the commissioner. None of us will ever breathe a word of it—if you so elect.... Don't interrupt. I'm not wasting time. Every word of this is necessary to show you how this ghastly nightmare happened.

"You're a revengeful man." It was a question in the form of a statement.

"I am," Temple gritted, "As you will damn soon find out." His hands, at his sides, clenched and unclenched. "I am hearing you out, but understand this—I am not swayed by sentimental appeals. Whatever you think you will influence me to do—it's useless, by that means. My life has been geared too high, for years, to give in to any sickening sentimentality—"

"I know it. Here is my question. If, for the sake of argument, your wife had made a cuckold of you, with the assistance of—well, say your brother, the Lothario—would you have killed them had you discovered it?"

Temple went perfectly rigid. Only wild dilation of his nostrils gave sign of emotion. His voice was even, husky, deadly. "You will pay for that insult."

"Answer the question."

"The answer is, no."

"You would have taken a more subtle, deadly revenge than that, wouldn't you? You would have kicked them out, bag and baggage. You would have closed the door of your mind on them, when you did the door of your house. The situation they faced would have meant nothing to you—ever. The desperate position they would be in—being who they are—would never have touched you again emotionally! You are that kind of a person—aren't you, Mr. Temple?"

After a second, Temple said evenly: "If such a thing had happened, you have probably said exactly the truth. Now—"

Drago took his eyes away from the ramrod-like gray man. "It's as well you're as hard-shelled as you are—and it makes it unnecessary for us to hold back any longer the fact that you have lost your son."

IT WAS a full second before the stunning horror crashed into Bryson Temple's eyes—and the strong man's shell had cracked. He choked out hoarsely: "Peter! Good God! You mean—"

Drago's hands were flat in his pockets, his eyes blazing. "But it's nothing to get excited over." His hand went into his pocket again, took a paper from the glassine envelope. "Do you know what this is?"

Temple snatched it, flung wild eyes over it. "No! What's happened to Peter? In God's name—"

"This paper," Drago drove grimly at him, "is a blood-grouping test, made by Doctor Anton LaPlace, some years ago—of you, your brother, your wife—and your son. Pardon me. Stuart Temple's son—for that is what this test shows. *Peter is not your son—he's your brother's.* The boy can mean nothing to you—emotionally. He's an imposter—a fake—with no reasonable claim on you."

Temple leaped, grabbed the detective by the lapels. His gray face was twitching, wild. "Where is he—what's happened to him? Answer me—before I...."

Drago backed away. "Did you hear me? He's *not your son!* He's your brother's son. He's no part of your life! He ceased to mean anything to you when you saw that report."

The stockbroker's face went mad. "You maniac! Where is he? I'll kill—"

Drago fought himself free. "He's all right, physically. The police have him under guard. They're bringing him here!"

Temple stood, half numb, shaking visibly. "In God's name—what are you doing? Is he or isn't he all right?"

"Sure. But I'm telling you he isn't your son."

"Good God—I didn't ask that. That—that we can straighten out later...."

Drago's voice leaped. "Oh, no we can't! We settle it here and now. Because both these killings—your brother and your wife—were engineered to prevent that kid ever finding out the truth of whose son he was. And to prevent you finding it out and kicking him into the gutter!"

"What!"

Drago faced him across the table, leaned his brown hands on the wood and put his dark face closer to the stockbroker's. "Now I'll tell you the truth—all of it!"

His voice whipped, rushed, spilled it out. "Your brother and your wife were killed by one person—the only person that could possibly have done it—*by your wife herself!*

"I see it this way. You've been married ten years. You're business-crazy. Women have funny impulses—and most men cater to them. Not you. Not a megalomaniac like you. Well, you're not the first. Your wife got tired of it, after, apparently, three years. She let her eyes stray. Your brother—according to your own story—could get any woman he wanted. The rat wanted her—and he got her.

"She went for him. I don't know your wife as well as you do, but I'm guessing it didn't last long. What she thought was romantic at first, must have revolted her almost at once. She was too fine and straight to be able to stand it very long.

"From what I saw of her, I'd guess that she would have come clean with you—then—except that she found that it was too late—that the boy was on the scene. She had no money. She knew you. She knew exactly what you'd do. And that left the kid with a swell future—publicly branded illegitimate, the son of a worthless, rum-soaked weakling who couldn't support even himself; and a wife who'd been thrown out of your house, and who would have to face your enmity the rest of your life.

DRAGO WET his lips. "Besides, there was evidently some doubt in her mind—about the kid—because that test was made when he was two years old.

"LaPlace kept her secret—he was the family doctor. Unfortunately he had pulled something shady in Europe, and a blackmailer got hold of it, milked him dry. When he was dry, in a fit of panic at the blackmailer's continued threats of exposure, he turned this secret over to him in lieu of money. This blackmailer, Savard, was a badly wanted man. He was desperate for money himself. He tried to dicker with your wife, but she had nothing. She knew that he'd go to you. So she planned the murders.

"She put the poison capsule in your brother's medicine. She boned up enough occultism out of your books on the subject, to make the notes sound queer. She had the poisoned dart—curare, did you say it was?—ready and hidden. She went through the whole farce, staged it to the end—went through all the searching we gave her—and then calmly picked up her hidden needle—we could not possibly have foreseen that—and killed herself.

"And she did it for only one reason—because she knew that if you found out—from the blackmailer—what had happened, you'd throw them all out, and the kid would go into the gutter with them. But she figured that if no one knew but you—and she and the rat who cheated on you were dead and out of your way—some spark of life in that piece of stone you call your heart might cause you to give the kid a break—to accept him as your own son, both publicly and privately.

"She died for that. I forced the blackmailer—yes, I caught up with him—to kill himself so that there'd be no talking mouths. I've told you I am the only one living that knows the truth—except you, now. I'll have to tell the commissioner—and he'll shut up the investigation. The newspapers will swallow the extortion story—with the confession I forced from Savard, and your uncompromising endorsement to back it up. The name of Savard is sensational enough to make them lose interest in anything else. I've gone a long way to back up your wife's gesture. Wild, mad, and hare-brained as it sounds, she went about it calmly and quite bravely. It's got me, in here"—he touched his chest—"and I salute her.

"And that covers everything if you want to give the kid a chance—back my lying story. There's a certain other officer—Craven—who might make trouble. We'll cut him in on the credit. He'll take the glory and shut up. Nobody else will ask any questions. The truth will never come out. On the other hand, if you want to be even more of a heel than your wife thought you—say the word and I'll phone the whole truth to the commissioner.

"Make up your mind. Do I call the commissioner and let him give out the real truth—or do I call in the newspapers here and now and give them the lie?"

Temple collapsed in a chair. His face was ghastly. He mumbled: "God—she didn't have to do that! I'm not a monster...."

"Which?" Drago thundered.

Temple looked up, could not meet his eye. He buried his face in his hands. "Get the newspapers in here, of course, and—"

IN THE commissioner's office, Drago sat on a huge leather chair, neat, brown, shining, one of the commissioner's cigars between his fingers. "Of course, you see the joker in the whole thing."

The white-haired commissioner turned his head away. "Joker! My God!"

"An unfortunate word, maybe, but—don't you see, sir? I've got only a hazy idea of the Mendelian laws of heredity—and I'm going to take good care not to learn any more. Because the way it looks to me now—why should Bryson Temple's blood be different from his brother's? My guess—and I'll take care never to know whether or not it's right—is that they weren't real brothers. Mrs. Temple, Senior, must have had friends of her own, too."

THE CORPSE THAT DIDN'T DIE

FROM THE MOMENT THE MURRAY ARMS' DOORMAN WATCHED THAT BLOOD-CRAZY KILLER PIN DR. ERSKINE TO HIS OWN THRESHOLD LIKE A BUTTERFLY ON A COLLECTOR'S CARD, THE THREE THREADS THAT LED TO THE SOLUTION OF THE BLACK-SCARAB MYSTERY BEGAN TO TIE THEMSELVES INTO THE TIGHTEST KNOT DRAGO HAD EVER HAD TO UNRAVEL.

CHAPTER ONE
DRESSED TO KILL

IT TOOK just four minutes to happen—and Raymond Colimo saw it all. Ironically, until two minutes past midnight—which was the moment when the yellow cab lurched into the dark block—the weedy, long-nosed little doorman at the Murray Arms would have sworn he was alone in the wet, shining street. He was out on the sidewalk, away from under the lighted building canopy, and in deep shadow, himself.

The rain, after an eight-hour downpour, had just stopped, and Colimo was estimating its probable effect on Belmont Park for the second race the next day.

The street was one-way and the taxi, perforce, turned in from the corner of Lexington, came panting and grinding up the slippery, narrow roadway between the phalanx of parked cars which flanked either curb. The block—like a dozen others in the Murray Hill district—slanted at a considerable angle down from Park Avenue, two doors above, to Lexington below, and the gutters of Park were still sending streaming overflow fanning down the dark little canyon. The cab, by its sound, was having hard going.

Colimo's interest became pointed only when the cab slid to a scudding stop, directly opposite him, obviously to disembark its fare before the white sandstone house across the street. That modern, little three-story stone building, sandwiched between two larger, dark ones to allow a postage-stamp lawn, was the property of Doctor Ralph Erskine. There was a strong morbid streak in Colimo's nosy little soul; he was interested in anything that

Drago blew a blast on his
whistle, and a circle of bluecoats
closed in from the woods.

came out of a midnight taxi to enter—or preferably, be carried into—the doctor's.

THE ONLY illumination at this end of the block came from a street-lamp placed around the corner of Park. It stood, unfortunately, in such a way that it rays fell on Colimo's side of the street, rather than the doctor's. The passenger who alighted from the taxi was in deepest shadow, till he stepped up to pay the cab-driver. Then, in the glow from the hack's dashlight, Colimo was disappointed to see the familiar and distinctive wide-brimmed, black, felt hat of Doctor Erskine himself. He caught the glint of his glasses, saw the leather handle of the stick the youngish physician habitually carried, tucked under his slickered arm.

It was just then that Colimo saw the small man in dark clothes and dark peaked cap, in the roadway. He seemed to have risen up out of the dark, gleaming pavement, to stand motionless in the road, a glowing cigarette cupped in his hand, watching from just outside the line of parked cars—watching, evidently, the doctor.

Colimo blinked curiously from one to the other. From where he stood, he could see the short gray ribbon of the little fieldstone walk that bisected the doctor's minute lawn and led to his arched, oaken front door. From behind yellow blinds on the second and third stories of the white house, light glowed very faintly down.

The doctor headed for the curb as the cab rolled away. He had to pass behind a parked car to reach the walk. Colimo saw him turn into the short walk, saw him stop.

His first impression was that the doctor had doubled in size in the moment he had been behind the car. Then a quick, guttural voice said huskily, "Not a word, Doctor! Don't stop! We'll talk inside!" and it dawned on the doorman that someone had swung in behind the doctor in the dark.

Colimo's startled eyes jumped to the roadway—the slight, hunched man in the peaked cap was still exactly where he had been.

The doctor and, evidently, the man who had joined him, moved up the walk in silence, till they were in a well of intense gloom before the arched, oaken door. For just a moment, in the rim of glow from the windows above, Colimo saw that the man behind the doctor wore a gray hat. Then they became just two darker shadows against the door. There was a mumbled monosyllable, then silence while Colimo assumed the doctor was fitting his key in the lock. Then—lashing, sudden movement in the dark—a threshing arm—and a muffled, metallic *thunk!*

Colimo went cold. Without the faintest comprehension of what was happening, horror touched him.

For one flashing, split second, the gray-hatted man sprang backward into the glow, swooping with incredible speed to snatch up a fieldstone from the walk. He jumped in again, arm drawn back....

Clank! The stone hit metal. Then again—*clank* and a thudding bump.

The fieldstone dropped, rattled on the pavement in the dark as the gray-hatted man spurted out of the shadow, hunched over, and raced across the lawn to the sidewalk. He whirled up to the corner of Park and vanished.

IN THE second that Colimo stood numb, a strange fear clawing at his stomach, he saw that the small, peaked-capped man had vanished, also.

He sprang for the doorway of the Murray Arms. There was a police-alarm button set in the facade. He did not even hesitate about jamming it home.

When his eyes jerked back to the white sandstone house opposite, he saw that one of the second-floor window-blinds was held aside. In the aperture, the white-coated figure and black face of Gulliver, Doctor Erskine's Negro house servant, peered out. Colimo's eyes strained toward the dark figure that still seemed to be standing in terrible silence against the arched, oaken door. Then the plate-glass entrance of the Murray Arms bulged out behind him. He grabbed hastily at a stanchion of the canopy. Giles, the telephone operator, on whose switchboard the red signal had flashed, burst out.

"Hey, what the—"

Colimo gulped. "Something… over there… Doctor.…"

Giles' neck craned out and he searched the darkness. "Where? I don't.…" He edged out into the street hesitantly, Colimo hovering at his back.

Gulliver's face disappeared from the window above as Giles and Colimo stepped hesitantly across to the stone-bordered walk. Giles cleared his throat. "Uh—Doctor!"

The dark figure made no answer. They stood rooted.

From behind the oaken door came the sound of latches being thrown back and Gulliver's querulous voice. "Jes' a minute, ge'mmans, please! Jes' a minute.…"

The door swung inward, letting out warm light.

Colimo choked. "Mother of God!"

The Negro did not see it for a second. Then his neck arched like a cat's back and he stumbled back against the hall wall, his hands beating at his mouth, his eyes almost pure white, fixed on the body that swung like a sack of meal, to the door, pinned through the throat, with a greenish, steel dagger.

Blood was still pulsing, spurting from the slashed throat arteries, cascading up against the door. The doctor's black hat was flattened on the back of the hanging man's head.

The Negro screamed: "Doctah! Oh, dear Hebbin!"

The flattened black hat fell off.

The hair underneath was carrot-colored. To have been the doctor's it would have to have been gray-black.

Colimo choked wildly. "God! That ain't the doctor! That ain't the doctor! It's his clothes, but it ain't—"

Giles dived forward, his face livid, his eyes tightly closed, and grabbed the handle of the knife, jerked and tugged.

"No! No!" Colimo gasped. "He—he hammered it in—"

The street behind them suddenly became a funnel, into which screaming police cars poured at both ends.

THE SIMPLE facts were easily established. The killer had lain in wait, in utter concealment, in the blackness. He had waited till the victim's back was turned, then swung in behind him and forced him up the walk. He had snarled him into silence, addressing him as—and quite obviously thinking him to be—the doctor, till he was against the wooden door. One terrific and unexpected blow of the greenish steel dagger had sliced both neck arteries and windpipe, and driven the knife's point at least an inch and a half into the oak. Two blows with the fieldstone had driven it in to a depth of four inches, and hung the victim by his jawbone, while his life gushed out. The last blow with the stone had been to the victim's head, to render him unconscious and silent.

No one knew for what purpose the carrot-headed man had been impersonating the doctor. The dead man had had no chance, so swiftly had the murderer struck, either to be seen closely by, or heard speaking by, the killer. Reenactment of the ghastly drama, under Colimo's prompting, removed the last possible objections the detectives could offer to the inescapable conclusion: Whatever ghastly cross-current had caused the red-headed man to be playing the part of the physician, it was Doctor Ralph Erskine and no other whom the killer had thought he was murdering.

And—at first investigation—to cap everything else— Doctor Ralph Erskine appeared to be missing.

The questions as to whom the redheaded masquerader was—and why he had been impersonating the doctor— still remained, along with that of the identity of the creature whose attack on Erskine had resulted in the grisly death of the impostor. Was the savage method of killing the result of some terrific emotion, pathological degeneracy or insanity? Or if not, what motive could call forth such an attack on the well-liked, rising young practitioner in the first place? And—what would the murderer do when he found out the terrible mistake he had made?

All these questions blended together into one huge interrogation mark that hung quivering over the city, from the moment of the first broadcast of the sensational details. But even without them, it would have been a first-page newspaper story. For up jumped the name of General Leon.

One of the few barons of America whom publicity really infuriated, he was the vicious delight of the New York papers. Long since retired, with his thundering steel fortune, to Philadelphia, his silencing influence no longer quite reached to metropolitan city-rooms, but every last one of them remembered irritably when it had. Somehow, he had created the impression that he considered the aristocratic name of Leon a little too majestic to be bandied to the public. This, of course, was a red flag in reporters' faces, and very little excuse was more than enough to spread his name like a rash, across every newsstand in town. The general, realizing this, as far as humanly possible took precious good care that even that little was usually lacking.

But Doctor Ralph Erskine, as it happened, was engaged to be married to Margaret, only daughter of General Leon.

It was bonus day for reporters.

If the general's influence could not touch the press, it definitely could make itself felt at police headquarters. The new commissioner, a civilian, had, in some past war, served under General Leon, and was a great respecter of the arrogant little Croesus. He weighed the situation swiftly, literally within minutes of the first appearance of the news on the teletype. Without the faintest conception of the tangled, sultry web of intrigue that lay behind the horror, he issued an ill-tempered edict that the case must be closed, wiped from the books, within forty-eight hours, or every man and department-head connected with it would feel his, the commissioner's, hand.

Inasmuch as Inspector McTigue of the headquarters squad was, through no volition of his own, very directly connected, he made anxious haste to add the tactful Drago, to the investigation.

CHAPTER TWO
DOCTOR'S DILEMMA

DRAGO WALKED into the lobby of the Alameda Hotel, on lower Broadway, exactly thirty minutes later. He was plump, shortish, brown, with his round dark face shining under the brim of a soft brown hat, his eyes two sparkling chips of black agate. He walked unhurriedly, hands in the slash pockets of his belted trench-coat, toward the two elevators.

The dingy little lobby was so full of thick pillars that he could hardly see the desk, tucked away in a rear corner. Frayed rugs covered the tile floor, and the smell of stale cigar smoke mixed with the aroma of a vast array of black leather couches and armchairs. A drummer's hotel, Drago noted idly, with the staircase easily accessible from the street door obviating the formality of passing inspection at the desk en route. The same was virtually the case, in reaching the elevators. The Alameda, too far downtown to be classed as a Broadway hotel, and too far run down to be a first-class hostelry, was evidently forced to make an attraction of its broadmindedness toward guests.

But only toward guests.

When Drago stepped into the elevator cage, the mulatto operator deliberately turned back from his lever and ran dull, insolent eyes over the detective, till Drago opened a gloved hand and showed his shield.

On the fourth floor, Drago caught sight of Lieutenant Craven's giant form, immaculate in dark clothes, disappearing around the corner into a side corridor. The big homicide officer had a bulky brown-paper parcel under his arm.

Drago turned into the corridor after him, called softly. The hefty lieutenant looked back over his shoulder, then turned and stood spread-legged till Drago came up. He was red-faced, red-eyed, and the hair visible under his expensive light felt hat was carroty red. A shadow came into his eyes and he looked Drago over through narrowed lids. "Exactly what the hell," he wanted to know, "has the H.Q. squad to do with this?"

"Just to bring a couple of suggestions," Drago said. "After all, it was my boss, Inspector McTigue, that Doctor Erskine phoned to announce that he was in a jam here in his underwear."

Craven scowled. "How did he get here, anyway?"

"That's the first thing we ask him."

"Does he know the inspector?"

"Met him."

"What are these suggestions you're supposed to gimme?"

Drago hesitated. "Let me get this straight first. What did you learn at the house?"

"Nothing to learn, yet. The M.E.'s got the body. Some rum-dumb, dressed in the doctor's outfit, was killed by mistake for Erskine. A wop doorman saw it, but can't describe the killer. I thought I'd hop over here an'—"

"There was no question but that it was the doctor the murderer wanted? I mean—the rum-dumb couldn't have been killed on his own account?"

"Hell, no. Where'd you get that brainwave?"

"I'm just asking. You've been at the house. I haven't."

"Well, don't make any mistake about that. Some guy was lying in wait for Erskine, and not for anyone else. He called him 'Doctor' before he gave it to him. Even if the street's so damn dark that he couldn't have seen his face, he killed him because he had the doctor's clothes on, because he was walkin' into the doctor's house, and—because he thought he was the doctor."

"Anything to show why the rum-dumb was going into the house?"

"No. To prowl it, I figure."

"Then why all the trouble to impersonate Erskine?"

"Hell, I don't know yet! Didn't Erskine tell your boss anything on the phone to open this thing up?"

"No. Mac didn't tell him about the murder."

Craven's eyes popped. "Didn't— Why the hell not?"

DRAGO EXPLAINED. "Erskine called up a little while back and said he'd just came to, in this hotel room, in his underwear. He'd got in a jam with the house detective when he tried to put in a phone call to his home, to get some clothes. The house dick wouldn't let him make the call, and was all for calling the wagon. But he did let him call Mac. Erskine wanted Mac to identify him, and to tell the house dick that he was good for a little something that he'd promised the dick for not calling the wagon, and for keeping his mouth closed. Mac realized then that he didn't know about the murder. To keep him from calling the house and being told about it, he volunteered to get some clothes sent over himself. You'd already left for Erskine's house, so Mac got your boss to call you there and arrange it."

"What's the idea of not telling—"

"So he'll come out with the real truth—fast—if he knows it, behind his being here."

"Ye gods! With that kind of a killer walking the streets wanting to murder him, you think he's going to tell us bedtime stories?"

"He might," Drago said, "if he knew he was talking into a front-page murder case. If it's just a quiet little matter of trying to find who snatched his clothes, he'd believe that we'd keep it mum. Knowing it was murder, he wouldn't believe we could keep anything mum. And rather than make one extra inch of newspaper space, I think he'd close up like a clam."

"If he does, he's asking for what the rum-dumb got. If we don't nail this butcher and trail him quick, he's going to be taking another crack at—"

"Even so," Drago cut in, "Erskine might prefer to take his chances. Let me get to my point—which is General Leon. Do you know about that angle?"

Craven grunted. "The doc's engaged to his daughter and the general don't like his name in the papers. Yeah."

"You haven't quite got it. The old man is a maniac on the subject. His daughter the same one that Erskine's engaged to—was engaged to a Spanish count a year ago. The count didn't have any money and that made good copy for the papers. Not much though, because the general stopped it. He stopped it by turning off the Spaniard and washing up the engagement."

"So?"

"So Erskine faces the same thing, if there's too much noise about him. And if he's got an enemy that he suspects might want to kill him like this, it isn't going to be any cheap criminal. From what I hear, he's a clever doctor and a clean liver, a pretty fair sort. If he has an enemy of that kind there's bound to be juicy newspaper copy behind it. Rather than risk losing his girl by disclosing it, he might let us stew in our own juice,"

Craven thumbed his red jaw, frowned down at the hall carpet. He looked up suddenly. "Hey-maybe he'd talk more freely if he didn't know there was any murder!"

Drago nodded slowly. "You've got an idea there. Incidentally, my orders are to spare him every possible line of publicity."

"So are mine."

"Tell him that"

The house detective opened the room door. He was a thin, red-faced turkey of a man with boiled blue eyes. He ran a finger ingratiatingly inside his gates-ajar collar and smiled with wide, thin lips. He was plainly nervous. "E-everything O.K. boys?"

They strolled by him without answering, into the cheap bare hotel room, done in green and muddy taupe. Nothing seemed out of place save a tumbler with a dry whitish residue in the bottom, now on the carpet by the bed.

Doctor Erskine stood up from the shabby counterpane to meet them.

HE WAS pale, but completely poised. Forty or less, Drago guessed. Clean-looking, lean, with high temples and a little gray along the sides of his dark hair. Fine breeding showed in the lines of his face, and in his steady, somber gray eyes. Even in his underclothing, with a sleazy hotel blanket draped on his shoulders, he had dignity. There was a red welt over his right ear.

Craven fastened a companionable smile on his red face, went over and dumped his parcel on the bed. "Everything to a clean hanky, Doc," he said. "Now tell us all about it."

Erskine blinked a little anxiously, his gray eyes on the sergeant's red ones. "I—really, I don't wish to enter a complaint, officer. I'm very grateful to you and this other gentleman for bringing my clothes, and if you'll give me your names, I'll show my appreciation properly when I reach home. But I—well, I'm sure, if you would speak to Inspector McTigue—"

"That's all right, Doc," Craven said heartily. "We understand the whole situation. The inspector told us to go all the way in keeping this thing confidential, so you needn't worry about that. I—"

He broke off and turned to the house detective. "You can ramble, Malloy—and if you open your yap, I'll braid your ears."

The house detective flushed, went out.

"Now, Doc?"

Erskine's forehead V'd. "Really, sir—I prefer to say no more about it. My only wish is to dress and leave this place as quickly as possible. Please call the inspector and—"

Drago's quiet voice flowed in smoothly. "We ought to know what happened, Doctor Erskine. Otherwise, it might be very uncomfortable for everyone. You can trust our discretion to the limit. I happen to be Inspector McTigue's assistant. I was sitting beside him when your call came in. We appreciate the delicacy of the whole matter, including the situation between yourself, Miss Leon, and the general. I think you will find that we'll handle it to your satisfaction. But we have to know what happened."

The doctor sat down slowly on the bed, accepted a cigarette from Craven, looked anxiously from one of them to the other.

"There's really very little to—to tell," he said finally. "You know that I am engaged to be married. At ten-thirty or so tonight, a man's voice phoned me, giving the name of Sam Wells. He claimed to have known me when I was at school at McGill University. I had no recollection of him whatever, but he mentioned—well, convincing incidents and that sort of thing. He told me that my fiancée was in danger from a former friend, and offered to provide me with the means of protecting her.

"He would not come to my house, nor discuss it further over the telephone. He asked me to meet him in my car, at a street corner just below here. I did so, and he urged me to come to this hotel, to see certain documents. He induced me to walk up three flights of stairs, because he said he was behind in his room rent and did not want to be seen by the employees. He led me to this room and, the minute I was inside, hit me from behind, rendering me unconscious for a few minutes.

"When I regained my senses, he had stripped me of my clothes and was wearing them himself. He was standing over me with a revolver wrapped in a bath towel. He offered to shoot me, claiming that the towel would muffle the report, unless I drank the glass of liquid he offered me. I drank it. It contained chloral hydrate. There is the glass.

"He then told me that we had entered this room illegally—with a skeleton key—that the room was unoccupied, as far as the management knew. He pointed out that, should I attempt to use the telephone, I could not help getting embroiled with the management, which, at the very least, would make a ludicrous story for the newspapers. If you know the extraordinary situation in which I am placed, you know that I cannot afford that. He promised to return before midnight and return my clothes. He—well, he didn't return. I waited till after midnight, and, in desperation, tried to call my house. I could not get the switchboard girl to put the call through, and—well, Mr. Malloy, the house detective, came up, and the rest you know."

"When you saw this Sam Wells, did you recognize him?"

"No."

"Did he continue to pretend he was Sam Wells, your old college chum?"

"He—as a matter of fact, he didn't say any more about it."

"You realize that he took your clothes for the purpose of impersonating you, don't you?"

THE DOCTOR looked concerned. "Why—he didn't resemble me in the slightest. His figure was about the same as mine, but he was a very dissipated-looking man, with little deep-sunk eyes that looked—well, humorous and evil at the same time, if you know what I mean. And he had very red hair. He—but I can't see how he could expect to impersonate me."

"He even took your spectacles," Craven pointed out. "That's the clincher. Can't you think of any object he might achieve by passing himself off as you—say, at a distance, at night?"

Erskine's fine forehead furrowed. "Really, I can't."

Craven took a thoughtful turn up and down the room, planted himself again, frowning. "Doc, I don't want to alarm you, but this sounds like a scheme—or part of a scheme."

Erskine's worried gray eyes came up. "A scheme?"

"Yeah. Say you have an enemy that wants to rig you into some sort of trouble. Say that Sam Wells is working for him, maybe. The way he worked doesn't sound like any joke to me. You may wake up and find they've jockeyed you into somethin' damn serious. Now who do you know that might want to make things unpleasant for you—say somebody that really hates you? Name me one or two."

Erskine's eyes were aghast. "I—I can't. I don't know anyone."

Craven massaged his jaw vigorously. "Well, let's tackle it from another angle. Nothin' personal, y'understand, Doc, but—I got to ask you this. You weren't maybe drinkin' a little tonight, were you?"

The doctor's forehead flushed. "I haven't had a drink in fourteen years, if it's any of your bus—"

"Hell, I got to ask," Craven said hastily. "No offense. Another thing—what is there in your house of great value?"

"Why—nothing. Medical equipment and instruments, but they would hardly—"

"No big sums of cash? Jewelry? Securities? Documents that might be worth something—either to you or somebody else?"

"No. No. Nothing of the sort. Please—don't bother about this any more. I—"

"How about drugs?"

"I have practically no drugs. Really, you are wasting your effort. There is nothing worth stealing in my house. No thief would find it worth his while even to walk in an open door, much less engineer a scheme like this to gain entry."

"Well," Craven said, "this one did."

Erskine's head snapped up. He stood up swiftly. "Did! You mean you caught him?"

Craven turned his head, rolled his red eyes to Drago's. Drago nodded slightly.

"We didn't catch him," Craven said. "But somebody else did. The fact is, Doc—just about the time you were coming out of your drug here, this man in your clothes was murdered. He was murdered in front of your house as he tried to get in. And he was murdered by a man who thought it was you he was killing!"

Erskine's face went gray. "You—you—is this true?"

"Just as true as that he's lying in your house now, waiting for you to identify him before we shift him to the morgue."

"Who—who killed him?"

CRAVEN'S RED face was intent now. "You tell me! It amounts to this: Who hates you enough, or has reason enough—to want to kill you?"

Erskine gasped. "Why—nobody."

"Wrong answer! Understand this, Doc—somebody tried to kill you tonight! And it wasn't a pretty death he picked out for you. That somebody got away. To protect yourself, you've got to help us find him—fast. You know who your enemies are! Tell us their names. We'll dig up which of them did it, dig up the evidence and close the case. That'll leave the newspapers holding their necks. Mr. Drago and me'll tell them nothing."

Erskine said desperately. "I know of no one—no one at all that would—"

"How about this count—Count—"

"Lilli? That's absurd. He's a splendid chap. Great heavens! His engagement to Margaret was just the usual thing—his title and her money. They weren't in love with each other. When it was broken off, neither of them got emotional about it. And certainly there's no animosity between Lilli and myself. We're all friends together, so to speak—he and Margaret and myself. He squires her around when I'm not available. Even to consider him as wanting to do me injury is—well, he's the very last person that merits your suspicion!"

"Who's the very first?"

"I tell you I don't know!"

Craven's red face was flushed, his eyes hot. "Doc, you don't seem to realize that a killer's marked you down—a mean killer. We can protect you only so far, unless we know who to protect you from."

Erskine nursed his hands, his eyes wide on the rug. "I—I do realize it—now. It must be as you say. But I know no more than you!"

Craven blew out breath. "All right," he said grimly. "Get dressed as quickly as you can and we'll go down to your house. We're holding things up."

Drago pushed himself up from the writing-table against which he had been leaning, strolled over to the room's one window. "How was this Sam Wells dressed when you picked him up, Doctor Erskine?"

"I—I really didn't notice closely, except that he looked shabby. Dark clothes—yes, a dark overcoat, I think, at any rate—and a dark gray hat, I believe."

"When he put your clothes on, what did he do with his own?"

"I—I don't know."

Drago examined the windowsill, shot the window up, put his head and shoulders out. He was there for nearly two minutes. Then he drew back in and asked Craven: "Have you a torch, Jack?"

Craven whipped a powerful flashlight from his overcoat pocket, crowded in beside Drago at the window. "What...?"

"Just an idea. A whole outfit of clothes is a bulky parcel to sneak out with," Drago said. "I was wondering—"

Craven sent the powerful beam downward. He uttered a startled exclamation. They were looking down on the roof of a store that fronted on the side street. It was a square, one-story building, from the front of which red neon light glowed up. On the roof of the building were sprawled dark shapes.

THE OWNER of the delicatessen store held the ladder while Drago followed Craven up to the roof of the store five minutes later. The ladder creaked and swayed under the homicide giant's weight. As he swung himself over the top, his flash beam swept the roof.

"They're here all right—the whole works—even shoes. He must have thrown them out in a ball."

He was going through a pair of trousers as Drago climbed from the ladder. He grunted in disappointment, dropped the trousers and stepped toward a coat and vest. Drago picked up the shiny blue serge trousers.

He struck pay dirt almost at once. Even through the tan gloves that covered his short fingers, he could feel a tiny, soft, cylindrical lump somewhere in the garment. Puzzled, he searched the pockets without success, till he realized that the trousers had that rare feature—a second watch pocket, on the left-hip, side. He fingered out the small cylinder from that pocket. As nearly as he could make out without attracting Craven's attention, he had a calling card with a few lines of spidery writing on it, rolled up tightly. He kept it in his gloved hand, put his hands again in the slash pockets of his belted trench coat.

Presently Craven stood up and kicked the heap of garments. "He cut all the labels and emptied the pockets, damn him."

Craven carried the clothes back to the hotel with him. As they entered the lobby, Malloy was hanging far back in the rear, eyeing them through the forest of pillars. Craven waved him up, and said to Drago: "I want to tell this keyhole-peeper exactly where he stands. You go get the doc and we'll take a cab down to his place. Or, come to think of it, the doc must have his car around here somewhere."

On the way up to the room, Drago had a chance to examine his rolled-up card. It bore no printing, but the handwriting, in faded ink, read—

Monette Moreau
19 St. Hyacinthe St.
Chapeau Falla, P.Q.
1922

Lying back in the tonneau of the doctor's sedan as they sped across town, Drago tried to find a hypothesis that would admit this unknown French girl to the picture, but gave it up when they came suddenly abreast of a Western Union branch office. He called abruptly: "Doctor—stop here a minute!"

When the car pulled to the curb, he asked: "What's your telephone number?"

"I have two—a private one and a listed one."

"The private one?"

Erskine gave it to him and Drago went into the telegraph office, put the rolled cylinder flat on the counter and asked the shirt-sleeved, gawky youth behind the counter: "Have you any idea where this address is?"

The youth adjusted his spectacles, consulted a book, and finally said: "P.Q. means Quebec. Chapeau Falls—sure. We got a correspondent office there. You want to send a message?"

"Yes. A rush."

He sent a wire to the chief of police at Chapeau Falls, Quebec, asking him to phone Drago at the number the doctor had supplied. He asked for any information available about a Monette Moreau, who lived—or had lived there, in 1922 perhaps. He signed the message with his name and shield number.

Then he sent a second wire—this one to the chief of police in Montreal, asking for any information in the files about Sam Wells. It was this second wire, only, that he mentioned to Craven as they drove southward again.

When they were three blocks from the doctor's house, Drago suggested: "Why not park at the next available space and walk the rest of the way? If you draw up in this car, there'll be no chance to avoid reporters."

They parked two blocks away, walked wet, slick sidewalks, till they rounded the corner into the still considerable crowd in front of the doctor's white, sandstone house. They breasted clamoring reporters, in silence.

CHAPTER THREE
THE SCARAB RING

IT WAS a neat, small house, done in dark-paneled wood within. The ground floor was a narrow hall that ran straight through to the rear, with rooms opening off its left wall. The rooms, in succession, were the doctor's waiting-room, office, dispensary and surgery.

The slim young Italian who admitted them at the front door was Barry, of Craven's homicide squad. He announced: "Hey—we got the dead man identified, chief."

"Hold it for a minute," Drago cautioned.

"Maybe we have, too."

They went down the hall to the last door, where detectives and photographers were wandering in and out. Craven led the way into the gleaming white surgery.

The M.E.'s man was still there, in short-sleeves, smoking a cigarette over the body. It was laid out on an operating-table, a towel draped across the torn throat. The M.E.'s doctor said: "A damned lucky stroke, in my opinion. It slashed the windpipe and the arteries together. The man literally drowned in his own blood."

Erskine took one gaunt look at the redheaded, lumpy-faced dead man, and said: "That's Sam Wells."

As they started out again, Drago asked Erskine: "Where is this private phone?"

"Upstairs in my library."

"Hey, wait!" Craven suddenly checked himself. "I want the doctor to see the stuff that was in his pockets. Maybe there's something there that wasn't the doc's—something we can go to work on."

"Let's get out of this madhouse," Drago suggested. "Why not round the things up and bring them to the library upstairs."

"Well, O.K."

As Drago and Erskine swung round the foot of the stairs by the front door, they compared notes with Barry. The Italian told them: "Name of Sam Wells. He was jugged in connection with a racing-tip fraud a year ago, on the Coast—a post-office rap, but he wriggled out of it."

The second floor of the house had a hall identical to the one downstairs. Opening off it were in succession, two large, high-ceilinged rooms, tastefully and quietly furnished in Colonial style, with the cream walls necessary for light. The rooms were respectively, the living-room and dining room. Behind the dining-room was the kitchen. The end of the dining-room—a third of it—had been walled off and turned into a library. This was a tiny, book-lined retreat, with a flat-topped, red-leather-covered desk and three wing chairs, also done in scarlet leather, to contrast with the black rug. Erskine snapped on a green-shaded desk lamp and dropped into a chair, wiping his face with a handkerchief. Drago was no more than inside the room, when the phone on the edge of the desk rang.

Erskine started, reached for it, but Drago said: "That may be mine," and took the instrument.

The operator said: "A long-distance call from Chapeau Falls, Quebec, for Mr. Drago."

"This is Mr. Drago."

A VOLATILE, Gallic voice came on the wire, obviously the French chief of police of Chapeau Falls. He spoke perfect English, but with a strong intonation. After elaborate greetings, he said: "I have just received your wire about Monette Moreau. What do you wish to know, exactly?"

Drago sat down at the desk, produced a notebook and pencil. "Everything you can give me," he said.

The Frenchman drew a long breath and rattled off: "She was born in this town. She has four brothers and eight sisters, still living here—*habitatants*—farmers. In Nineteen twenty-two she was on our list of missing persons for a while. She left home unexpectedly and without notifying anyone. We found that she had bought a railway ticket to Greenville, Maine.

"We tried to trace her. We thought she might have run away with some—man. We even notified the Maine police, to see if their Mann Act might be involved. But we found no trace of her. She has never been back to Chapeau Falls, but her mother received a letter from her, three years later from Paris, France. We removed her from our list and that is the last we have heard of her. May I ask you what inspires your query?"

"The name cropped up here in rather a big murder case."

"Mon Dieu! You would wish, perhaps, that I cable my colleagues in Paris? There might be further word there."

"I'd appreciate it a lot. It may be very important."

"I can reach you at this number all night?"

"I'm not sure. It would be safer to call me at headquarters. If I'm not there, the message will be relayed."

"It shall be done. Would you care for a description of the girl?"

When he had noted that down, Drago said: "There is just one other thing. Did you ever have anything on a man named Sam Wells?"

After reflection, the French police chief decided not. Drago thanked him and hung up.

He studied the notes he had made, asked Erskine: "Do you know where Greenville, Maine, is?"

The doctor nodded. "Yes. I have never been there, but it is about two hundred miles from my home town, Marlborough, also in Maine."

"Do you think Sam Wells could have come from Greenville?"

Erskine looked anxious. "I'm sure I don't know. I—I don't know anything about him."

"Excuse me. I meant, in reminding you of incidents connected with your schooldays, did he give any intimation that would connect him with Greenville?"

"No. The allusions he made were only connected with Montreal. McGill University is in Montreal, you understand."

Drago fingered his smooth, round chin. "You're absolutely sure you don't remember him—I mean, remember him as an acquaintance of that time?"

The doctor shook his head. "I'm sorry.

I don't."

"Did you ever hear of a person named Monette Moreau?"

The lean doctor's gray eyes were mystified. "No. I don't believe I ever heard the name. I presume you mean, in Montreal?"

"Or a place called Chapeau Falls. She seems to have some connection with Sam Wells."

"Where is Chapeau Falls?"

Drago said, "Skip it," hastily, and restored the notebook to his pocket as the door swept open to admit the red-faced Craven.

Craven kicked the door to behind him, stepped to the desk and set down a shoe box. "Just take a look at these, Doc, and point out anything that wasn't in your pockets when you lost the suit."

WALLET, KEYS, handkerchiefs, cigar-case, change, a cigar-lighter, and a folder of cards and licenses—the usual contents of a man's pockets were in the box, gruesomely spattered with purple bloodstains. Erskine's anxious eyes dwelt on them for a considerable time before he said with finality: "Not only is everything mine but, as near as I can tell, nothing is missing, either."

"Ah," said Craven, "but how about *this?*" He opened his big, red, clenched hand suddenly and displayed a small gold ring, set with a black scarab.

Erskine reacted as though he had received a blow in the solar plexus. His breath went out in a gasp and his eyes were white-rimmed. His throat worked. "That—that's not mine," he said hoarsely.

"But you've seen it before, eh?"

"No. No. I never saw it before."

Craven grunted. "Your face tells a different story, Doc."

Erskine ran a finger inside his collar, stared obliquely at the ring with hot eyes. "I—I once knew a man that had one like it. That's—all."

Drago took the ring from Craven's big palm. He slipped the glove from his short, brown, left hand, as he examined the ring closely under the light. He tried to slip it on his little finger. It barely could be squeezed on the extreme tip.

"It's a woman's ring," Drago said.

"Ha!" Craven rubbed his red hands together. "Now we're getting somewhere!"

He towered over Erskine, fists on hips. "What woman's, doctor? We'll have to know—confidentially."

Erskine was hunched over in the chair, looking at his palms. He got up and walked the length of the room twice. He finally faced them with his hands clasped behind him. His face was gray. "I—I gave that ring to a young woman who cannot possibly have any connection with this."

"Well, it was found on the edge of your walk, just now," Craven said bluntly. "At the very least, she'll have to explain how the ring got away from her."

Erskine's forehead was thinly beaded. "Lieutenant—it is impossible that she could be involved in this. I—I cannot give you her name—tell you anything about her."

"You mean you won't!"

Drago said soothingly: "Be intelligent about this, Doctor. It's nothing to us how many private friends you have. We'll have to get in touch with this lady. We're not going to let the press in on what we find, of course, no matter what the situation may be between you and her—"

"There isn't any! Gentlemen, I give you my word—that was all over months ago."

"We believe you. But we still have to see her, anyway. We'll have to trace that ring. It's the only breath of a lead we've got, so far. But no one will even know we talked to her. We'll make absolutely certain that no one sees us make the visit. We'll shield her completely—unless she's actually guiltily involved. If she's one of those who are trying to kill you, you'd hardly want to protect her—would you?"

"My God—she's just a child. You don't know how insane such a supposition is!"

"We will," Craven promised, "after we've seen her. What's her name?"

"Renée Laverne."

"A French girl?"

"No. She—she is a Gypsy."

"A Gypsy! What was she doing in this country?"

THE DOCTOR looked sheepish. "She—was hoping to get employment as an entertainer. She had just come to New York when I met her. She fell on the icy pavement outside my office, and tore a ligament in her wrist. She came here for treatment. I took her home. I called on her—after that."

"And?"

Erskine nursed his hands. "It—just wore out. She felt the same way I did. She was a charming, honest child. We parted the best of friends. I forced—yes, that is the word—forced her to let me help a little financially."

"Can you describe her for us?" Drago asked.

"She was very dark, with black hair. She was small—really very small—small-boned, though she was—well, I guess you'd say, well-rounded. She had dark eyes, of course—long lashes. Her ankles and wrists were very small. She was a lovely picture, Mr. Drago—very young."

"How tall—as close as you can make it?"

"Certainly not more than an inch over five feet, if that."

Drago felt a blank feeling. The natural idea that had sprung into his mind, that the Monette Moreau of 1922 was the Renée Laverne of 1936, collapsed completely. For the description of Monette Moreau in his inside pocket, gave her height as five feet six inches. She could hardly have shrunk five inches in the interim. They were two separate and distinct girls.

And it was here that he realized there were two separate, distinct, and apparently unrelated threads to the inquiry. One led from Monette Moreau and Sam Wells; the other from this Gypsy and the scarab ring.

"When did you give this Miss Laverne the scarab ring?" Drago asked.

"Early—early in the time that we were friends."

"Don't be too delicate at a time like this.

You don't mean friends, do you?"

Erskine flushed. "No."

Drago held the ring under the light again. "May I ask where you got this ring?"

"Where? In one of the curio shops around Sixth Avenue."

"How much did you pay?"

"My Lord, it's years ago. I don't remember exactly. Maybe twenty dollars, maybe less."

Drago's jet-black eyes were merry and friendly. "You're a liar, Doctor. This is a genuine Antibes scarab, and it's worth thousands." Erskine's face went dead white and his chin came up. "That may be so. I got it, nevertheless, exactly as I said."

There was a sudden light tapping at the door. Craven reached over and yanked it open.

Barry, the slim Italian detective, said, "Headquarters on the wire downstairs, chief," then added, "Important."

Craven hesitated, scowling, got up. "Hold this till I get back," he told Drago, and went out.

CHAPTER FOUR
THE THIRD GHOUL

WHEN THE door closed, Drago said rapidly: "There's one less to hear it, if you want to tell it now, Doctor. No—don't repeat what you just said. I dislike to threaten anyone, least of all a man like yourself. But you've told us too much now to hold anything back. We're trying to keep you from being killed. We're on your side. If you are killed, it's professional disgrace for us, and we don't want any. Rather than let you hamper us—me, I should say—I'll turn up all you've told us, and make public the fact that you won't cooperate, with the reasons. I mean that. If you want to die, go and shoot yourself in the bathroom. We're not working for you, remember. We're trying to save you from being murdered, and the city pays us for it. I won't stand for you, or anyone else, hindering us by keeping secrets. We've so wretched little to go on that the slightest clue looks like the breath of life right now. You've got about three minutes left. Don't waste time. Get it out. And don't try to lie any more. You don't seem to be much good at it. Now—what's the secret behind that ring—quickly!"

Erskine sat down and held his head in his hands. "In God's name," he croaked, "what kind of Pandora's box have I opened?"

"Murder usually works that way. When it lifts the lid, all sorts of things swarm out.... I'm waiting."

Erskine raised his haggard face. "Mr. Drago, it has to do with a madness twenty years ago. But—but it could ruin me not only with Margaret but in the profession. You've got to swear never to reveal it. It—*this,* at least—has no bearing on what happened tonight."

"You don't seem to think anything has. But go ahead—unless you want to wait till Mr. Craven—"

"No. No."

"I was in medical school at McGill. One of our classmates—an Egyptian boy—died. I—we—did quite a lot of drinking. We—myself and two others of my class—were drinking heavily, a night or two after Joel died and had been buried. We—it sounds insane, Mr. Drago, but I think all medical students *are* insane—we convinced ourselves that the attending physician had diagnosed the cause of Joel's death erroneously. He was a small man—a tiny man, you might say. That ring which you claimed was a woman's, did, in all truth, come from Joel's finger."

"Wait a minute," Drago said incredulously. "You mean you—dug him up?" Erskine nodded stiffly, his eyes on the floor. "As I say, we were drinking heavily. Someone suggested that we exhume the body and perform our own post-mortem. We—we did just that.

"It was nearly dawn when he finished it, and we were coming to our senses by then. We were afraid to take the risk of reinterring the body. We cremated it, in—"

Drago jumped in his chair. "You what!"

"We—we had to dispose of the body, so we cremated it in an electrical furnace in the chemical laboratory. I—I kept that ring as a souvenir."

"My God! Didn't you ever hear— Never mind—excuse me. Did anyone ever find out what you'd done?"

"I'm sure no living person knows. The other two students were killed in a train wreck, some years ago. Joel's family were wealthy but illiterate people—desert folk. He had met some white man in the desert—a doctor—and became obsessed with the idea of coming to Canada and getting a medical education. His family wouldn't listen to him. He stole some valuable jewels from them, and ran away. The jewels, of course—this ring was one he hadn't cashed in on—paid his tuition. But he had cut himself completely off from his family. They would probably never even hear that he was dead, and certainly they weren't likely to have sent for his body. There was no other way as far as we—"

"This train wreck that killed your fellow students. Exactly what happened?"

ERSKINE LOOKED down at his hands. "It was a ghastly accident. They—they were pinned underneath burning wreckage, and—well, they couldn't get them out."

Drago coughed quickly, as the room vibrated to heavy footsteps outside. "I'll not tell Mr. Craven about that," he said. "Now—about this gypsy girl. You didn't give us her address."

"I—I don't know the number exactly," Erskine stammered. "I could point it out if I saw the house. It's down in Greenwich Village—on Morton Street—"

The door of the room swept open as he was saying the last of it. Craven began gustily, "Well, things are beginning to open up. We..." and stopped. He turned a puzzled red face to Erskine. "What were you saying about Morton Street?"

Drago answered. "This Gypsy girl, Renée Laverne, lives on Morton Street, in the Village."

Craven looked at the slip in his red hand. "Good God! What number?"

"He doesn't recall the number, but he can point out the house."

"Sam Wells lived at Number Seventeen-A, Morton Street!" Craven crowed. "Doc, you'll have to come with us and see if it's the same house the jane lived in!"

Erskine blinked. "Now?"

"Now? Of course, now! We don't ever waste minutes in murder cases. Hell, I was beginning to think there was never going to be anything to get my teeth in on this job. If that cheap tout and this Gypsy jane were living together— Well, come on! What are we waiting for?"

Erskine began desperately: "Lieutenant, I shall have to ask you not to refer to Miss Laverne in that manner. And as far as going down there now—with the reporters hanging around the front door, as they are—" He choked. "You— you promised to make a secret call on Miss Laverne, if you made any. You promised no reporter would know about it. Now you propose this!"

"Well—" Craven scowled, rubbed his red chin.

Barry knocked again at the door. "Inspector McTigue is downstairs," he told Drago. "He doesn't want to disturb anything, but he'd like to see you if you've got a minute."

"I'll be right down," Drago said, and got up from the swivel chair. "As far as ducking the reporters to go down to Morton Street, I think we can leave by the rear and get through the building behind here. That will let us out on the next street above, without being seen."

"Exactly!" Craven echoed. "That's the ticket! And if the reporters haven't discovered the doc's car, well use that, so not even a hack-driver'll know our business!"

"I'll be just a few minutes," Drago said. "I'll meet you at the car."

MCTIGUE'S LONG Irish face and shining bald head gleamed in the light of Erskine's office downstairs as Drago came in. The grizzled old inspector's china-blue eyes were worried. "Anything yet?" he asked. "I was just knocking off, and I thought I'd run by. Not that I—well, you know—we're all worried a bit about this one."

Drago's black eyes were clouded. "That includes me, chief," he said. "Listen to this."

He told him of the scarab ring, and of the Egyptian medical student whom Erskine and his classmates had dug up in Montreal, twenty years ago.

McTigue looked at him in consternation. "Well, it was a mad thing to do, but I don't understand why it worries you. I don't see any connection with this present situation—"

"The scarab ring is the connection. It was found out here on the walk—presumably dropped by the murderer. Erskine gave it away some time ago. Certain people might have traced Erskine by that ring—or they might have been inspired because somebody else saw that ring—to dig up the whole ugly business of the Egyptian boy."

"Wait a minute. You mean that friends or relatives of the boy himself might have, one way or another, found out what happened to him, and be waging some sort of campaign of revenge against Erskine?"

"Possibly something like that."

"Keep your feet on the ground, man. After twenty years, you mean to say that—"

"I don't mean to say anything, chief. Except that it's a possibility. As far as the lapse of time goes, it might conceivably take twenty years for the kind of people the Egyptian boy's were, to find out the truth and locate Erskine."

"Even so! Concede that. Concede that, in some way, the ring that Erskine gave away, furnished the line that would lead these desert people to him. Don't you see what you're building on? Revenge! Revenge for what? Erskine didn't do anything, certainly, to merit the kind of death that somebody tried to hand him here tonight. It isn't as though he killed the Egyptian boy."

"No, it isn't," Drago said slowly. "It's infinitely worse. That is—it is if what Erskine said was true—that these people are desert folk, illiterate. If they are, then what Erskine did was the most ghastly offense he could have committed."

"What do you mean—digging the boy up?"

"No. Cremating him."

"My God! What are you talking about?"

"Mac—they're waiting for me to go downtown. I'll try to explain it to you, quickly. If the Egyptian family of that student were desert people, they were more than likely believers in the old Hermetic religion."

McTigue blinked anxiously. "The—the what?"

DRAGO LEANED forward. "It was the religion in Egypt before Christianity. I won't go into it deeply, Mac— but believe every word I say. They believed in reincarnation. They believed that when a soul left a body, the soul went to a state of—well, heaven. The soul stayed there for a certain time, in an exalted state of happiness. The body, meanwhile, decayed and, in due course, evaporated, went back to a sort of cosmic reservoir of matter. However, it did not stay there. In the course of some fifteen hundred years, the matter of the body would come out of that reservoir and draw together again. When the body was ready, the soul was jerked out of its heavenly state and forced to come back and inhabit the body. Inasmuch as the Egyptians called—and believed—this world to be hell, you can understand that the last thing they wanted was to reincarnate.

"That is why they invented the process of mummifying a body. The assumption was that, if the vital organs were removed and the body thus made incapable of sustaining life, and then the body matter were frozen, so to speak, where it was, the soul would be free to stay in heaven. Don't tell me it's fantastic. I know that as well as you do. The fact remains that it was part of their religion. They believed it, as utterly and completely as you believe that I'm standing here. Even the poorest beggars were given some sort of mummification—anything to prolong the time they could avoid coming back to this earth.

"That's why curses are promised, on Egyptian tombs, to anyone who opens them, and thus lets the body inside decay and get back into the stream of life. Get it into your head, Mac—Egyptian people worked and slaved all their lives to get enough money together to have the best mummifying process performed on their bodies when they died. It was everything to them—their whole existence was a feverish striving to arrange so that when they got out of this world they could stay out as long as possible. And get this, too—criminals and outcasts—people who had committed the vilest crimes in the calendar—were sentenced to be cremated, because cremation was the fastest known way to send the body back on the path to reincarnation!

"Now, in the light of that, add up the possibilities. Erskine cremated the body of the Egyptian boy. The person who tried to kill Erskine tonight was driven by some sort of frenzy—otherwise he couldn't have done the thing he did. I don't say the answer is inevitable. It isn't. But, by Judas, chief—it can't be ignored as a possibility."

McTigue mopped his head. "I—it's the craziest thing I ever heard."

"Crazy or not, if we are up against the relatives of this student, we're facing a fury that you and I couldn't understand except in terms of religious fanaticism. In other words, reasonable considerations won't stop them. And if they do get Erskine—"

"Hell, surely the New York Police Department can protect him against a mob of Egyptian hill-billies."

"I hope we can."

"Drago! For God's sake, snap out of it. You act as if—"

"I don't like it, chief—and that's a fact. But probably this is all fancy. There are a couple of other possibilities just as good. We're on the way to look one over now. I'll try and give you a full report in the morning. Do you mind if I don't go into it any more right now? Craven is just as likely to run off without me, if the idea ever struck his thick head."

McTigue nodded. "All right, but—well, the thing's in your hands. Run it your own way."

"Thanks," Drago said.

CHAPTER FIVE
THE DOUGH IN THE
DOPE-SHEETS

IN THE tonneau of Erskine's car once more, as it rolled downtown, Drago's eyes were sharp, alert, on the road behind and ahead, alternately. Certainly, by now, the savage murderer, whoever he was, must be aware that his attempt to kill Erskine had miscarried. Was his urge to kill strong enough to make him strike again—at once—in spite of the obvious police surveillance around the doctor? Drago wondered.

There was no answer to that, until he could put his finger definitely on the motive that drove the killer. And now there were three threads instead of two, to any one of which the motive might be tied. There was the thread from which hung Sam Wells and Monette Moreau—certainly a bare one so far. The one on which were strung the black scarab ring and the Gypsy girl. And finally, grimmest of all, this new thread—the Egyptian one—pointing to a group of religious maniacs.

Drago threw the alternatives around in his speeding brain. Could two of the threads be combined into one? Would the present visit establish any contact between Sam Wells and Renée Laverne? Somehow, Drago was reluctant to believe so. He was not so reluctant to believe that Renée Laverne, self-styled Gypsy, with a French name, might, in truth be an Egyptian. In fact, he was eager to believe that. Unfortunately, there was not yet a shred of evidence to support such a theory. The three threads were as yet, completely separate.

They turned into narrow, crooked little Morton Street and Craven said hastily to Erskine: "Easy. Maybe we better leave your car here. We don't want to frighten her."

"My car won't frighten her," Erskine said bitterly.

"Well, don't stop as we go past, anyway. Point out her place and then go down and turn the next corner."

By the time they were safely around the next corner and parked at the curb, Craven was jubilant. "It's the same house, all right! The one you pointed out as the jane's is Seventeen-A! Now we'll have a little talk with Miss Laverne."

"You'll let me come up with you?" Erskine asked.

"Sure, if you promise not to butt in. Drive up to the patrol box on the next corner."

Erskine, his hand on the clutch, stiffened. "Patrol box!"

"Sure. I got to get a couple men from the precinct and sew the place up before we go in! Get going!"

Erskine made no move. His teeth clicked in the darkness. "Sergeant, you gave your word that no one but you and Mr. Drago would know so much as Miss Laverne's name."

Craven cleared his throat. "Now, Doc—you don't know this work like we do—"

"I know that you don't need any squad of police to surround the house. If you're afraid she'll escape, or some such madness, Mr. Drago can watch in front while we go up. Her apartment is on the second floor, in the front. There is no way she could escape except through a window and down the fire-escape in front. My God! Isn't it bad enough, breaking in on her at three in the morning, without treating her as though she were a criminal?"

Craven rubbed his red jaw, threw a sidelong glance at Drago. "You still seem to be pretty sweet on this twist," he told Erskine.

Erskine flushed, said nothing.

"All right," Craven said. "Go around the block and park in front of the house."

IT WAS a shabby square gray-brick building, in total darkness, save for a dim light behind the frosted glass of the front door. The whole narrow street was dark, but a street lamp at a distant corner gave just enough light for Drago to be sure no one could descend the fire-escape without his seeing it.

Erskine said, "That's the window," and pointed to a dark pane on the second floor at the left.

Craven said, as he climbed out: "Give us about three minutes, before you take your eye off that window, Drago. You coming up then?"

"Yes."

Craven and Erskine went silently up the walk.

Drago lit a little cigar and sat hunched on the edge of the seat, watching the window above. The frosted-glass front door of the little building opened to receive Erskine and the big lieutenant, closed behind them.

Minutes passed, with no sound from within the building. Drago's eyes started to ache from staring at the one spot so long. He shifted and eyed the silhouette of the silent building against the glow of the uptown sky. It was a queer place, neither converted residence, nor conventional apartment house.

Nor was that all that was queer about it.

For one thing, the building was rocking slowly from side to side, even as he looked at it. It varied this, by jumping up and down.

Drago made a queer, sucking noise in his throat.

The building began to dance, teetering from one side to the other in a jovial sort of jig. Drago shook his head, tried to get the heaviness out of it, then looked again.

His jet eyes suddenly became startled, muddy. He looked sharply at the little cigar in his hand, tried to call out in a thick voice and slumped to his hands and knees on the bottom of the car.

HAMMERS WERE banging at Drago's head. There was a roaring in his ears, and a faint ringing. An iron band seemed to be closing around his stomach. The tonneau of the car was a thundering pinwheel of light as he tried to raise a hand toward the door handle—and his hand weighed a ton. He put out every effort he could summon in flopping himself at the door, his clasped hands clawing at the shininess of the handle. Fortunately, it was of the lever type, with a four-inch curved handle projecting from the upholstery of the door, and operated by being dragged downward. If it had been any other type he would have died there on the floor of the car.

The door burst open and he pitched out onto his face on the wet, dark grass at the curbside. He flopped over and hit on his side, one gloved hand clutching a tuft of grass while his stomach heaved up again and again.

Presently he lay still, panting, and his senses got control of themselves once more. He turned weakly over onto his back and stared up through dizzy eyes at the building. The second-floor window that he had been watching was wide open and a bright light was burning inside.

The door of the house burst open and Erskine, his gray head bare, came running out. The big figure of Craven pounded in his wake, ten yards behind.

Erskine dropped to his knees, his hand going inside Drago's trench coat, feeling the detective's heart. "Mr. Drago! Mr. Drago! What's—what's happened?"

Drago said quietly: "I'm all right, I think. Just give me a minute. What happened up there?"

Craven swore. "Nothing. Nobody home. Looks like the dame's moved out. There's only men's things there. For God's sake what happened to you?"

"I'm not sure." Drago sat up, propped on slanted arms. "I seem to be all right. I thought somebody'd doped one of my cigars, but..."

He rolled slowly to his feet, felt all right, walked over to the car and pointed his pencil flash into the tonneau. His little cigar smoldered on the floor. He reached in to pick it out—and his forehead V'd. The air in the lower part of the tonneau was very cold.

He moved his hand around. It got colder as he approached the back of the front seat. Then his head began to ache again. He jerked back quickly, eyes sharp on the rug that hung on the rack. He reached in, caught an edge of it, jerked it free of the rack. His flash beam centered on the large, square flap-pocket on the back of the front seat. In the pocket was a black cylinder, tilted at a sharp angle. An inch or two of its plain black top struck out above the pocket. There was a hole in the side, near the end, about the size of a dime. Wrapping his hand in the motor rug, Drago reached in and lifted it out, flung it on the ground behind him, then knelt down beside it. He lit a match and drew it slowly across the hole. Blue flame came alight. He snuffed it with his hand and stood up. His dark face had the sheen of lead.

"Liquefied carbon monoxide," he said grimly. "There's probably a tippet valve fallen down inside it. As long as the tube stood upright, the valve blocked the hole. The minute it tipped over, the valve slipped out. The liquid evaporated, expanding to twenty times its volume, and poured out of that hole. It was the car's motion that tipped it, I guess—which seems to be what was intended. Somebody put that tube in there since we were in the car last."

Craven's red eyes shone. "Trying to kill us all off, now!"

Drago eyed the doctor. "Still think you're not in danger?"

Erskine's teeth chattered. "I—I'm not insane."

Craven's jaw snapped. "We got to get this guy now—before he gets us. Come on, maybe there's something here." He swung again toward the building. "Standing here gawking won't buy us nothing."

IT WAS two rooms and bath—and kitchen cubicle. The room they entered was at the front. It was a living-room with black-painted woodwork, a hideous gray rug, a fireplace with black mantel, an oaken, circular dining-room table directly under the single brilliant incandescent light that hung shadeless from the ceiling. A pack of race-track programs, a cheap tablet of paper and a pencil lay on the round table. A vase of pencils and a pile of Daily Racing Forms six inches high and bound flatly with two bands of string, lay on the black mantel beside a cheap alarm clock.

The bedroom opened through a frame of black wood that had once housed sliding doors. Maple dressed, low studio bed covered with a brown blanket, a black chiffo-robe in place of a clothes closet, were its furnishings. The kitchen and bathroom cubicles were side by side, off the bedroom's rear wall.

Craven plowed into the bedroom while Drago's shining black eyes circled the living-room. There was no place of concealment. He picked up the pack of programs, riffled through them, spread them out, examined the tablet, peered into the vase of pencils. He picked up the tied stack of Daily Racing Forms to look under them—and his eyes sharpened.

He put them down on the table, tried to run a hand into the middle of the pile, but the string bound them together too tightly. He used a penknife to cut the strings, and lifted off the top half-dozen papers.

Save for possibly ten papers, at top and bottom of the stack, the center of the pile was cut out neatly, to form an oblong box, six inches by four.

And the box was full.

On top of the contents was a small, clear, glossy photograph, miniature size—two inches by two. Drago bent over to examine it—and instantly moved round the table so that his back was to Erskine. Craven, in the other room, was yanking out drawers.

The photograph was the picture of a ruled, large sheet of paper, evidently a page of something, for on the upper righthand corner was a faint 86, presumably a page number, and across the top of the page a crabbed hand had written—*3.5.22.* Apart from the numbers, only one line of the page was written on. That line read—*Russell Brown and Monette Moreau.*

With the same motion that he used to poke a gloved finger into the pile of stuff under the photo, Drago palmed the picture swiftly. Next on top of the pile was a note written on a scrap of the paper from the cheap tablet on the table. The note, in pencil, read—

Ike:

   Will have the other grand for you, I think, tonight. Wait for me here, if you come in before I do. Keep this little memento, in case of a tie.

                                                          S.W.

Under the note was a thick stack of twenty-dollar bills and nothing else.

Drago called: "Jack—look here!"

He stood back as Craven pounded in, and Erskine crowded up to the table. Drago put his hands in his pockets casually, his dark face expressionless as the red-faced lieutenant's fierce eyes and Erskine's bloodshot gray ones, raced over the note.

Craven blew out breath. He clawed the money out of the recess, flipped it through his big thumbs. "There's all of a grand right here! And one of Wells' pals—the one he owes it to, by the looks—is coming here to collect, tonight! By God! And he speaks of this grand as a memento! Or is it the dough that he means?"

"What else could it be?"

Craven was suddenly a bundle of bustling energy. He swung round on the room, the window. "Hell and damnation! We got to get this light out! He might walk in here any minute!" He reached high for the cord, jerked the incandescent to darkness. "Hey—Doc—you stand over there by the window. Close it, and watch out. If anybody comes—even into the street—give me a shout. Drago—watch the hall, huh? I'll go through the rest of this joint with my flash."

Drago said nothing, but went over and stood in the open door to the hall. Rustling, creaking sounds came from the bedroom.

In less than three minutes, Craven's husky whisper called, "O.K., Doc—come on. I'm through," and the three of them left the apartment.

IN THE downstairs hall, Craven whispered sharply: "Now, wait a minute! I got something good here—I got to figure it carefully."

Drago asked: "You mean you found something else in the bed—"

"No, you chump! I mean this guy that's coming here! Let me get my hands on him and I'll clean this thing up fast!"

It was on the tip of Drago's tongue to point out that, if Wells' friend had not shown up at this late hour, and had any guilty knowledge whatever, it was a safe bet that news of Wells' fate had reached him by now and that he would be speeding out of town by the fastest route.

Drago said nothing, however. Another thought had occurred to him. It was now well over an hour since his conversation with the French-Canadian police chief—time enough for a cable to go across the Atlantic, and almost time for its answer to be back.

He said: "Jack—I've got to go down to headquarters on a matter. If you don't mind, I'll leave this to you—"

"Oh, yeah? And leave me to take the doc home? Not much, wise guy. I get it. Pull me away, so you can walk around the block and come back to nab this accomplice of Wells. Am I laughing!"

Drago's forehead wrinkled. "Use some reason, he said. "You're not going to catch anybody important here. I think personally—"

"Uh-huh. I know all about what you think. How many times have I found myself holding the burlap because I listened to what you thought—or what you said you thought? No, sir. Little Jackie Craven is sitting right here on this nest. This is the break of the case, and I know it. This Ike, whoever he is, has got dough coming—more than just the grand that's here, from what the note says. He's not going to pass it up, without at least a look-see. You can guard the doc home, Mr. Drago—with my compliments."

Drago was silent. Finally, he said quietly: "All right."

"Always the gent," grinned Craven. "There's a rooming-house right opposite here. If there's a vacant front room, I'll take a plant there. Will you send Barry down to spell me, or do I call him myself?"

"I'll send him down," Drago said.

Drago went out, gave the street narrow inspection before he allowed the doctor to emerge. A sheet of newspaper in the gutter caught his eye. He retrieved it, and, using the paper as a wrapper, picked the black tube from the grass, shook it. Its liquid contents had now completely evaporated. He laid it in the tonneau.

For the first ten blocks of the trip back uptown, Drago was too intent on watching the road, both before and behind them, to do anything else, but he could discern no shadow. At last he got the photograph from his slash-pocket and examined it covertly in the light of the dash. Having made sure that nothing on the pictured page had escaped him before, he glanced at the back—and his eyes shone brighter. There was penciled writing—obviously an address—in Wells' loose handwriting—*corner Lindstrom and Hazlitt Blvd.*

If he had not been anxious enough to get to headquarters before, he was now. He knew of no such address, did not believe it was in New York. Yet only the traffic squad could give him a definite yes or no. And they could do more, in all probability. If it were in the United States, they could tell him where, in a very short time.

He shoved the picture back in his pocket. "We'll go in the back way—the same way we came out," he told the doctor. "I'll have to hurry right away, but I'll see there's plenty of law there so you can rest easy in your mind, before I leave. And if you want me any more tonight, I'll probably be at headquarters."

CHAPTER SIX
"I DIED TEN YEARS AGO"

DRAGO CARRIED the wrapped black tube into the house. The white sandstone residence seemed strangely empty—almost deserted—after the crowd that had been there before, even though Barry, Crowinshield and Whitehead, of Craven's staff, were still keeping guard in the lower hall.

As Barry closed the back door after letting them in, the Italian said: "Hey—there's a couple of visitors for the doctor."

Drago blinked. "Who?"

"Miss Margaret Leon, and Count Lilli. I'm afraid I pulled a bull. When they came—about twenty minutes ago—I thought I thought I ought to keep them for you or Jack, and I let them think the doctor was here. When they found he wasn't, they were all for leaving, but I kind of didn't let them."

The doctor gasped, his eyes jerking upwards. "I—if you'll excuse me—"

"I'm right behind you," Drago assured him, and to Barry, as he put the wrapped tube in his hands, "Send this down for prints and tracing when you get a chance. You didn't pull any bull. I'll square it."

He followed the hurrying doctor up the stairs into the high-ceilinged living-room.

A tall, beautiful girl, purest blond, was sitting in an armchair. She wore an evening dress of white sequins; her white ermine wrap was flung over the back of the chair. She had an anxious look in her cornflower-blue eyes; her face was a little pale under her rouge.

A DARK man in full evening dress stood beside her, his hands behind his back. He must have been three inches shorter than the girl, swarthy, his hair a gleaming skullcap of black, his large, almost bulbous, brown eyes smoldering in his pinched-together face.

Erskine went into the room, saying: "Margaret— Tommy—what are you doing here at this hour?"

Drago lagged, just inside the door, laid his hat on an end-table under a gilt mirror. He eyed his shining reflection hastily, ran a hand along the side of his rippling, neat black hair and removed a glove in case anyone should want to shake hands with him. The girl said, a little nervously: "We're being detained by the police, at the moment. We are at the Fisher's dance and people started calling us up and telling us—well, everyone had a different story. Somebody said you'd been—injured, and I couldn't get an answer from your phone, so I got hold of Tommy and made him drive me over."

Erskine's forced laugh was hollow. "What nonsense. A—a burglar was trying to get in, and one of his accomplices... He turned to Drago, desperate appeal in his eyes. "This is Mr. Drago—the police officer who is working on the business... Miss Leon... Count Lilli."

Drago ignored the appeal. He made a little bow and his soft voice said smoothly: "I'm very sorry you've been detained this way. I left orders to admit everyone, but not let anyone leave. I didn't have any idea that any of the doctor's friends might come, but I'm glad, in a way, that you are here. One of my colleagues has the idea that this burglar was killed in mistake for the doctor, by some enemy of the doctor. I have to ask everyone if it sounds at all logical to them."

The girl stared at him blankly. "For heaven's sake, who would want to—"

Drago's quick smile took the rudeness from his words "That is the question I was going to ask you."

"Me? Good heavens, I never heard of such a thing! I—I'm sure I don't know."

Drago's shining eyes moved somberly to Lilli. "I don't suppose you could suggest anything, Your Highness?"

Lilli's mouth came open in surprise at the unexpected form of address. His stiff resentment wilted. He said with anxious sincerity: "I'd like to help, Mr. Officer, but I can't imagine how you would expect me to know."

Drago bobbed again. "Thank you. If you, Miss Leon, or you, sir, should think of anything, I hope you will communicate with me."

"Oh, rather."

Margaret Leon got up. "May we go now?"

"By all means."

The count jumped for the girl's wrap, and when it was around her, she went over, put up her lips for Erskine to kiss. There was real fright in her blue eyes. "I'm sure I don't understand this, but everything will be all right won't it, Ralph?"

"Oh, of course. As—as Mr. Drago says, one of the other officers got the idea—shall I drive you home, dear?"

"No, no. Dad is in town and we're staying at the hotel tonight. Tommy will drive me over."

"I—then I'll call you in the morning. May I?"

Drago followed them out into the hall, made a signal to Barry below, as Erskine escorted them down. Drago did not follow; just stood gazing thoughtfully down after them.

WHEN THE doctor came back up, Drago said: "When you're ready to turn in, let Mr. Whitehead know. He'll hang around near your bedroom. Don't be alarmed. It's not because there's any danger that I know of, but more to relieve your mind completely."

Erskine said hesitantly: "Very well. Thank you."

"You'll hear from me in a few hours," Drago told him, as he went down the stairs.

He drew Barry down the hall out of earshot. "Call another of your squad to stay here till morning. Then you go down and report to Craven." He told him where, then pointed to the doctor's office. "Get your phoning done fast, and send that tube down. I want to use the phone after you."

"Oke." Barry pulled open the office door—and stopped at the threshold, grinned over his shoulder at Drago and jerked his head.

Drago looked in and saw Gulliver, the Negro house-servant, his blue trousers wrinkled, his collar wilted, his white jacket crumpled and dirty, with the thin line of bloodspots across its front—blood that had showered him when he swung open the door with its grisly burden hours earlier. He sat sprawled in an armchair, his hands folded over his stomach, his mouth open, snoring gently.

"I guess the boys asked him a few questions," Drago said.

They woke him and he yelped and cringed, scuttled upstairs, still terrified.

Barry phoned, hung up, vacated the doctor's swivel chair and Drago reached for the instrument, had his hand on it when from upstairs, came the bang of a door. Then Erskine's hoarse voice, faint through intervening walls and floor: "Mr. Drago! Mr. Drago! Hello! Mr. Drago!"

Then Gulliver's echoing yelp: "Mistah Dargo!"

Drago ran out of the office, his heart in his throat, and tore up the stairs. When he flung round the newel post at the top, the Negro was standing in the open door of the living-room, waving with one arm and pointing with the other. "The lib'ary! The lib'ary—in the lib…" he stammered.

Drago had a gun in his hand when he reached the library.

Erskine was standing inside, holding the door open with one foot, bent over. He had the phone in his hands, was jiggling the hook, frantically. His face was ashen as he choked into the mouthpiece: "Operator—trace that call—quickly!"

Drago dropped his gun in his pocket, took the instrument and added, "Police business!" gave his shield number and ordered, "Call back here at once," before he hung up.

"What is it?"

Erskine licked his lips, fought for poise. "A—a man's voice—as soon as I lifted the receiver. He didn't address me by name or anything. He just started talking. He said that I seemed to have a—a protective aura around me, and that some of his organization think not being able to kill me in two attempts is an omen. They are willing to let me live if I pay them ten thousand dollars at my Northport house tonight."

"Where?"

"I—I have a house at Northport on Long Island. Some time during the day I'm to get ten thousand dollars without the police knowing about it. I'm to go out there all alone, at nine o'clock tonight. If—they say they have a person watching my house out there now, and that if there is any sign of police activity, or if they have any reason to believe that I've told the police anything, they will withdraw my chance to live. I'm to go alone to my house, with the ten thousand dollars—and the scarab ring!"

DRAGO'S EYES glowed. He whipped off his hat, dropped into the chair before the desk, but the phone rang even as he grabbed it.

The operator said: "I'm sorry, but that call must have come from a dial phone. I have no record of it."

Drago hung up slowly, his jaw tight.

Erskine's frightened eyes dragged at him. "What—what should I do?"

"Get the money," Drago said, after a minute. "You can?"

"Yes, yes, but—am I to—"

"We'll decide the rest when the time comes. I—" He clamped his lips. There was a disturbed look in his black, shining eyes as he stared at the phone. "The rats are jerking time out from under me. Well, I've still got a few hours."

"You have reason to think—you mean you're expecting to learn something—today?"

Drago reached for his hat, his eyes heavy-lidded. "I'm going to be a sick man, Doctor, if I have to go up against them without learning more than I know now. Where is this house of yours in Northport?"

"It's just on the outskirts. I have about four acres of woods, and a cottage in the middle. It's at the intersection of Lindstrom Avenue and Hazlitt Boulevard."

"What!"

Drago's hand dipped into his pocket and he brought out the small photograph, stared at the penciled address on the back. "Now it begins to pile up," he said half to himself. He suddenly looked at his watch, said, "Excuse me," and dropped into a chair, again reaching for the phone.

When his office answered, the patrolman that sat in Drago's chair when he was out, said: "Oh. I was just wondering where to get you. Did you have some truck with a chief of police at Chap—"

"What did you hear from him?"

"Well, he called about half an hour back. Something about a girl you wanted him to trace. This cable was the answer, which he said he got from someplace. Sounded like France, but—"

"Read the cable, you pinhead."

"Well, I ain't got it. All he said was that this jane left Paris— Wait, here's the name—Monette Moreau. Yeah. She left Paris a month ago, and left a forwarding address at the hotel she was at. This is the forwarding address—care Henri DeRussy, Junior, Eighteen and a Half West Sixty-fourth Street. That's just off the Park, in case—"

"I know." Drago hung up, swung for the door, stopped and told Erskine: "You can sleep till I call you. Mr. White-head's going to be right beside you. But get that money."

"You've learned something?"

"I know where to go to learn something."

IT WAS graying toward dawn when he left his cab on the corner of Central Park West. He approached the little apartment building from the opposite side of 64th Street, till he stood directly opposite. It was an odd little build-ing—dingy and ancient, like the rest of the bedraggled near-tenements on the block. But Number 18 1/2 sported an orange canopy, lighted, and he could see a lighted lobby within, as though it were aping the exclusive apartment buildings along the Park. He crossed over and went in the open lobby door.

In a niche in the wall of the gaudy little lobby, behind a switchboard, a uniformed Negro with neat tufts of pure white hair and old-fashioned square spectacles. His eyes widened at the sight of Drago's badge, but he answered the detective's quick question, with: "No, sah—he not live here."

The vein on Drago's forehead stood out. "Dammit, he must live here. Look at your list of tenants."

The old man shook his head. "No need to look, suh. I been here goin' on eight years and I knows evr' tenant in the building. Mr. DeRussy—he ain't been here in mo'n two years."

"You mean he used to live here then?"

"Yes, sah, I regret to say, he did."

"Regret? Why?"

The Negro shook his head forbiddingly. "No one comin' to my good end what fools around with sperits. They was suckin' him, Mist' Officer—suckin' him pale—and him just a boy. They wasn't no blood in him—him and his sissy face."

"You mean he was a spiritualist? A medium?"

"Thass what the people used to call him. I dunno what he call hisself."

"Where did he move to?"

"Lawd, Mist' Officer, I dunno. We not a hotel."

Drago's eyes were strained. "Sam—I've got to find that Frenchman."

The Negro looked anxious. "What he done?"

"He hasn't done anyth— Look, does the building run a laundry service?"

"Yessuh, we always has."

"Can you trace back and find out for me what laundry mark they used on DeRussy's clothes?"

The Negro fingered his chin. "Why—I guess I could, suh—yessuh."

Drago slapped the counter with a gloved palm as he turned away. "I'll make it worth your while, Sam. I'll be back in a few minutes. I'm going over to the postoffice and make a try there. They might have a forwarding address or something."

He walked out the door, turned toward Columbus Avenue, intending to visit the postal sub-station a few blocks up. The street, in the dawn was utterly silent, bare in every direction. He hurried toward the corner, hands in the pockets of his trenchcoat.

The first bullet whipped under his chin before he heard the *crack* from across the street.

His head jerked back so quickly that he stumbled. His heel came against the single wooden step of a cheap, falling-to-pieces wooden rooming house he was passing, and he went crashing down on his back.

The gun *cracked* again, and glass snarled in a window of the room-house. Now Drago was a pinwheel of flying arms and legs. The man obliquely across the street—two houses nearer the corner of Columbus—stepped boldly into the road, pumping lead from an outstretched gun. His third shot struck wood in front of Drago, ricocheted up the detective's pant leg, leaving a line of fire along his thigh—and then Drago had his own gun free. He fired as fast as he knew how—twice—and gasped in relief as he saw the gun fly out of the gunman's hand.

He whipped up to his feet as the man dived after the gun. There was not the slightest cover of any sort around Drago. As the gunman jerked his weapon up again—now in his left hand—Drago had to shoot again. He saw the man wince, but his pistol spat pale flame and another bullet chunked into the wood at Drago's back. The gunman started to back quickly toward the corner, firing again.

DRAGO DROPPED to one knee, returned the shot. Now, for the first time, his assailant stood up out of his crouch and his face became visible. He was undersized, wizened, brown-skinned, with straight, shiny black hair. Drago saw him sag in the middle, fall up against the building beside him, but he somehow kept erect—and then he literally fell around the corner and was gone.

Drago swore, jumped to his feet, his short legs pumping as he raced in pursuit.

He flung round the corner—and faced a blank sidewalk stretching ahead of him. His eyes dropped to blood spots on the pavement, and he saw that they slanted off the curb a few feet ahead. He looked up—across the street—just in time. The brown man was steadying himself against a barber's pole across the street. His gun barked just as Drago dropped, but before the detective could fire, the gunman had lurched through a door that led to flats above the block of stores opposite.

Drago counted, as he darted across the street after him—and realized that the man's gun must be empty. He didn't even hesitate at the door but dived through found himself at the foot of narrow wooden stairs. Thick blood splashes led upward. He ran up to the dim second floor, jerked his gun up.

"Don't move!" he warned sharply.

The brown man had no intention of moving. The hall was a blank rectangle of closed doors, save for the stairs. The flight leading to the third floor was a few feet away, around a large closet. The brown man lay there on his back, his heels on the floor level, his back on the slant of the stairs, knees jack-knifed. He had obviously tried to get up the stairs before his strength failed, but could not make it. The gun was still hanging from one hand, but the man was too far gone to use it. Blood was pouring out from under him, dripping down the steps. His wizened, walnut-brown face was completely without expression, but there was a faint flicker of life in his tiny brown eyes.

Drago dropped to one knee beside him, ran quick eyes over the bullet-riddled body and then told the brown man somberly: "I'm afraid I've finished you, Mac. Why not tell me who sent you? You're going to die."

The brown eyes blinked slowly once. The man's lips moved. Drago held his ear swiftly down to catch the breathed words.

The man got out with difficulty: "I—died ten years ago. It isn't—my soul—you've released...." The words ended.

Drago jerked his head up to look sharply at the small brown eyes. They were already glazing, and as Drago jumped to his feet, the last of the man's life drained out of him.

Drago pocketed his gun, his face livid. He stepped to the nearest of the closed doors in the hall, pounded on it.

"Police. Phone for—"

He found it unnecessary to finish. A siren was whining to a stop in the street outside.

HE HAD finished searching the dead man, was stepping back empty-handed from the body when a gaunt sergeant burst up the stairs, bluecoats streaming up at his back. The sergeant threw down his service gun on Drago. "Up, brother—fast, or—hell, it's Drago! What the hell?"

Drago slid his hands into the slash pockets of his trench-coat. He nodded out at the street. "I shot him over there on Sixty-fourth. He came over here and died."

"Yeah?" The sergeant leaned over the body. "Hold-up or something?"

"No. He just stepped out of nowhere and started blasting as I came along. I know what it's about. Put it on your report as a hold-up though, for now."

"O.K. What the hell is he—an Armenian?"

"I think he's Egyptian. There isn't a scrap on him. He'll take some tracing. Look—you handle it, Polk, will you? I'm trying to rig a miracle, by tonight. I haven't a tenth enough time as it is. I've got to move along. Later, I'll—"

"Gentle Annie! Look!" Polk pointed down. "You're not going nowhere, mister!"

Drago's eyes went down to his feet. A neat little pool of his own blood had run down and collected at the side of his brown shoe. More was trickling down his leg.

Polk yelled: "Martins! Hey—give Mr. Drago a hand—"

"Never mind," Drago said sharply. "It's just a nick." He jerked a handkerchief from his breast pocket.

"Now, wait a minute," soothed Polk. "Don't get excited. You got to have that looked at. What is it you got to do in such a hurry? Maybe we can do it for you, while—"

"Thanks, no," Drago said shortly. "It's something I—"

Then he closed his mouth.

"On second thought," he said, "you can. At least, about three of your plainclothes reserves can. I'm getting a little hot in the head, I guess. Yes—it's not a one-man job. I've got to trace a Frenchman—fast, Polk. Could you throw three good men right at it?"

"Like shooting fish. Just take it easy."

CHAPTER SEVEN
THE THREE THREADS

I T WAS nine when Drago left the hospital; ten when, barbered, bathed and in fresh brown clothes, he ran up the long steps of headquarters and to his office; eleven when he had finished a series of phone calls.

The black tube that had contained the carbon monoxide with which the murder attempt had been made the previous night, was on his desk, with a note from the "I" bureau stating that there were no fingerprints, and the apparatus had evidently been fabricated from a common type of lubrication gun, and the chances of tracing it were a little less than nil.

When, at twelve, Inspector McTigue came in anxiously, mopping his long, grizzled Irish face and bald head, Drago, forehead propped on his hands, was so deeply absorbed in worry that it was a minute before he realized his chief was in the office.

McTigue cleared his throat. "Uh—how's it going—"

Drago's head jerked up. His eyes were a little red-rimmed from lack of sleep, and McTigue's voice took on concern. "Nothing's happ—the doctor's still all right, isn't he?"

"Yes. I just talked to the house. He's sleeping."

"Where do we stand?"

Drago told him what had happened.

"By God!" McTigue said. "A pay-off after all! That tears it! We'll get them at Northport!"

"Maybe."

The phone rang on Drago's desk. It was Barry, of Craven's squad, phoning from a drug-store. He complained: "Hey—what do you advise me to do? Craven's supposed to spell me, on and off, four hours apiece, while the other one sleeps. The big ape's gone so sound asleep now that I can't even wake him."

Drago said: "Better stick with him. When he does come to, suggest that he try tracing that Renée Laverne, through the janitor or whoever runs that apartment house. Not that I think he'll get anywhere, but he might as well have something to play with. All I need right now to put me in a padded cell is to have him in my hair. Keep him off me, Fred, and I'll buy you a dinner—if I'm around."

When he hung up, McTigue asked anxiously: "What do you mean—if you're around?"

"Well, they seem to be trying to rub me out, don't they? They might succeed."

"Why do you say 'maybe' about catching these rats at Northport? Hell, it's the only way to crack this thing."

"It won't be as simple as all that. Personally, I'm only hoping that Polk's precinct men turn up this DeRussy in time—and that I can reach this Monette Moreau."

"What for? That doesn't sound like much of a lead to me!"

"I didn't say it was. But it's the only lead."

"All you've got on her is that some time in the past she was associated with Sam Wells. The fact that her old address was in his pants proves to me that he didn't know her present one. Where are you if it turns out that she hasn't seen him in years?"

"I hate to think where I'll be if that's the case," Drago said.

HE GOT up and walked the office. "Add up what we've got. As I told you, I see three separate and distinct lines. One of them leads to this cheap tout, Sam Wells, who snatched the doctor and, for some as yet unknown reason, impersonated him. The only chance of finding why he impersonated Erskine, is to find some of the tout's acquaintances and see what he was mixed up in. Obviously, this Monette Moreau did know him at one time. I'm reasonably sure that whatever this page is that's shown in the photograph we found, the Russell Brown signature is an alias. It sounds like an alias. It's probably Sam Wells. All right. I admit there's only the slimmest hope of getting light on that line. On the other hand, it might be that Sam Wells had her old address because he had been tracing her. We know that she left Paris within the last thirty days. She may have left because she was coming here to go into this job with Wells, in which case you'll admit that she's a vital witness, at least. For if we knew the whole story behind Wells' impersonation of the doctor, we might get wind of the second half of the mystery—namely, who killed him in mistake for the doctor? Thin—yes—but it's something, isn't it?

"And what is there on the second thread? Only the fact that this 'Gypsy' girl, Renée Laverne, was Erskine's mistress. And, of course, she did have that scarab ring, and it was found at the scene of the crime. But there is absolutely nothing else to tie her to it. And there are several ways that she could be utterly clear. For one—she was in the entertainment business, and having a precarious time of it. She might have sold the ring. For another—she occupied the apartment that Sam Wells later moved into.

Maybe she lost the ring in the place and Sam Wells found it after she'd vacated. At any rate I've had a couple of men trying to locate the girl, ever since last night, and she seems to have disappeared. I just now suggested to Barry that he put Craven on the same lead. However, I don't think we'll find that girl. For, if she has the slightest guilty connection with this mess, I think she'll be far out of our reach by now. Oh yes—there is a way that she could be in this up to her neck. I mean, if she had some connection with the third thread—the one that ties to the situation regarding the dead Egyptian that Erskine dug out of his grave."

McTigue mopped his head.

DRAGO SPREAD his hands on the desk, sat down. "If the girl—instead of being a 'Gypsy' as she claimed— were an Egyptian, then what?"

McTigue blinked rapidly. "She—you mean—"

"I mean she might know of the origin of that scarab ring and the very fact that it was in Erskine's possession might have told her the whole story. Possibly her loyalties would induce her to send word to the people in Egypt, and they came to fix Erskine. But in that case, it's a certainty that the girl would be far, far away by the time anything happened. However, I don't put much faith in that possibility. There's another one that's a little easier to swallow.

"Say that some Egyptian who happened to be in New York, happened to see that scarab ring on the girl's finger. Say that the significance of the thing was apparent to him at sight. Say that he bought the ring from her, and that he sent the word along. Maybe the girl even told him—in all innocence—what the doctor had told her about how he got the ring. Certainly, in that event, it is probably that the revengeful Egyptians would see that the girl was in the clear before they did anything.

"So—if the girl did have anything of value to us—we would hardly be able to find her anyway. If we had days instead of minutes, we might, but we haven't. So that thread is blind, as far as I'm concerned. And the third thread—the one that ties up with the Egyptian religious fanaticism—"

McTigue looked uncomfortably at his big hands. "I can't seem to believe there's anything to that angle," he interrupted. "It's too fantastic, even to bother thinking about, when you come right down to it. It—"

"How about the old Egyptian that tried to kill me this morning?"

"Well, maybe it was just a coincidence."

Drago shook his head. "You don't believe that any more than I do. That old man was sent to kill me. We've traced him. He's been in this country about twelve years. He's run a business in cotton—a straight business, according to the cops in his precinct. But he's been an absolute hermit all that time. Has no friends—rarely speaks to anyone except in terms of straight business. Even his next-door neighbors—he lives above his shop—don't know what his first name is. That presupposes a man who feels set apart from the people around him, and that setting-apart could just as easily be traced to a religious angle as not. Certainly, I can see no way, except some emotional one, that would turn an honest merchant into a free-lance killer overnight."

McTigue scratched his bald head uncomfortably. "What do you make of what he said to you when he went out—that he had died years ago, and that it wasn't his soul that you were freeing or something?"

Drago's shining round face was pinched for just a minute. "If I knew that, chief, I think I'd have the answer to this whole business—or at least a way to clear it up quickly. Certainly—even you will admit this—that remark came out of some mystic belief. And the old man was absolutely in earnest when he said it."

"You're definitely going through—or letting Erskine go through—with the payoff?"

"I'm afraid not to. I'm afraid to let loose of the one sure chance of being in contact with the murderers."

"We ought to have a platoon around the place, so that—"

"If we do that, I'm afraid there'll be no pay-off. Don't tie me down to plans yet, chief. I'll handle it, somehow. I'm praying I won't have to make any plans till after Polk and his men turn up this Monette Moreau for me—or, rather, this DeRussy."

"My God, you've only a few hours left."

"I know it. Polk's simply got to find the Frenchman in time."

At three the phone rang. "This is Doctor Erskine, Mr. Drago. I—I got the money."

"Good. I'll call later. Don't move out of your house."

The hours fled. At five, in a light sweat, Drago called the precinct house from which Polk's men were operating, but there was no report.

At six he gave up, went to the phone with a cold feeling in his spine and put into effect the only precautions that he could think of. He ordered a car without insignia or siren from the garage for the two hour drive to Northport.

At six-thirty, just as he was about to leave the office, the phone rang again.

Sergeant Polk said: "We found your DeRussy—through the laundry mark. I only hope to hell we haven't made it too late for you, Mr. Drago."

DRAGO REACHED the apartment on Christopher Street within ten minutes. It was a modern elevator building, with a surprisingly luxurious lobby. He almost ran in, at five minutes to seven, rode up eight floors in the elevator. Even the minute that he spent waiting for an answer to his ring at the door of 8-A was agony by that time.

The door was opened by a dark youth in morning coat and Ascot tie. He was obviously French, his coat flaring, in the French fashion, over his hips. His face was small, dark, with liquid brown eyes, his hair a neat, black pompadour.

Drago said: "Mr. DeRussy, junior, on a matter of urgent importance." The youth stepped back in silence, closed the door after Drago had entered. He indicated the way along the little foyer into a large living-room, luxuriously furnished, with somber reds and blacks predominating. Three table lamps, each of which had a red shade of one sort or another, lit the room. One was on a baby-grand piano, one on an end table beside a long, black sofa, one beside a red-brocaded armchair.

THE YOUNG man stood in the entrance of the foyer. Drago put his hat on the table and turned up a palm holding his shield. "Well, get Mr. DeRussy!"

"I am Mr. DeRussy"—he had a pleasant, light voice—"and I may say that I will not endure the police persecution that I did three years ago, Mr. Officer. I am able to have competent lawyers look after my interest now, and—"

Drago made a slashing gesture. "I'm not here for that. I don't care about your racket—except indirectly. I want to get news from you about a girl named Monette Moreau."

The youth's eyebrows rose—almost hopefully, it seemed. "She's—she is in trouble?"

"We don't know. We're trying to find out—with your help."

"She is in this country?"

Drago sagged. He countered doggedly: "You know her well?"

The psychic shrugged. "We worked together for a year in Paris. She has a remarkable gift—second only to my own."

"What kind of a gift?"

"Astral projection. She—"

"Where is she now?"

The youth's dark eyes clouded. "I'm sure I don't know. She was in Paris three months ago when I left there."

"You have not seen her since?"

"No. I asked you if she were in this country and you said 'no.' What are you trying—"

"I didn't say 'no.' She is in this country. As forwarding address in Paris, she left your name and old address on Sixtyfourth Street. She has been in town at least two weeks and it's nonsense to expect me to believe she hasn't looked you up."

"If she wanted, to, perhaps my change of address may have—"

"Sure, I know. Mr. DeRussy, I've an urgent appointment, for which I'm late now. I'd like to talk around corners with you for hours. I can't. You know what I want. This is damned serious business. If for any reason you know where Miss Moreau is and don't feel that you should tell me—forget it. She is in no danger if I find her—but in grave danger if I don't."

"What—what kind of danger?"

Drago hesitated, made a last desperate stab, as the hands of his wrist watch pointed their grim warning. "Did you ever hear of a man named Sam Wells?"

The youth's olive face became concerned. He half turned toward a newspaper on the couch. "I—you mean—"

Drago nodded. "That's the man—he was murdered last night. We have reason to suppose that Miss Moreau's name is in the hands of the same people that did that. We don't know what for."

The psychic was silent, looking troubledly at Drago's shining black eyes. "I—I might put personal advertisements in the papers. If Monette were in town, she might see them and call me—"

Drago clamped his lips, picked up his hat. "Do that," he said through tight teeth. "And don't leave here. I'll be back—later."

There was a drug-store next door to the apartment house. From there he phoned Erskine and told the husky-voiced physician: "Take the money and your car and drive over the Queensboro Bridge. Drive alone. Take Route Twenty-five-A. Don't look for me, but stop and pick me up at the place they call Five Corners."

"You—then you've been in Northport—"

"I've been in touch with someone who knows it."

"What—what are we going to do?"

"Put an end to your danger, I hope."

"I—I haven't any firearms, Mr. Drago. If there's any—"

"I'll lend you a gun."

Between the apartment house and Northport, Drago made just one stop—to pick up Inspector McTigue at the near end of the Queensboro Bridge. He told the grizzled, worried inspector: "If some speed cop picks us up, don't flash any badges. It's almost a certainty that Erskine's car will be followed. We've got to keep whoever's following him from any hint that cops are coming, too."

"Ye gods! You're letting him drive out alone—unprotected?"

"I've got reason to think that nothing will interfere with his getting to Northport."

"You"—the inspector gasped—"you've learned something?"

"Maybe. Did you bring that extra gun from my desk?"

"Yes." McTigue fished it from his pocket. "What—what did you learn?"

"Don't ask me questions. I've only a hunch. Let me concentrate on driving this crate. Northport is two hours away. We've got to make it at least twenty minutes better than that."

CHAPTER EIGHT
THE MAN INSIDE

THEY TURNED off Highway Twenty-five-A, onto the road that looked out over the dark, glittering harbor of Northport, at twenty minutes to nine, exactly. They sped down the sloping road and in a minute turned up the main street. Before rolling through the brief, abbreviated little shopping district, they changed seats. After about a mile they were at the place called Five Corners.

Drago's heart jumped.

The spot was the intersection of five country roads—desolate, heavily wooded. There had been no ambiguity about the road on which Drago had told Erskine to meet him. But the dark corner was deserted—in pitch darkness.

Drago said, "By God—if I've made a mistake—" and touched the horn button once as the puzzled McTigue let the car coast.

The lights of the blue sedan blazed on suddenly, under an overhanging tree by the roadside. Drago cursed in his throat, sprang from the police car and it rolled away without stopping. He ran around to climb in beside Erskine in the sedan.

The doctor's teeth were chattering. "I—I'm sorry. I thought it best to hide where they couldn't see—"

"You were followed?"

"I'm almost positive—a black touring—"

"Drive faster. We've only minutes."

Erskine gulped. "We—this place of mine is a lonely spot. My property is about four acres, mostly woods. The cottage is in the middle—a clearing there."

"I know. It's on a wooded corner where two highways intersect. There's a road leads in from each of them, through the woods to the property. You told me that."

"I know, but"—Erskine's damp face in the dashlight's glow was haggard—"I hope I'm not a coward, Mr. Drago, but don't you think—I mean, just the two of us going in there—even with the man who was driving your car—"

Drago passed him the gun. "I know it's scary. But you know what they said: Any attempt to surround them would send them running. And there would be long-nosed reporters, if there were any sign of a cordon, anyway. Keep your chin up."

Erskine suddenly slowed the car. "There—there's the road in to the—there, through the woods there."

"Turn, then," Drago said.

They drove a mile through even thicker, higher woods, that seemed to close overhead. Drago had a flat, black automatic pistol on his knee.

"Stop about three hundred yards from the clearing," he told Erskine, and the doctor braked at once.

For a second they sat there, lights and motor dead.

Erskine whispered huskily: "I—a little way back, there's a moss path I know. It would take us through the woods to the edge of the clearing. They might be watching the mouth of the road—"

Drago nodded, and they slipped from the car, walked back sixty yards and the doctor's trembling hand urged

Drago into a path that was completely invisible in the darkness. Soft moss underfoot made their going almost noiseless.

Presently they were in the clearing.

THE SKY overhead seemed surprisingly light, after the inky blackness of the woods. But the small house in the center of the clearing was only a dark, formless blur.

Drago took the doctor's arm in the darkness, pulled him close enough and whispered: "Are you game to walk into the house—alone? I'll be within a few yards of—"

He stopped in mid-sentence as surprise dumbed him. He felt Erskine stiffen and quiver.

A light had blazed on, inside the tiny cottage that centered the clearing. The light was in the living-room, and there was a door from the living-room to the outside. That door faced exactly where they were standing, and the door was wide open.

For what seemed an eternity, nothing happened. Then the ghastly, rushing climax was on them so swiftly that he had no time to think.

Inside the barely furnished living-room, there was suddenly a man's shadow on one wall. The man who cast it was invisible, but he was in the end of the room opposite to the staircase. To get to that staircase, he would have to pass a large window and then the open door.

The shadow started moving, slowly, hesitantly.

The man came abreast of the window, and Drago sucked in breath audibly. The man wore a polo coat and pigskin gloves, his uncovered hair shone like ebony. In one hand he gripped a blue pistol, rigidly. His pinched-together, swarthy face was protruded forward. The man in the house was

Count Lilli, the Spaniard, the former suitor of Erskine's fiancée, Margaret Leon!

Erskine's gasped whisper rattled. "Good God! It's Tommy!"

Drago's swift hand closed like iron on the doctor's sleeve, kept him motionless. "Don't give us away. He isn't our killer! God knows why he's here, but we're waiting for someone else...."

The man in the living-room seemed to be at a loss. He stood framed in the window, staring uneasily around the room, one hand on the long refectory table whose jutting end Drago could see through the open door.

The Spaniard's eyes went to the staircase. He gripped his revolver more firmly, inched toward it.

Erskine groaned in Drago's ear: "Catch him! For God's sake—catch him—don't let him get away!" He tried to shake off Drago's inflexible grip.

"Stop it!" Drago ordered.

The man in the house moved into the open doorway, was past the end of the table now. Something on the floor seemed to attract his attention. His head jerked round, tilted downward, and he seemed to stiffen. Drago took a quick step sideways, in front of Erskine to try to see what it was.

On the bare floor of the room, he saw something crumpled and green. It was a second before he realized that it was money—a wadded bank-note.

The Spaniard stood over it a second, frowning, then stooped and reached a gloved hand toward it.

Fire and thunder belched from the ceiling—the two-toned roar of a double-barreled shotgun. Count Lilli's head was blown into a shattered, frightful horror driven down between his shoulders, the terrible impact of the discharge pounding him to his knees.

THERE WAS a second of blank, stunned silence. Then Erskine was crying in a hysterical voice in Drago's ear: "Good God! Get him! Get the killer—Mr. Drago!" His hand pounded wildly at Drago's back, sent the detective stumbling wildly toward the house. A loose vine caught his ankle and he pitched forward to one knee. Erskine, completely distraught, was beside him, dragging at him with frenzied fingers. "God—he'll escape—the back— don't let him get away, Mr. Drago—they'll—the back…."

Drago slashed out furiously, as the unstrung doctor again attempted to hurry him. The doctor caught the blow on the neck, staggered sideways, and tripped, fell heavily, moaning.

Then hell opened the night.

The little house shot forty feet in the air on a pillar of blazing, eye-searing light. It dissolved into flying sticks. The dreadful roar and concussion was so terrific that Drago's senses went momentarily numb. He did not feel himself slammed to the ground.

Then he did feel once more. He felt blistering heat, and he felt clutching hands at his shoulders, jerking at him. He opened his eyes and saw the mad, staring face of Erskine, as the doctor tried to tug him away from the blazing house. Erskine gasped out in terrible relief, as he saw Drago's eyes open: "Oh—thank God! I thought—"

Drago spun and staggered to his feet. Where the house had been, there was now a leaping, crackling pillar of fire, lighting up the center of the clearing like day.

Erskine screamed suddenly in Drago's ear, "Look!" and pointed toward the side of the clearing. Half-way between the house and the edge of the woods, a dark, formless figure on the grass was weaving drunkenly erect.

The figure resolved itself into a small man in a dark, belt coat and a black soft hat. The small man staggered to his feet, shook his head, then resumed the flight that he had evidently been making when the explosion knocked him down. He flung a white, frightened, unrecognizable face over his shoulder toward the fire, then sprinted for the woods like a bullet.

The hysterical doctor whipped up his revolver and fired—then ran furiously after the fugitive. Drago jerked a police whistle from his shirt front and plunged after Erskine. He blew three short blasts, which mingled with the fruitless, banging reports of Erskine's gun.

Suddenly, four huge floodlights blazed—one from each of the four corners of the clearing, flinging dazzling, blinding candle-power into their faces.

The running small man in the black hat was flung back as though the lights had been a physical force—and the flying doctor dived at him. They went down in a threshing heap, the doctor screaming: "I've got him! I've got him! Help!"

Drago blew a single shrill blast as he ran up. A circle of bluecoats stepped from the edge of the woods as he side-stepped the struggling pair on the ground.

The doctor was on top, trying to tug his arm free, still shouting, "Help! Help!" and suddenly the gun Drago had lent him flashed in the firelight. The doctor had it pointed squarely at the head of the wriggling dark man under him.

DRAGO'S ARM, from behind, whipped across the doctor's chest, under his gun wrist, jerked up to send the muzzle of the gun skyward as it exploded. Then Drago heaved, lifted the hysterical, yammering physician right off the small man, and with a shunt from knee and chest, flung him a few feet away, where he lit in a squirming heap.

Drago looked down at the sweating, terrified, smooth features of Henri DeRussy, the psychic. The medium's brown eyes were white-ringed, and he huddled to the ground, looking up obliquely, like a trapped animal.

The doctor flung himself to a kneeling posture, sobbing, yelling shrilly: "Damn you! Damn you! You're helping him—helping the fiend…!" He flung up his gun, aimed squarely at Drago's head.

Drago ducked instinctively, as the doctor's left hand shot flame. Then, before he could prevent it, a police positive in the hand of one of the running bluecoats exploded. The gun flew out of Erskine's fingers and the doctor was knocked over backward, fell on his back and lay moaning, sobbing, clutching his wounded shoulder.

The circle of bluecoats was almost around them. Behind the ring, McTigue's shining bald head and frantic Irish face loomed. Drago stooped and grabbed the lapels of DeRussy, still huddled on the ground, and even as he lifted the medium to his feet, he called to McTigue: "Mac—the doctor's wounded—an accident. Get him to his car and we'll take him to a doctor I know!"

He swung on the commander of the Northport police cordon, without loosing his grip on DeRussy's lapels. "There's a man in that burning house! He was dead before the fire started, but use your best efforts to get the body out!"

McTigue, breaking through and dropping down beside Erskine, could not take his eyes from the shrinking, cowering, little DeRussy in Drago's grip. He asked Drago in a hoarse voice: "Is that the killer? Who in God's name is he?"

Drago snapped: "Get Erskine out of here before he bleeds unconscious! He's got to help us some more yet! No, this man isn't the killer, you chump!" He turned his shining brown face down to stare squarely into DeRussy's stunned brown eyes. "This is Henri—he's been working undercover for me. Now, move!"

McTigue's face was twisted in anxiety, but he forced his lips closed, flung an arm around the moaning doctor, half trotted across the clearing with him. The commander of the Northport police was barking orders to his men. Three of them ran off at a trot.

Drago's shining black eyes bored into the little medium's frantic ones. "Stay close to me and don't lose your head," he clipped in an undertone. "I'll get you out of this if you do."

The medium gasped: "I—I'll do anything you say!"

The commander of the Northport contingent ran over. He panted anxiously: "Drago, nobody got through my cordon! I swear—"

"They did," Drago said, "but it wasn't your fault. It's all right. There's a smart officer on his tail right now. You did a great job—exactly what I wanted, Lieutenant. You're in charge here now. I'm going to the doctor's with Erskine and McTigue. I'll send the coroner out if you like."

"But—but wait—what's it all about? What'll I tell—"

"Either McTigue or I will be back here in a short time," Drago assured him hastily. "Come on, Henri."

They caught up to McTigue and the wounded Erskine just as the veteran inspector was trying to load him into the blue sedan. McTigue said: "Where do we—"

"I'll show you. You take him in back with you. I hope to hell the wound isn't too serious."

CHAPTER NINE
THE CORPSE THAT
DIDN'T DIE

TWENTY MINUTES later, McTigue, DeRussy and Drago sat anxiously around the local doctor's waiting-room and the medico put his head out. "Just a minute or two now and he'll be able to come out and talk," he assured them.

Almost as the words left his mouth, the phone in one corner of the waiting-room rang. McTigue, who had already been in touch with headquarters answered, but it was for Drago.

Drago's dark, shining face was puzzled as he picked up the receiver.

McTigue said hastily: "It's Craven. I guess they told him where we were."

Drago put the instrument to his ear and Craven's bull voice boomed: "Well, Monsoor Drago—I've got a little news for you! What do you think? The janitor of that place in Morton claims no jane named Renée LaVerne ever lived there! So she must of been going under a phony name. Listen—is Doc Erskine with you now...? Then ask him if the girl could have been known as Marie Petoske, because that's the name the girl that had the place before Sam Wells—"

Drago said: "Hey—did you just find that out?"

"No. I been looking for you for about an hour, wise guy—"

"If you didn't find it out till an hour ago, you certainly must have been doing something funny. You haven't been sleeping on the job have you?"

Craven's voice snarled: "Never mind the wise cracks. Find out what I asked you—"

"Call me back in ten minutes," Drago said. "The doctor's been hurt and we're waiting till he gets his wound dressed. Then I'll ask him." He hung up hastily before Craven could reply.

The door of the surgery came open, and the Northport doctor helped Erskine, pale-faced, his arm bandaged under his coat, out into the waiting-room. Drago sprang to help, guided the weakened physician quickly to a small writing-desk in the corner. "Just take it easy," he told him swiftly, as the haggard-faced Erskine attempted to speak. "I know. You lost your head. I would have, too, in your place."

Erskine croaked huskily: "The killer—he—he got away?"

"In a way. But he's well covered. We'll have him in minutes. But I've got to get you to write me a note."

"A—a note!"

Drago whipped writing-paper from the desk, laid it, with his fountain pen before Erskine. "Just write what I dictate. Your right hand's all right, isn't it?"

"Ye—es, but—" The doctor picked up the pen, looked apprehensively at Drago.

"Write this," Drago said. *"Russell Brown and Monette Moreau.* Write it as though—well, as though you were dashing it off on a marriage register."

Every eye in the room was on the pen that rested on the sheet of paper before the doctor.

The pen did not move.

Erskine laid the pen down, dropped his lax hand in his lap, stared down at the blotting-pad. His voice was very low.

"All right," he said. "You've got me."

MCTIGUE'S IRISH face gawked open, then closed, as Drago's gloved hand slashed warningly. Drago pressed the doctor. "Write it," he urged. "It can't hurt you now."

After a minute, the doctor wrote, dully. Drago snatched the sheet literally from under the pen. From his pockets, he dug a large photograph. It was an enlargement of the small picture that he had found in Sam Wells' apartment— the picture of the book-page bearing the same names that Erskine had just written. He compared them at a glance, passed them to McTigue.

"The page in the picture," he said, "would be a page which is probably missing from the marriage register at Greenville, Maine, around May, Nineteen Twenty-two. And Mr. Russell Brown, as the writing will point out, is Doctor Erskine."

McTigue gasped. "Then—then he was married— married to this Monette Moreau under a phony name?"

"Was?" Drago said. "He still is. Aren't you, Doctor?"

The hunched physician seemed to come out of a trance. "What? Oh, yes," he said dully.

"Then—then—" McTigue groped.

"Sam Wells knew about it. Sam Wells had a picture of the page of the marriage register that proved it. Sam Wells, on his uppers, saw the announcement of Erskine's engagement to Miss Leon and decided to cash in. He popped up and tried to blackmail Erskine, so Erskine killed him.

Then—when Erskine realized I was on the right trail—
that is, that I was seeking Monette Moreau—he tried to
kill me. When the first attempt failed, he called on a friend,
the old Egyptian, to make another try. When that failed, he
decided to use this trap in his cottage on me, and, apparently, he decided to include all his other troubles as well.
First, Count Lilli, whom he still suspected to be a powerful
rival for Miss Leon, in spite of all the camouflage—and
on which I think he was undoubtedly right. Secondly,
Mr. DeRussy here, who, on my instructions, posed as a
representative of Monette Moreau. Erksine got them to
come here, on promise of a cash settlement. The plan, you
understand, was to get us all in the house at once—then
wipe the slate clean."

"But—but—"McTigue spluttered. "The—Egyptians—
and this Renée Laverne—"

"They never existed,"Drago said, his shining black eyes
never leaving the doctor. "They were just charming little
fictions invented by Doctor Erskine in a nimble-witted
way, to confuse the issue."

"But—if they never existed—"

"Perhaps I shouldn't say that. One Egyptian certainly
existed—the cotton dealer that tried to gun me. I have a
hunch that he was the germ in the good doctor's mind
from the first—the germ that blossomed into the fantastic
story he made up from there. For some reason, the poor old
man must have been willing to do anything for Erskine.
When Erskine felt things closing in, he decided to get the
old man to kill me, so he built up the fantastic background
of the dead medical student. A man that never existed, a
corpse that never died. So far, I can't understand why a
respectable merchant such as the Egyptian, would—wait

a minute! Doctor—yes, I've got it now! Did you ever give him a blood transfusion, Doctor?"

"Yes," the doctor said thickly. "How—you must be a mind-reader—or did he tell you?"

"He told me—but I couldn't make sense of it," Drago said. "He said he, himself, had died years ago, and that it was someone else's soul that I had liberated. That clicks perfectly with the old Egyptian belief—that the soul of a man lives in his blood stream. Good Lord, why didn't I see that at once? That, then, was the reason he was willing to do anything you told him to?"

THE DOCTOR nodded listlessly. "Yes. He had a congenital diathesis—a form of haematuria. When I was a student at McGill, he was brought in to the clinic. I gave him two quarts of blood. Since then, he has followed me wherever I went—not personally, exactly, but he always let me know he was in the background and that he—well, that he was at my disposal. He—he gave me that scarab ring. I had no idea it was worth so much money—not until the moment when you told me." McTigue's dazed blue eyes jerked to Drago's. "How in God's name did you get onto this?"

Drago's smooth brown forehead V'd. "To tell you the truth, I'm a little ashamed that it didn't hit me sooner. It's the only explanation that doesn't hit some discrepancy. When Craven and I were at the hotel, the doctor blurted out unthinkingly that he had stopped drinking fourteen years ago—or words to that effect. That made it back in Nineteen Twenty-two. I know—it's probably the fluffiest clue that ever broke a case, but try and argue around it! When I started to put together all the things that happened in Twenty-two, how could I miss it? Obviously, Erskine had, through drinking, got himself into some sort of jam, in that year. And here was a register, dated then. When you consider that Erskine wound up getting engaged to a wealthy, socially prominent girl, it's not too far a stretch to imagine that he'd planned something like that, years back, as a boost to his career. But, according to my information, this Monette Moreau was an ignorant, backwoods, French-Canadian girl, who would have wrecked any ambitions of that kind."

He was silent, burning black eyes on the huddled figure of Erskine by the desk. "Want to tell us about it, Doctor?" he asked cordially.

The doctor roused, slowly. "There's nothing left to tell. Wells was an acquaintance of mine in Montreal. He was a sponger, and I used to take him on—well, sprees—with me. Then, as you say, after a two weeks' drunk, I woke up in Greenville and found that I'd picked this girl up in a little Quebec Village, taken her across the line and married her. She was, as you say, illiterate, ignorant—she couldn't even speak English. I could see myself as a backwoods doctor all my life.

"I got Wells to go and tear the page out of the marriage register and bring it to me. It was the only record of the thing. I destroyed it. I gave the girl some money and lit out. I didn't think she even knew my real name. And, of course, I never suspected that Wells had taken a photograph of the page before handing it to me.

"After fourteen years, I thought I was safe, and I became engaged to Miss Leon. Then I found out that fourteen years wasn't long enough. As soon as my engagement was announced it drew both Wells and, as I thought, Miss Moreau, down on me like vultures.

"I laid this trap in my cottage for Wells, originally. It was an electric-eye device that would discharge the shotgun when a person crossed the beam. I trained both beam and gun on a certain spot on the floor, and laid a thousand-dollar bill there. As soon as the shotgun exploded, a second device blew up the house, to wipe out all traces of the gun and so forth. But, unfortunately, I couldn't get Wells to come here.

"I gave him a little money, but I told him I had no more—not enough to meet his demand. I said I could borrow it, but that I was being watched night and day by detectives in the employ of General Leon, who thought I was a fortune-hunter. I dared not go to the money-lenders and have it reported to the general, or he would break off my engagement. I urged Wells to impersonate me, by wearing my clothes, thus drawing the detective off my track. I arranged the hotel business. I know—it wasn't a very clever plan, but it was the best I could think of at the last moment, when he balked at the other. And he wasn't a very clever man."

ERSKINE CONTINUED in a monotone: "I changed clothes with him in the hotel, then, when he went out, I followed him. He must have found keys to my house in my pockets and had the brilliant idea to prowl the place. At any rate, as soon as I, following him, realized that he was heading for my house, I beat him there and was waiting for him, and—did what I did.

"Then, when you got on the case and started talking, to Chapeau Falls, and asking me if I knew Monette Moreau, I knew that sooner or later you would come to the truth. I invented those stories, as hastily as possible. I was in a panic. I knew I had to divert your attention, till I could silence you. I tried to kill you with that carbon monoxide, after jockeying to get you left alone in the car. And, as you say, I got the Egyptian to try and kill you. By then I was

desperate. I thought I might as well gamble everything—
to be either in the clear, or lost. So I tried to get all these
people out here—and I tried my best to push you in close
to the house, after the shotgun went off, but—well, that's
all."

"You'll make it easy for all of us, won't you, Doctor?"
Drago asked quickly. "You'll be tried for the killing of
Count Lilli, first. You don't mind writing a full confession and all that, do you? In return, I'll promise you every
comfort that there can be, while you're in—"

The doctor made a weary gesture. "I can face a beating,"
he said dully. "I'll sign all the confessions you want."

Drago drew McTigue aside. "Play it that way, Mac. Try
him for killing Count Lilli. He'll be convicted. Then the
other jobs can be written off against him. Not that the
killing of Wells wouldn't stand up. It's a perfect case, too,
if we can find this Monette Moreau, but that might be a
job. God knows where she is."

McTigue looked keenly at Drago. "So you were giving
me the run-around about this DeRussy guy? I thought he
was supposed to be a lead-in to the Moreau girl."

Drago covered up hastily, "I was afraid you might peep
to Erskine. I'd suggest that you take Erskine down to the
local station-house and then go back out to the cottage and
explain to the Northport lads. I'll see you—" He broke off,
as the phone rang.

At Drago's nod, McTigue answered, held monosyllabic
conversation, then covered the mouthpiece with one hand.

"It's Craven. He thinks he's broken the case. He just
grabbed a bookmaker named Ike Sehotterman, going into
Wells' apartment. The bookie claimed Wells owed him
money, and—"

Drago picked up his hat. "That's probably the truth. That bookie may have been intimate with Wells, but he's not in on this job. You explain to Craven, Mac—I've promised to get Mr. DeRussy back to town by midnight, in return for the valuable help he's given us. I'll leave it up to you from here on. Break up Craven's pipe-dream and tell him what's happened. I'll see you at headquarters."

As they climbed into the doctor's blue sedan for the ride home to town, Drago told DeRussy: "I've sure done a lot of lying for you."

The white-faced medium's eyes were apprehensive in the dashlight glow. "I—I know it," he said huskily. "I—I can't understand why you did it."

"But you're grateful, though—?"

"My God, yes!"

"Are you grateful enough to buy me a drink in your apartment when we get back—and not ask any questions till then?"

"Of—of course."

THE WHITE-RIMMED eyes of fear were still in DeRussy's small, olive face when they entered the medium's apartment. Drago walked unhurriedly into the living-room, put his hat on the table and turned to face DeRussy. The detective's dark, shining face and rippling black hair put an aura around his head.

"Never mind the drinks," he said quietly, as the youth turned toward the kitchen.

Drago said: "I'm curious to know what happened to Monette Moreau after being deserted in Greenville, and so forth."

DeRussy's liquid brown eyes were a little dark with question. He said: "A French girl can always get along—

even an ignorant, illiterate, backwoods French girl, left in a position where she dares not go home. She may get a little wise in the process—a little shopworn, perhaps, but she can get by, somehow. Even, perhaps, become not quite so illiterate"

"I was wondering if Monette happened to be vindictive about Erskine."

The medium shrugged. "She was for a while, but time cools those things. And our business is the most harrowing kind of show business, you know. Especially for a girl. One uncomfortable contretemps follows another so quickly that there is little time to worry about old wrongs. I think Monette would have liked to take a financial bite out of Erskine, and make him squirm a little, but that's all."

Drago's shining black eyes squinted a little. "How do you mean your business is harrowing for a girl?"

DeRussy fumbled out a cigarette case, looked down. "Any kind of business where a girl tries to go it alone, is harrowing," the medium said. "Especially when the business happens to be called illegal in most places."

"I see," Drago said quietly. "You mean that men make it tough for such girls."

DeRussy nodded.

"That might explain," Drago said thoughtfully, "why some girls in that line masquerade as men."

DeRussy's eyes jumped, shifted quickly back and forth between one of Drago's shining black ones and the other. The medium's pleasant, light voice was almost a whisper. "You—"

There was a moment of silence.

Then DeRussy finished. "You guessed that from the first?"

"No. Not till darned near the last." Drago took a flat package from the inside pocket of his coat, laid it on the table without losing the psychic's eyes. "Doctor Erskine was thoughtful enough to draw ten thousand dollars from the bank. I happened to take it from his pocket, in trust for you, of course."

"For me?"

"Yes. You're his widow, when you come right down to it, aren't you?"

Monette Moreau looked down. "Yes."

From his coat pocket, Drago took the scarab ring, laid it on top of the money. "I shouldn't return this to you. In the first place, it might be called in evidence, though I doubt it. In the second, you're too darn careless with a valuable ring—dropping it around where people are killing each other. But it's yours, isn't it?"

She looked dully at the ring. "Yes. That was the ring we—used as a wedding ring. I—when I went to call on Ralph, last night, I was afraid he might not recognize me in my boy's clothes—"

"With peaked cap."

"Yes. With peaked cap, I took the ring to make sure he would have no doubts. I was waiting for him—when that thing happened. I didn't know, of course, who had done it, but when I went up the walk, I saw what had happened, and I—I ran. I dropped the ring, then."

"Then that's that," Drago said cheerfully. He picked up his hat, strolled over to the door.

"Don't go," the girl said softly. "You've done so much for me. Won't you take half that money?"

Drago shook his head smilingly.

"Then—wouldn't you be curious to see Monette Moreau—as herself? She's not so bad looking—"

Drago guessed he was curious, at that.

VICIOUS CIRCLE

OUT OF DOCTOR KERN'S SHADOW-FILLED PAST CAME THE SKELETON IN HIS CLOSET—THE MURDERER WHOSE FACE THE MEDICO'S PLASTIC SURGERY HAD WARPED BEYOND ALL RECOGNITION. BUT WHILE FACES CAN BE CHANGED, BLOOD-GUILT CANNOT BE ALTERED ONE DEGREE, AS THE DOCTOR DISCOVERED WHEN HE SOUGHT TO WIPE OUT THE PAST AS HE HAD ERASED THE FEATURES OF THE KILLER, RABBIT PIRIE.

THERE WAS no long-drawn-out, agonizing deliberation leading up to Doctor Morris Kern's decision to murder. In the first place, the cold, brilliant brain that had brought him, at forty-two, to be ranked among the twenty top surgeons in the country, did not function that way. In the second, there was no time for any such thing, even had he desired it. The crisis simply bloomed up out of nowhere—out of a past that he had long since satisfied himself to be dead—literally between one minute and the next.

It was twenty minutes past six when he came reluctantly out of his office, to the door of his luxurious waiting-room, his hunched, tight body still in surgeon's white coat. His dark eyes went to the clock on the cool, green wall, in sour annoyance. That was all that was in his mind as he moved woodenly toward the insistently ringing phone on his receptionist's cleared desk and leaned across the desk-top to answer—annoyance at a call so long after hours. And even that irritation was not very deep. He was a stranger to ill humour. He was savoring the cream of life at this point, reaching toward the climax of his career. He was not conscious of having even the slightest shadow on his sparkling horizon. Certainly, the idea that *any* phone call could disturb anything vital would have seemed a joke.

And, in nine banal words, he was a criminal wanted by—and in real, momentary danger of being taken by—the State of New York.

A husky, anxious voice at the other end of the wire blurted: "This—this is Rabbit Pirie, Doc. You—remember me?"

As simply as that, his ghost came back, or—more aptly—his evil genius.

For a moment, his mind was chocked to a dead standstill, unable to absorb it.

It was not a simple thing to absorb.

THERE HAD been times, in the past, when he had regretted what he had done for Pirie, twelve years ago, when the frantic little killer had run to his dingy, ill-equipped office for help—and had received it. Those were the dark ages of plastic surgery. Few surgeons had even heard of it. Kern had heard of it as, even then, he had heard of most things touching his profession. He had studied what technique had been evolved on the subject. It was partly the enormous sum of cash Pirie offered, partly the consuming professional itch to attempt the then unheard of feat of disguising a hunted man's face by surgery, that had tempted him to alter the cowardly little murderer's appearance sufficiently to enable him to escape the country.

It had, obviously, made Kern legally a criminal. Actually, by one of Fate's more subtle twists, it had done far more than that. It had warped nearly every thread of his life—upward. It had in a way, brought on the emotional upheaval that had seared out of him, once and for all, all emotional feeling. There had been a woman—the one woman who had stirred the full, burning force of Kern's gaunt desire—and she had turned from him because of what he had done

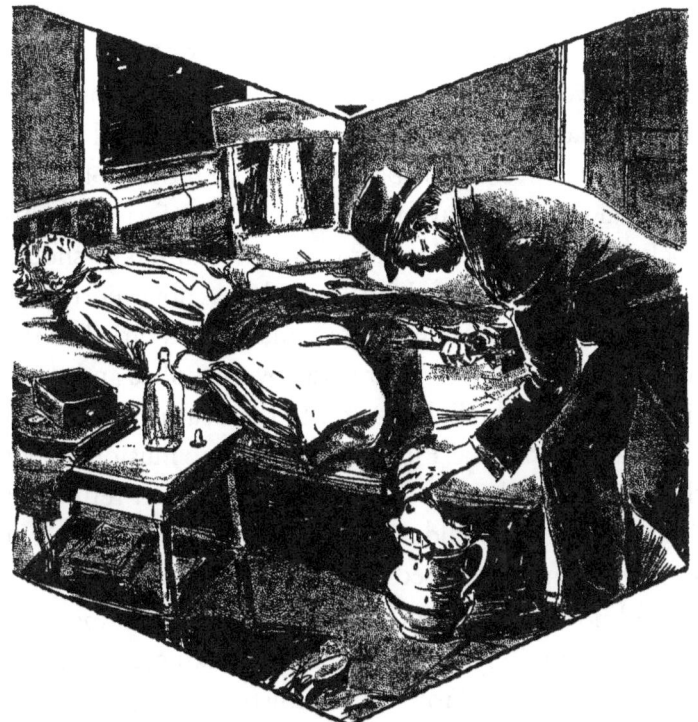

He propped the foot on the cake of ice which lay across the pitcher.

for the murderer. That had been like a bad amputation. There had been a period of emotional torture that tore him, burned him out. The woman had married someone else and been long forgotten. But the gnawing frustration that she left was the impetus that had thrown him with such fierce drive into his practice.

With Pirie's blood-money, he had been able to desert the dingy tenements, seek richer fields. And, because he was cold, he was a supreme surgeon. No sympathy, no impatience, no apprehension, nervousness, sentiment—no feelings of any kind ever distorted the brilliant, errorless logic of his mind, or the devastating directness of his thin hands. Success had almost seemed to flow toward him.

But never once, in all the time, had he ever considered what he had done for Pirie as ever being of actual danger to himself. Twelve years back, he had seen the rabbit-like criminal off on a boat for Holland, with a fortune in his pocket, and the electric chair waiting for him if he should ever again be caught in this country. It was not even a question of evidence. Besides the face of a rabbit, Pirie had the heart of one. If he were ever taken by the police and questioned, he would talk himself into the death chair even if they had *no* evidence. Pirie, himself, had no illusions about that. He knew that his only safety lay in never returning. That the little rat would return—ever—was something that simply had never entered Kern's logical mind.

And now he *had* returned—the living, breathing, and, what was infinitely more perilous, the talking, evidence of Kern's criminal act. From being a misty memory, he was, in the twinkling of an eye, solid human flesh at the other end of a phone—a supreme, momentary threat to all that Kern had, or was. Career, position, possessions—even, quite possibly, his life—were suddenly hanging by the desperate hope that Pirie might not be caught.

It was a jolt that even Kern's cold, driving mind could not take in full stride. Yet it faltered only a moment. Then he swallowed the incredible situation whole and faced the problem.

THERE WAS not a ripple on his dark, carved Indian face. He said, in a quiet, controlled voice: "Yes. Of course I remember you. Are you in New York?" He waited for the answer.

Words blurted over the phone—husky, desperate words.

"Couldn't stand it. Twelve years in them cold countries like you told me. Half nutty to see New York—hear good old U.S.A. Can't imagine what it's like, Doc. Guy goes off his onion, just sittin' there, thinkin' of the big town, achin' to see folks like hisself. Had to sneak back, Doc. After twelve years, figured there was no danger, but that's where I was wrong, Doc. Think some flatty spotted me—or something. Seen him watching my hide-out up on the Drive. Got to get away again, Doc. If the flatty was watchin' me, and goes to the joint and picks up my fingerprints, it's curtains. Got to get back on a boat, somehow—don't mind so much now. Had a whole month around the old town. All set to go back, Doc—only I'm broke, Doc. The cash I had is stashed in the apartment—don't dare go near the place. Nobody else to turn to, Doc—nobody else that's interested in seein' me get clear."

He gulped into tense silence.

By then, Kern knew all that he needed to know. There was only one way to insure, positively, that Pirie would never blurt out Kern's name in the back room of some police station. The factor of safety—of having Pirie in some distant country—had collapsed once, and it could never be trusted again. He knew he would have to kill Pirie—and kill him as quickly as ever he could.

His voice was unhurried. "Where are you now?"

"Now? You mean—where'm I holed up? A little hotel on Hunerd'n Twenty-Fi'th—Hotel Kalpa, corner of—"

"I mean, where are you phoning from?"

"A cigar store across— Oh, I get what you mean, Doc, but you needn't worry. Nobody's listenin' in. Listen, Doc. If you can leave me have five yards, I can get a boat that's leavin' tomorrow—a freighter. Then I'll be—you know—off your mind as well. Because if they catch me, and—"

"Have you made any arrangements with this freighter yet?"

"No—not yet. I got to have the money in my hand before I can go to—the party I know. But I can fix it. Oh, I can fix it all right, if—"

"How is the work I did for you holding up?"

"Huh? You mean my— Oh, it's swell, Doc. Yeah, it's swell. But, see—the copper knows it now and—"

"I'd like to see it," Kern said.

There was a second's silence.

"You—mean you want me to come down there?" Pirie asked huskily.

"No—no," Kern said. "That would hardly be wise. What kind of place is this Kalpa hotel? If I came there—say, late tonight—could I manage to get to your room without being seen by anyone? I don't mind letting you have the money, if I can do that."

"Sure! Sure you can, Doc!" Pirie said eagerly. "Hell, that's easy. There ain't no bell boys or like that, in this flea-bag. I'll figure some gag to get the clerk to come up at—well, whatever time you say. The lobby'll be empty, and you can walk in and up the stairs to the second floor. They don't keep no lights in the halls at night, and you can wait in the dark till you see him go down again. Then come up—my room's on the third, see? Three-two,"

After a moment, Kern said: "I see." His voice was dull. "You know you're pretty foolish to come back to this country at all, Rabbit."

"God, Doc—I know it! I've learned my lesson. I'll never do it again! I swear it—if you'll help me out now!"

"That's settled, isn't it? What time does that hotel quiet down? I mean, so that there would be no one in the lobby to see me?"

"Around midnight, I guess, Doc—though it's certain by one o'clock. God, Doc, I'll never forget—"

"I'll come then, at exactly one o'clock. You manage to take care of the clerk, will you?"

"Yeah. You—you won't forget, like, or—or anything?"

Kern's sunken, glowing eyes dropped down to his left hand, and to the heavy onyx-and-gold ring on his finger. It had not been there long. Two days. It had been specially designed for the puzzled Surgeon's Society, who felt impelled to grant him some recognition, without exactly knowing how. It had been a presentation, as its raised-gold lettering admitted, on the event of his birthday, the first of the month, for *Distinguished Service.* It constituted, very neatly and precisely, the full total and symbol of his success to date—exactly the things that Rabbit Pirie's very existence threw into imminent peril.

"You can depend on me, Rabbit," he said. "I'll be there."

HE STOOD beside the receptionist's desk, for five full minutes after he had hung up, his bent, powerful body motionless, his long arms propping him against the desk edge. His darkly carved, high-cheek-boned face, startling in its contrast to his flaming crest of long, silky red hair, was like a mask. His dark, blazing eyes only, were alive in the cool, green room. His cool brain drove on. That was an end to his hesitancy.

He plotted this murder with the same cold, unerring logic with which he had planned a thousand operations. But for once, he was not direct. On the contrary—he deliberately chose a method fantastic enough so that it might be expected to muddle up all police investigation at its very start. It was no part of his intention to have to submit to police questioning, or even suspicion, after the thing were done. Yet he did not for a moment ignore the percentage of possible error. Carefully, bit by bit, he conceived the pieces of his plan, checking and rechecking every item.

He turned and made his way back to the office. From a shelf, he took down various books on forensic medicine, and carefully checked his own crystal-clear memory against two items in their pages—

> Seven or eight grains of cocaine, by injection, will produce insensibility almost at once, which will last for several hours, but will not produce death.
>
> The application of more than a four-percent solution of cocaine to the abraded skin will cause death in a very few minutes.

When he was satisfied, he restored the books, turned unhurriedly into his surgery. In one wall, a white cabinet concealed an ice-machine. He opened it, inspected the ranks of cube-trays, drew out the top one, and emptied it. He withdrew the grid, and refilled the tray, so that presently it would produce a solid slab of ice.

He paused in front of the rank upon rank of narrow drawers containing his instruments. After a moment, he opened one and removed an oversized, coarse file. From another, he took a small hypodermic syringe.

He went methodically on into the dispensary, busied himself there for a matter of minutes. When he again emerged into the office, he carried a long case, with the hypodermic syringe, now filled, lying in it. He also carried a quart bottle, filled with a twenty-percent solution of cocaine.

He placed them all on his desk, sat down slowly in the swivel chair, regarding them woodenly, his eyes almost closed.

Finally he reached for a red-leather-covered book marked *Engagements,* and opened it at today—November third. His own crabbed handwriting told him that he was due to attend a dinner given by the Long Island Surgeon's Association at Long Island City this evening.

After rummaging in a drawer for a minute, he unearthed the original engraved invitation to the dinner, that had reached him a week before.

Among various announcements on the card, one caught his eye: *Doctor Quand Edgeworth, president of the Surgeons' Society and well-known hernia specialist, will be the guest of honor.*

Kern's eyes became unseeing on the announcement, blank with quick concentration.

Presently, he rose and went out to the phone on his receptionist's desk—his own was disconnected at this hour—and called the home of the pompous little president of the Surgeons' Society.

"I think I've stumbled on something rather important in your field," he told him. "Would you be interested in a method of turning practically any strangulated hernia into a reducible one *without* surgery?"

"Good Lord! You aren't serious?"

"Oh, yes. I'm not quite ready to show it to you yet, but I think I will be in a few hours. I called now to find out where I could be sure of getting hold of you later tonight—that is, if you're interested enough to—"

"But—but this is the night of the Long Island Association dinner! I've promised to speak. Aren't you attending it yourself?"

Kern hesitated. "I'd intended to, at that. This thing drove it completely from my mind. Not that I'm going, now—not with this thing in sight. Would you care— About what time will the dinner be over?"

"Eh? Around midnight, I suppose—maybe a little later."

"Are you interested enough to come down to the dissecting-room at Bellevue afterwards? I would meet you there, say, at one-thirty—give you plenty of leeway and time to get back."

"Yes—yes—by all means, my dear fellow! I'll come direct from the dinner. At the dissecting-room—one-thirty. You couldn't give me any hint now as to what you base—"

"I'm not sure enough for that, Doctor."

FLOPHOUSE WAS the only word to describe the Kalpa. A sagging, narrow frame structure, jammed in the middle of a sagging, sinister-looking block. Two fly-specked windows, behind which dim light glowed sullenly, announced in chipped enamel that rooms with running water were one dollar. Knifing, whistling November wind had swept the silent street almost empty of humans, and there was no one but Kern, a shapeless dark figure in dark slouch hat and swaddling dark coat, a brief-case under his arm, to read it, at one o'clock.

It was as if magic were at work for him.

There was no one to dispute his passage, as he slipped into the odorous cubicle that was the lobby, no one to interfere as his rubber-soled shoes went silently up the broad, bare stairs into the utter dark of the second floor. He had barely reached the point in the darkness which he considered safe, and was pulling thin blacksilk gloves over his hands, when the clumping steps of the clerk came down from above, vanished into the lobby below. Even the boards of the noisome hall refrained from creeking, and the steps to the third—and top—story.

As if by signal, as he mounted the topmost step, a door down the hall opened silently, letting out a wedge of orange light, and the furtive, incredibly thin figure of a man, whose head seemed too large for him, peered out. He turned his face at an angle, and Kern recognized Rabbit Pirie, in dirty shirt sleeves.

THE LITTLE killer had his hand behind him, at his hip, as Kern came into the light. He dropped his head, licked his lips and backed, in an invitation to enter, his little, furtive eyes desperately agleam. Kern entered the room, Pirie hurried the door closed, locked it behind him.

The room was a foul slot. A cot, covered with sleazy blankets, filled a third of it. A single, dangling, fly-specked bulb hung from a cord in the center of the ceiling. There was running water as advertised—a filthy basin. There was either a solid rectangle of dirt beside the bed or a carpet—impossible to tell which—also a rickety chair and table, holding Pirie's suitcase and magazines. Atop a peeling, gray-painted chest of drawers was a dark mirror and a fat water pitcher.

"God, Doc," Pirie burst out desperately. "You don't know how I hated to bother ya—only, I—I was at the end o' my rope. I been in this hellhole for ten days, starvin', you might say—tryin' to think how to—"

"You've no need to apologize," Kern said. "I've a lot of professional curiosity in seeing how you look."

He looked like a freak. He looked as if his body had been on a starvation diet for months, with a wasting disease thrown in. His scrabbly hair was almost all gray now, and the forehead under it seamed and lined. But from the eyes down, his face—apart from a pastiness—was fantastically youthful, firm and round, blooming. His shifty little gray eyes seemed to be surveying the world from behind an emplacement. He avoided Kern's burning, dark gaze.

"Guess—guess I don't look so hot, right now, Doc. I—I ain't had much to eat this last ten days, and I been—well, I ain't seemed to be able to get no sleep. I—"

"We'll take care of that, too," Kern said. "Step over under the light here and let me have a look at you."

Pirie backed obediently over, till he stood just under the light, no more than three feet from the bed, pulling at his shaking hands, stammering huskily: "Honest to God, Doc—don't get me wrong. I woulda done anything to keep from puttin' the bite on you. I ain't the kind of a guy to shake a party that done a favor for me. I ain't never forgot that, if it wasn't for you, I'd a burned long ago. I— Doc, so help me, even if the cops did get me, I'd—I'd try not to give them your name. I ain't never—not even once, drunk or sober, since that night—mentioned your name to a living soul, ya know that? Not even in them foreign countries, Doc."

"I'm glad to hear it," Kern said. "Tilt your head back, so I can see under your chin."

He bent his knees, stooped down a little, his left hand slipping out of his pocket, dropping almost to the floor. Pirie's chin tilted obediently to the ceiling. "It—it was only because I didn't have no place else," Pirie insisted at the light bulb.

"I know," Kern said, and slammed a perfectly scientific, timed uppercut, squarely under the little man's chin, lifting him completely from the floor, to crash down on the cot, cleanly knocked out.

Kern stood motionless, his heavy-lidded eyes sliding to the door, as he strained to catch any indication that the noise had been heard. But there was no such indication.

HE WORKED with sure fingers, his carved, glowing Indian face utterly impassive, his blazing eyes swift. He opened the briefcase, took out the syringe and bent over Pirie. He injected the full contents of the syringe, just behind, and under, the little killer's ear.

He stepped back and waited.

A minute went by—two minutes.

The wasted, shrunken little body suddenly shook, vibrated, then, in a sudden burst of wriggling, rolled off the bed to the floor, with a thump. Kern stepped forward calmly, and, with his black-gloved hands, picked the writhing little man up as if he had been a satchel, redepositing him on the bed. There were a few more convulsive twistings, some queer sounds in his throat—and then the fugitive relaxed into the full unconsciousness that would hold him for several hours.

Kern reached the fat water pitcher from the chest of drawers. Beside the cot, he lined up the heavy file, the quart bottle of violent cocaine solution, the water pitcher, and a square black thermos box.

He poured the cocaine solution into the fat water pitcher. From the thermos box he took the long slab of ice, about the size of a small book. He laid the slab of ice down, so that it rested across the top of the now one-third full water pitcher. He took up the rasp, hastily undid Pirie's shoe, ripped off his sock, and took the unclean foot between his knees.

In ninety seconds, the sole of Pirie's foot was a raw, bloody, lacerated sore.

He returned everything not in use, to the briefcase, strapping it shut. He took the bloody, raw foot and propped it on the slab of ice, in such position that, when the ice should have melted, the foot would drop down into the solution in the fat pitcher.

He took his watch from his pocket, stood with the briefcase under his arm, glowing dark eyes on the doomed man, checked again mentally, carefully, and swiftly, his calculations. The injection of cocaine would hold Pirie unconscious for at least three hours. In this hot room, the slab of ice would melt and let Pirie's foot touch the strong solution, in very little over an hour. Pirie would die within fifteen minutes after that. And no autopsy would be able to detect the injected cocaine after the lacerated foot once began absorbing it at the other end.

He looked quickly around the room. There was no telephone.

He unlocked the door, looking out into the hall. Halfway toward the stairs, on the wall, he could discern a wall phone.

He took the key from the inside of the door, stepped out and locked it from outside, slid the key under the door. No one seemed to be stirring throughout the entire hot, noisome building, as he walked silently down the hall. Without stopping, he lifted the receiver of the wall phone from the hook, left it dangling.

Far down below him, he could hear a faint, rasping buzz begin.

He was again in the shadows of the second floor as the cursing clerk climbed wearily up to the third. No one saw his dark, muffled figure as he slipped out of the dingy hotel, walking swiftly the four blocks to where he had parked his coupé.

When, minutes later, he angled his car in to a parking-space beside the side entrance of Bellevue Hospital, and climbed out, a dapper, white-goatee'd little man came bustling across the walk.

"Ah, Kern," Quand Edgeworth said eagerly. "You're exactly on the dot. One-thirty to the second. I've gotten old. Have to open up for us. Though I've been thinking and thinking over what you said, and I'm dashed if I don't think you're attempting the impossible."

"Well, maybe," Kern said.

WHEN DRAGO came, Kern was almost as shocked as he had been at Pirie's voice. When his office girl, at twelve-thirty the following day, came in to his office to announce, "A Mr. Drago—from police headquarters," it stopped his breath in his throat. There was nothing assumed in the utterly blank look he gave her.

"What in the name of God does he want?"

"He wants to consult you as an expert, he says, on the murder of a man with a paraffin chin."

It was almost a minute before he got control of his voice. But there was certainly only one answer to make.

"All right," he said. "Send him in."

Drago, brown, bland, in neat tan clothes, his eyes two twinkling specks of Jet in his round, shining face, came in smoothing his dark, rippling hair. His vermilion lips showed a thin flash of white teeth as he closed the door behind him.

"I'm looking for a man like you," he said cheerfully, "for murder." Then, as he looked at Kern's stiff, unsmiling face, he lifted a short, gloved hand. "Not you, I didn't mean—but a man like you."

Kern sat perfectly motionless. He actually had to struggle up through the fog of utter confusion. For the first time in his life, his cold, driving mind was trapped between two chains of logic. It was beyond human belief that this bland, brown man should be here by pure coincidence. It was equally beyond Kern's belief that he had left a single flaw in what he had done last night. He knew, as well as he knew his name, that he had left no trace of his presence in Pirie's room. He knew that it was humanly impossible that the crime could have been traced to him. He was, momentarily, flabbergasted. Yet, even while his mind churned and grasped at the incredible problem, his dark Indian face remained calm, frozen.

"Very enlightening and interesting, I'm sure," he said without interest. "May I ask exactly what you want of me?"

"About an hour of your time—maybe less. I hope less," Drago said politely.

"What? Just an hour?" Kern said with irony. "Just an hour out of the middle of the day? Why be so modest? I'm very sorry, Mr. Drago. It may not have occurred to whoever sent you here, but my time is worth money. I am afraid I must decline to offer the city an hour of it."

"I wasn't sent here by anybody," Drago said. "It just happens that Mr. Barry, of the homicide squad, who is handling this case, is a very close friend of mine. He's completely stumped. I'm just poking around, completely unofficially, to see if I can line it up for him. He doesn't know—no one knows—that I'm even working on it, yet."

A less acute mind than Kern's would have marked that, of course, to all intents and purposes, the man before him was a free-lance agent, for the moment, at any rate. Somehow, a surge of relief because of it—a return of his cold confidence—seeped over Kern.

"Very touching, I'm sure," he said dryly, "but I am also unable to sacrifice an hour of my time to you, personally."

Drago's round face became anxious. "Doctor, I know it's unusual, but you're about the one man that can help me. None of our regular experts are qualified. You—well, of course"—he indicated the onyx-and-gold ring with a faint gesture at Kern's hand— "I guess everybody that reads the papers these days knows that your knowledge is about as broad as possible. And I've built up a theory to such size that I've simply got to have someone check me. I didn't expect you to do it for nothing. I wouldn't want you to think that. But, say, for a fee?"

Kern blinked dully. "For a fee? Yes, for a fee, you or anybody else can have an hour of my time. For a fee of about five hundred dollars."

In a movement so smooth and efficient that it seemed startlingly fast, the neat, bland detective extracted a wallet, fingered out five one-hundred-dollar bills, laid them on the desk, and sat down in the chair. He put the tips of one gloved hand on the edge of the desk, and said: "I'd like to go into every detail of the murder—even if it seems a little labored to you, and, when I get to the questions, I'll ask them."

Kern struggled to take his eyes from the bills. After a minute, he shrugged. "All right—if you feel it's worth it. A man was murdered."

Drago leaned forward, talked quickly, almost naively up at Kern. And, in two minutes, Kern realized that he had made one ghastly mistake—the mistake of underestimating police brains. His stomach went taut.

DRAGO SAID: "An old-time lush worker and burglar, named Rabbit Pirie, was the victim, in a flophouse. He was killed last night between two and three, the M.E. says, by having his foot scraped raw and immersed in a very strong solution of cocaine. Did you ever hear of that method of killing a person?"

Kern shook his head. "I can't say that I did."

"Neither did the M.E. Neither did I—or any of the men on the case. However, this murderer knew it—and that pegs him, as far as I'm concerned, as a doctor or a chemist. I can't imagine anyone else knowing about it. Since there was no sign of the container in which the cocaine solution was brought into the room, or the instrument that hacked up Pirie's foot, it's a safe bet that the killer brought them in—some time between two and three last night—made Pirie unconscious somehow, and put his foot in that stuff before he came to, and then took the things out with him. I'm not worried about that part of it. But there's another queer angle.

"The dead man looked no more like Rabbit Pirie when he was found, than I do. It was his fingerprints, only, that identified him. He'd had his face changed by plastic surgery. The M.E. got him down to the morgue, of course, and tried to reconstruct the face as it used to be, but his skin was so thin—almost pathologically so—that it ripped and tore all over the place. But—and this is the significant item, Doctor—the material used to build up his cheeks and chin was paraffin. How long ago did plastic surgeons stop using paraffin for that purpose?"

There was no avoiding the answer. "About ten years ago, I guess," he heard himself say.

"That's what the M.E. said. So the surgery must have been done at least ten years ago. Well, about twelve years ago, Rabbit Pirie hit a man on the head, too hard, in a dark alley. The man happened to be a gambler, with a lot of money on him. He died. Pirie was named for it, but he absolutely vanished off the face of the earth.

"In Pirie's effects, at the flophouse, there was not one article that hadn't been purchased in some foreign country. Not even so much as a handkerchief. It's a cinch he's been out of the country, for a long time, and just returned. Add all that up, and what have we got?"

He answered his own question. "We've got Pirie, on the run from a murder charge, having his face altered, twelve years ago and skipping the country. We've got him coming back now, and being murdered by, presumably, a doctor. I don't see any avoiding the probability that he was killed by the doctor who changed his face twelve years ago."

"I—" Kern began.

"Wait—there're other things to be considered. Pirie was desperately broke. He'd been away for twelve years. He had no underworld contacts left. He was still wanted for murder. He had to raise money somewhere. He'd hardly have forgotten the name of the man who fixed his face.

"That doctor must have been a smart man to know how to do such a first-class job as long ago as twelve years—so the M.E. says. If he was smart then, he's probably smart today. And, if he's been smart for twelve years, he probably amounts to something today. Maybe—in fact, this is what I think—maybe he's even outstandingly prominent. Assuming that to be so, he'd be both the best and the worst target Pirie could choose to blackmail for the funds that he needed. The best, because he'd have the money—the top men in your line make plenty. The worst, because he'd have more to lose if Pirie were ever caught, and talked. And, if he knew Pirie at all, he must have known that it was inevitable that just that thing would happen sometime.

So he killed him to seal his mouth permanently. Where's the flaw in that?"

Kern felt as though he'd been blackjacked. This—this was the police inquiry that he had expected to befog hopelessly at the very inception! His whole secret lay ripped open at his feet. In the one long stroke, the bland, round detective had swept away everything he had counted on for concealment. How had— But the soft insistent voice had already explained, in deadly, devastating detail, exactly how he had arrived at the dangerous truth.

For the first time in many years, he suddenly felt emotion—an almost superstitious, disorganizing fear, crawling up inside him for this plump, brown man.

KERN TRIED desperately to grasp at his slipping confidence. There was still his alibi—he was aware of that, every minute. It had not been broken, or he would be in handcuffs now. But, in the grip of unreason, it suddenly seemed to him to be pitifully weak—a scant thing to stand between himself and the electric chair. If the shining, coal-black eyes opposite him had penetrated everything else in these few hours, how long would the alibi hold up under their scrutiny? He tried to tell himself that there was no evidence—no evidence whatever—to connect him, in any way, with the murder of Pirie. Drago was shooting into the air by coming to him at all. Or even-yes, it was possible, by some fantastic coincidence, that he did not suspect Kern at all—that pure chance had brought him here.

He had to clear the huskiness out of his throat to say: "It's a reasonable theory, all right. Tenuous, but I can't say I see a real flaw in it."

"Then"—Drago leaned a little forward—"the whole thing resolves itself into this. I must find a surgeon of some prominence, who was obscure twelve years ago—he must have been obscure or he would never have touched the job on Pirie. It's quite probable that he branched out a bit, after that job. Pirie was well fixed, and he could have collected plenty. That's what I want. A prominent surgeon, who was obscure twelve years ago, but who branched out just about that time—had some sort of accession of prosperity."

"And was in a flophouse murdering this criminal, between two and three last night," Kern added.

"Yes."

Kern looked at his hands. "As it happens," he said, "I, myself fit that description—in all but one particular. I happened to come into a small legacy just about twelve years ago. At least, I think it was about then. You might say I've won a little prominence lately. And I certainly was poor twelve years ago. But, between two and three last night, I was with Doctor Quand Edgeworth. Rather difficult for me to be off in this Pirie's hotel murdering him at the same time, eh? I wish I knew how I could do a trick like that, though."

It was sickeningly weak, and he knew it the moment it was out. The black eyes across the desk did not smile, did not waver.

"So do I," Drago said.

Then Kern knew. This policeman was perfectly certain that Kern had murdered Rabbit Pirie. He knew why. He knew part of the how.

Kern began to fight panic. His cold, clear mind was a mass of frightened confusion, his perspective gone. He felt that he no longer had any defenses.

Then Drago said: "I'm hoping you can name the man—from among your acquaintances. It would be nice if I could keep everything absolutely to myself, till I make an arrest."

Something hot jumped alive in Kern's head.

Queerly, a part of his mind recognized the clinical symptoms in himself—the psychology of the habitual murderer—the desperate grasping at the one sure means to solve every problem. Yet, to the churning part of him, it seemed his only salvation—to silence this man before he transmitted the disastrous information he had collected.

The hot thing blazed up. Even though this office were located in the busy Park Avenue section, murder could be done here. Every wall in the suite—gruesome thought—was thoroughly sound-proofed. There was a small automatic pistol—small caliber, but loaded with high-speed, long, hollow-point bullets—in the drawer by his right knee. The only window in the office—a small one—opened onto the delivery alley of the building. There were rubber sheets in the surgery behind him. There was a large incinerator whose mouth opened into the surgery—not large enough to take the body whole, but if it were cut up into bits....

He tried weakly to check the feverish line of thought. There was his office nurse, due to arrive in less than an hour. He could never hope to have the traces removed in an hour. There was no way of explaining what she would find in the surgery....

"I'm afraid," he told Drago, "that I don't know the background of any prominent surgeon that would correspond to that."

DRAGO WAS silent a while, his round face disappointed. Finally, he said: "Well, if you can't—you can't." Reluctantly, he took a handful of old envelopes from an inner pocket, began to sort them on the desk edge. "I'll just get you to sign a receipt form for that money, if you don't mind. Maybe I can retrieve it later. I've got an official form here somewhere."

Kern glanced down—and his head began to sing.

On the back of one of the envelopes was inked a name and address. The name was that of the one person in the whole world who knew of his relations with Pirie long ago—the woman who had thrown him over because of them.

Then he knew the vicious circle of murder had come round again. If Drago reached that woman, she would tell everything. If he left this office, he would reach her. That was cold, terrifying logic. If he had been told that Drago had already spent more than an hour fruitlessly questioning the woman, who, for purely sentimental reasons would say nothing incriminating to her former lover, Kern could not have believed it. It was not logical.

Nothing was logical, but that Drago must not leave this office. He felt the fever mounting in his head. Yet—the nurse? And there was Miss Craigie, the girl in the reception room. She had seen Drago come in. If she did not see him go out....

The phone at his elbow tinkled.

Miss Craigie's voice said diffidently into his ear: "Would it be all right, if I went to lunch now, Doctor? I'm supposed to meet my mother at the train, and—"

"Just a minute," Kern said stiffly. "I'll be right out."

He had to sit at the desk for another minute, bend over the drawer at his knee and pretend to be searching for a paper. When he walked out into the waiting-room, the gun was in his trouser pocket.

The flaxen-haired Miss Craigie looked up apologetically. He silenced her with a wave. "Just call my nurse before you go and tell her she needn't come in today. Take all the time you want for lunch. I've nothing for you to do."

He stood by her till she had called the nurse, and departed.

The hot thing was hammering in his head as he paused just outside the office door before reentering. The thing was to get the brown devil into the surgery, where blood could easily be wiped up—where all traces could be easily removed—and if they were not, what of it?

He went back in.

"I can't seem to find the wretched form," Drago said. "I wonder if you'd give me one of yours."

"Certainly," Kern said promptly, and nodded toward the surgery. "Just step in here."

Drago blinked, but Kern gave him no chance to demur. He turned and led the way into the surgery.

BUT DRAGO only came as far as the door. Maddeningly, he halted at the door. Kern, turning back, saw the shining black eyes sweep over the dazzling white-and-nickel room. They came to rest on the ice-machine and the grid, lying in full sight on top of it—the grid he had removed the night before to freeze the slab of ice.

"A very impressive lay-out," Drago's soft voice said. "What is that?"

"My ice-machine," Kern said hastily, and nodded toward the closed door of the dispensary beyond. "If you'll just step in here—"

But Drago was not listening. His eyes, momentarily, had swollen.

"Ice!" he muttered in sudden illumination. "And it never occurred to—"

Abruptly, he disappeared from the door, back into the surgery.

Kern, stung to panic, whirled and dived after him, the gun jerking out of his pocket. Yet he had sense to keep his hand behind him as he swept into the office.

Drago was hastily scooping up the envelopes he had left on the desk, but he was on the other side of the desk now. He said gruffly, without looking up: "Sorry. Just remembered something. Got to rush away. Hope you don't mind."

Kern's throat tightened. He said, in a queer, slaty voice: "Mr. Drago!"

Drago looked up, his eyes granite.

"Let's stop this foolishness," Kern said.

"You suspect me. Why?"

Drago's eyes veiled. "That will come out, presently."

Kern jerked up the gun, and Drago stopped dead, his mouth coming open. Then he closed it. He said softly: "I suppose you know that this is all adding to the evidence against you."

"No," Kern said, and squeezed the trigger.

Flame and roar spurted, but they spurted a fraction of a second too late. They were preceded by the explosion of glass at the alley window and the dull, *thunking* report of an air-pistol.

Kern stumbled backward, cursing, clutching his shattered wrist, brought up against the wall, as the window swung inward and a lean, young Italian jumped into the room.

Drago rose from behind the desk. For a second, there was silence. Then Drago said: "Well, I guess that does it, Doc. That ice gag was all we needed. What we had wasn't evidence—unless we could explain away your alibi."

"Explain? I don't know what you're talking about! I've done nothing. If you're still talking about that Pirie—"

"Keep it for your lawyer, Doc," Drago said. "The old vicious circle got you. You started your career on Pirie's paraffin chin—and you wind up right there. As I told you, he had a very thin skin. He'd been in that overheated hotel for ten days, almost continuously. The paraffin couldn't take it. It softened. When the M.E. peeled the skin away, there was a hazy impression. We couldn't make anything of it till we got the old black light to work. Then we had no trouble. We could even see the impression of the mesh of the silk gloves you wore."

"My God, what nonsense is this?"

"Let me finish. There was also a very distinct and readable set of letters. Maybe you can guess what they were? No? They read: *For Distinguished Service to Surgery* and, underneath, your birthday date—the first of this month."

He gestured with a short, gloved finger toward the heavy onyx-and-gold ring on Kern's hand. "From what Doctor Edgeworth told me, there isn't another ring like that in existence. They had it made especially for you. Kind of a vicious circle all by itself—if you think it over."

MURDER ON MARGIN

THERE WAS ONLY A RING OF KEYS LYING IN THE SNOW BESIDE THE COP KILLERS' VICTIM, BUT WITH THEM THE LITTLE BROWN MAN FROM HEADQUARTERS SET OUT TO UNLOCK THE RIDDLE OF THE TIPSY DEAD MAN WHO BOBBED UP OUT OF THE BOWELS OF THE EARTH, TO ENGAGE IN A MACABRE DEVIL-DANCE, ARM IN ARM WITH TWO DRUNKEN COMRADES.

CHAPTER ONE
BLOOD ON THE SNOW

THERE WAS nothing wrong when Patrolman Charles Birn rang in at four o'clock. On the contrary, high spirits had him in such fettle that he ignored the viciously bitter, cold morning—even to the point of giving out song. The smash line of the second stanza of one of the more robust squadroom ballads burned the sergeant's ear as he came on the wire.

"Ah," he said grimly, " 'twould be young Bernstein, yippin' for help."

"Bernstein? Hey, where do you get that stuff—"

"That'll do from you, ye cocky young bantam. Make your report and spare your betters' ears."

"Patrolman Birn reporting that everything is okey-doke, hi-de-hi, and copessettic."

He banged the call-box shut, ranged on up the inclined side street toward upper Broadway, grinning. The future looked just about as rosy as anything the youngster could possibly imagine. He had a reasonable right to be pleased.

Behind him, icy, knifing wind whistled in fitful gusts along Riverside Drive, and down the incline of the cross streets. At this dead hour, no soul stirred abroad. The black, motionless pavements were covered with thin ice; snow was banked up at curbs. It bothered Patrolman Charles

Birn not at all. In his present frame of mind, the warmth of his own burning enthusiasm would have kept him comfortable in a graveyard. His probationary period was well behind him. And he was free at last from the nightmare that pursues every fledgling cop—he was out of debt.

He touched the breast of his greatcoat. The envelope underneath crackled. Lacking only a stamp, the letter was ready to be mailed—the letter and money-order. The money-order was the final payment of the loan which had paid for his equipment and uniforms, ten months before. It had been no small effort that had enabled him to squeeze it out in so short a time. It had been lent him—forced on him, really—by his father's old side-partner—sergeant then, but inspector now, McTigue.

THERE WAS a bit of emotion concerned in the swarm of thought that occupied Patrolman Birn, as he stared happily into the black slot. Presently, he swallowed his feelings, moved on. The deserted pavement of Broadway stretched on into the distance ahead of him. There were more blue street lights here and the shining sidewalk was not in shadow, as far as he could see. The rubber of his shoe soles squeaked faintly on the packed snow.

It was about then that three men's heads suddenly sprouted out of the sidewalk, a half block ahead.

He was so startled that he stopped dead, his mouth opening.

The three heads became three busts, then three figures. It was exactly as if the ground had suddenly opened and was spewing the three slowly forth. There was even the pile of earth, flanking out, that they displaced.

Then he realized what he was actually seeing, and his white teeth showed in a smile.

She kept him covered every second.

The pile of earth was not earth but was a wing-door of iron, folding upward from the sidewalk. It was folding upward because the loading-elevator under it was rising, bringing the three men up on its platform. There are thousands of such elevators in New York, where alley space is practically nonexistent. Bulky deliveries can hardly be carried through stores full of customers. These elevators are the answer. Deliveries are taken at the curb, lowered into the basement of the store.

The three men were coming up from the basement of one of the stores in the long, two-story block-building a half block ahead.

Birn resumed his walk unhurriedly, a little curious, but in no way disturbed. The store, if he recalled it, was a butcher store, in which nothing of value was stored overnight. The three men stepped out on the icy sidewalk. One of them turned back and leaned down.

The elevator sank quietly again from sight. The bent man straightened, rejoined his tipsy companions—tipsy, Birn assumed, because they had their arms around each other's shoulders—and they moved off.

They had gone only a few paces when something dropped from the clothes of one of them. It was metallic, happened to catch the beam of light from a street lamp, and flashed in Birn's eye. It was impossible to know which of them had dropped it, or, at thirty paces' distance, what it was.

He quickened his pace, however, as the three roisterers sailed on for the corner ahead. He picked up a ring of keys from the gelid white snow, straightened, when the losers were only a few yards from the corner.

He whistled sharply, to attract their attention. Queerly, it seemed to have no effect. They passed on. He started after them, dangling the keys at arm's length.

"Hey, wait a minute!"

It seemed as if the third man—the one detached from the other two—flung a white face over his shoulder, just as Birn broke into a trot, still waving the keys.

The patrolman called impatiently: "You, there. Wait a minute. You dropped these—"

Then the shocking thing happened.

There was absolutely no warning. The third man suddenly wheeled around and faced the approaching patrolman, legs spread. The third man's hand jerked up, holding something that glittered.

Flame and roar exploded from the gun. The penultimate of agony ripped through Birn's face—a bullet tearing up the side of his teeth, ripping out every nerve.

He screamed, dropped the keys, his arms flying over his pain-maddened face, knees sagging. He staggered three steps in a wild circle. The man at the corner was cruelly careful. He fired again, his pistol held at arm's length—and again.

Lead splashed into Birn's cheek, into his forehead, and he pitched forward, arms still clawing over his head in the mad agony of that first shot. He plunged forward on his head, his body raised itself at the middle, then sank slowly sidewise and died in the snow, red streamers raying out from his face in the white.

The car around the corner thundered away, screamed as it skidded into the Drive below, roared again in frantic acceleration, and its sound died away in the whistling wind in a matter of seconds.

CHAPTER TWO
COP-KILLER CRUSADE

ONE MAN in a darkened fifth-floor apart-ment-house window had seen it, but he could give no descriptions. He phoned police, and prowl-cars were screaming to the curb in less than four minutes, disgorging bluecoats. They found the letter addressed to Inspector McTigue and called the old man. That was how Drago came into the picture.

The veteran, bald-headed inspector nearly went berserk. He tried to get out of bed in the hospital. A nurse had to fall on him, yell for orderlies. It took three of them to pin the big-framed man in bed and he gave up struggling only when they made the phone call he yelled for.

The call caught Drago just getting in from a bachelor dinner he had attended.

Tears streamed down McTigue's weathered, seamed old face as he shouted into the phone: "Go out and get whoever did it. Get them—but don't take them in. Bring them to me. I'll give them a taste of hell before they get there. They won't let me out of this damned bed or I wouldn't put it on you. But for God's sake, boy—if there's a spark of loyalty in your brown hide—track down what's behind this, and bring *who* is behind it, to me. I'll kill them with my bare—"

"Take it easy, Mac," Drago said. "I'm hitting it now."

The prowl-car he commandeered whirled onto Broadway, a block from the scene no more than twenty minutes from the first shooting, and Drago had it all from the radio by then. The tense driver said: "You're Drago from H.Q., ain't you?"

"Yes."

"The town'll go on fire over this. Them guys must be kill-crazy. Now, anyway."

"Eh?"

"I say they'll be kill-crazy now, anyway. If anybody gets close to them, they'll shoot fast. They got to. By now they're thinkin' what they'll face if they're taken. They'll be beaten to death. On the other hand, they can kill every cop in New York and lose nothing. They'll be dynamite to take. Why do guys kill cops?"

"I wonder."

"If the kid stumbled on some crooked work, it must be some racket—to be worth blasting cops. That angle strike you?"

"Yes."

The street was alive with police cars. The big black homicide squad-car was just screaming to a stop as Drago's prowlcar flung in behind it.

Drago and Lieutenant Craven dived out of their cars, together. Craven, red-faced, red-eyed, was a giant. In double-breasted gray guard's coat and muffler, gray hat on the back of his fiery red thatch, he towered four inches over Drago's neat, brown blandness.

"Ha—Drago!"

Drago swung, oblivious, toward the swarm of hunkered-down cops surrounding the dark figure on the sidewalk.

He walked into the road, then crunched across the curb's snow-bank and peeled a patrolman out of his way.

Craven bellowed, "Drago!" and ran up the sidewalk, scattered the men in his way, till he faced Drago over the fallen body. His voice was hoarse with fury.

"Get out of here. This is a man's job. We don't need any of your wise pussyfooting. I'm taking charge. Keep away from that body, damn you. We intend to find the rats that did this."

"Close your fat head," Drago said. "I've got my chief's orders."

"McTigue's off duty. He can't give orders. You keep away from that body or I'll crucify you. You hear?" He swung toward the squad-car. "Mac! Harry! Move, damn it!" He gestured impatiently at the staggering photographers. They came running with tripods. "You, Drago—you heard me."

Drago had words in his throat. He closed his mouth on them. By one of Fate's queer twists, he had found the keys.

HE DID not know that he had found them. Up to here, no one had mentioned keys, the single witness having been too far away to see what article Birn had waved at the killers. All Drago knew was that, in the piled snow at the edge of the sidewalk, he was standing on something hard and jagged—something that gave a fresh metallic gleam when he moved his foot and glanced down.

He put his foot back on the object and stood motionless, his gloved hands in the pockets of his coat, his smooth, dark face stony under the snap-brim of his brown hat, slightly oriental eyes downcast.

The cameras staggered up. Men milled around. Drago looked back a few yards. The butcher store, before which yawned the loading-elevator, was ablaze with lights now.

The precinct men were prowling about inside it, and also in the dentist's office that comprised the second story of the store. A precinct sergeant emerged from the store, his broad face dissatisfied, roamed over to the group around the body, as flashbulbs boomed.

"Anything?" Craven snapped at the sergeant.

"Nothing. They broke the padlock on the elevator and got in that way. There's nothing to show why they broke in. The butcher's on his way from his home now, and I've called the dentist above to come down."

"What do you think he'll tell you?"

"Nothin'. Neither will the butcher. But those are the only two places they could break into through that elevator."

A drab, black morgue wagon chugged in to the curb behind Drago. In the confusion, he got his chance. He bent quickly down and his gloved hand closed on the ring of keys. He backed out into the street with the keys in his pocket.

He thought, wrongly, that he had been unobserved. He walked quickly back to his own prowl-car, held his find in the glare of a headlight. His dark, liquid eyes were intent as he counted over four keys. They might have been the keys to any spring-locks. But the oval-shaped, bronze tag that also hung on the key-ring was only one possible article. On one side, in relief on the dark metal, was the name of Lamborn's, one of New York's largest department stores. On the reverse, also in relief, nothing—save a series of fat figures. The numbers were 563894.

They were burned into Drago's remarkable memory in the instant of reading, fortunately. He had, of course, recognized the tag on sight—a credit tag issued to the store's charge-account customers to expedite their shopping.

He heard the nasal muttering behind him, and snow crunched. "Snaked something from the snow, right near young Birn's head."

Before he could turn, Craven's breath hissed in his ear, and the homicide man's beefy red hand snatched down at Drago's wrist. Craven's teeth were tight closed as he bit out: "You—"

Drago jerked clear, jumping back a step. His hands ducked into his pockets, came out again. Over the glove of his left hand, brass knuckles shone dully. His right hand held out the keys.

"You can have these—or these. Keep your hands off me."

Craven swelled, his hands clenching into fists as he stepped forward. The thin-faced detective with the nasal voice grabbed hastily at his shoulder, swung him half round. He whispered earnestly in the big red-haired man's ear, and Craven's face got stony. He said in a slaty, tight voice: "All right. We can take this up later. Give me them keys."

Drago tossed them to him. As the others crowded round to examine the prize, he took two casual steps backward out of the light, turned and walked swiftly, silently, outside the line of parked cars, toward the corner above.

He turned down the side street. It was in his mind that one of the chief executives of the mammoth Lamborn's was a police buff—an honorary chief. Three doors down the side street, there was an unshaven man peering out of a vestibule. Drago ran up the steps and commandeered his phone. From the chief operator, he bullied the private phone number of the store executive. In three minutes he had roused him from his bed.

"Charge Account Number Five-six-three-eight-nine-four. I've got to know who it is, with his address, in a matter of minutes, sir. A cop's been killed, and this may be the killer. Can you get your credit man, at this time?"

"Call me back in fifteen minutes," the executive snapped.

And in fifteen minutes, he had it: "Charles Simmons. He lives in Suite Four-A, at the Graff Arms Hotel."

New York streets have a reputation of producing a crowd anywhere, at any time, in minutes. Broadway was struggling to maintain this tradition when Drago walked back to it. The bitter cold, icy wind, and late hour inhibited it but little. The crowd was forming now, led by the vanguard—night-hawk taxi drivers who were beginning to line curbs above and below.

He abandoned his prowl-car, took a taxi the half mile. When they swung into exclusive Fifty-seventh street, he crouched low in the tonneau, peering up and ahead. His eyes suddenly twitched. As they bowled over the street-car tracks on Seventh Avenue, he told the driver. "It's the next corner. Go on past and drop me on the far corner."

There was a light in the corner of the hotel, on what might be the fourth floor.

CHAPTER THREE
WINDOW OF DEATH

IT **STOOD** on the northwest corner of Essex and Fifty-seventh, a small, exclusive hotel. Drago stood on the howling corner opposite, braced against a police call-box, as the wind tore down from Central Park. He counted carefully. The light windows—the only lighted windows above the lobby—were definitely on the fourth floor. There were two windows lighted on the side of the hotel that Drago faced, and three along the front. There was better than an even chance that he was looking at Suite 4-A.

He stood completely motionless, hands in brown coat pockets, the wind whipping the snap-brim of his brown hat, his dark face shining. Quick, careful debate was in his oblique brown eyes.

He looked far down Fifty-seventh. Save for cars parked at the curb, nothing was on the street. Across from the front of the hotel glowed a neon tube including the menu of a hole-in-the-wall restaurant, and it was the only light for blocks, other than street lights, Essex, on which he stood, was equally deserted for the two blocks between Drago and the dark bulk of the Park. Far downtown, he could see a single trolley car—a tiny miniature.

He carefully scanned the small hotel opposite. He blinked slowly, dully, as he made out an oblong of deep black at the rear of the hotel—a tiny delivery alley, opening from the side street, or possibly a fire exit.

He hunched the brown coat higher on his shoulders and turned away from the call-box, toward the little alley's entrance. Halting in the gutter, his eyes fixed on the lighted windows above. For an instant, a man's thick head of black hair had flashed past the windows—first the rear one, then the front one. Even as Drago stood somberly watchful in the gutter, a second man—a thin, long-headed man whose hair was close-shaven and either blond or pink—scudded past the two windows. The second man wore a peaked cap.

Men wearing peaked caps indoors do not live in hotels like the Graff Arms. Warmth swept over Drago as he realized that his lead had really led somewhere. He started on, then turned back, his eyes swinging to the call-box behind him. He jerked out his keycase as he jumped back. He fumbled the box swiftly open and rang impatiently. Just as he got an answer, the man with the thick black hair flashed by the windows for the second time, high overhead.

"Drago, H.Q.," Drago said quickly into the box. "Send me three men here."

As he closed the box, the pink-headed man appeared again, briefly. A line cut Drago's smooth forehead. It looked for all the world as if the two men were performing some kind of a dance in the room above.

Then his eyes jerked wide. Something huge and black—something shaped exactly like a huge bat—suddenly flattened itself against the front window. It was there only an instant, then vanished. But it was exactly as if the Thing had spit out the window. For the first time, Drago realized that this particular window was open a few inches at the top. Through this slot, the bat-like entity had spewed out something—something that was only visible for a second in the window's glow and then vanished in the dark.

He heard it spat on the icy pavement opposite. Solidly parked cars blocked his line of sight. He did not move, but his curious, intent eyes jerked up and down, between the windows above and the spot in the darkness opposite. He waited three, four minutes. No one came out of the shadows to claim the thing that had come from above. No one showed again at the windows. Drago's hand was on his service gun in his side pocket now.

HE STEPPED quickly across the street, looking for an opening in the line of parked cars. They were solid, nose to tail, till he reached the clearance space of the alley behind the hotel. He swung up, started back on the sidewalk. The wind whistled savagely.

Over the wind, he suddenly heard a hoarse yell, from the blackness of the alley, "Hey, mister!"

He resisted the impulse to stop and peer in, by as narrow a margin as he ever hoped to miss anything. He was already checking himself on the icy cement when sanity caught up with him. He flung himself flat, on the mound of snow between sidewalk and roadway—and the alley became alive with darting, spitting orange flashes. Metal whanged and splintered above his head, as the car before which he was standing was riddled with lead.

He was soaked in sweat as he flung himself over the frozen mound of snow, rolled down into the gutter. The hammering of the lead above him was louder than the reports of the guns exploding into the wind. He spun himself desperately, scrambled out from under the other side of the car into the roadway, backed swiftly toward the corner.

A split-second lull in the wind whirled words at him. A hoarse voice shouting: "Get him! Get the—" Orange flashes spat and jabbered at him from the roadway. Drago steadied himself tight against the side of the car nearest, turned back and fired twice, carefully, aiming as well as the flashes of the pursuing man's—or men's—guns permitted. He heard a curse faint against the wind.

Then, from no more than a block away, came the shrill whining wail of a police siren. For a second, the flashes in front of Drago stopped. Drago started quickly back.

He flung himself again tight against a car. The shooting was suddenly redoubled, slamming, punching holes in the wind. No less than two automatic pistols with full clips were in front of him. He felt wind snick in his ear, twice, and tried to flatten himself still farther—then his foot slipped on the ice. He went down in a wild scramble of legs on the slippery pavement, his heart stuck in his throat, flipped wildly to face his assailants, his gun pumping.

He heard the police car scream around the corner behind him. Suddenly, the gun-stabs ahead of him ceased. A roaring thunder-bolt leaped out of the alley. The gun-flashes started again, tracing the course of the man who had jumped onto the thundering car's running-board. They whirled in a half circle, as the car swung northward, exhaust firing. Drago clawed out his flashlight and shield as he scrambled up, ran out into the middle of the road and sprayed light on his palm, waved the wildly skidding police car onward.

"Don't stop. Get them. Get that car. Cop-killers, I think."

He stood grim-jawed, breathing heavily, gloved hands in his pockets, his brown, oblique eyes hot, as the police car leaped in pursuit. In a flash, sound and sight were swallowed by the Park and the wind.

DRAGO TURNED back, walked up on the sidewalk and sent his flash beam creeping ahead of him. Two thirds the way to the front of the building, he saw a small, black pin-seal wallet. He picked it up and gave it cursory examination, without finding anything startling.

He turned back to the rear of the building, swung his light into the crevice that was the alley. It was just large enough to have held the car. Set flush with the cobbles of the little blind niche, was a fat steel door. He found the knob, and the door opened heavily. His flash showed the interior of a metal-lined stair-well. It was dark. He swung his flash beam around, located a punch-button and thumbed it. Light flared on all the way up the shaft, showing the stone-tiled stairs and metal banisters of the hotel's emergency fire-escape.

In the light, he examined the wallet more closely.

He found paper money, an identification card for Charles Simmons from the Voyagers' Accident Insurance Co., a four-year-old driver's license, issued to Charles Simmons at this address, three business cards from stationery houses—and four colored cards.

The colored cards were in a compartment by themselves. Two of them were buff-yellow, one of them pale blue and the other plain white. The white one was obviously a printed form, filled in with handwriting, reading to the effect that: This card would identify bearer, Charles Simmons, or his agent, who was empowered to act under full power of attorney in the following matters—to buy or sell, accept or make deliveries of, any cash or securities in the account of Seymour Rance, at the offices of Enderby, Throttle & Co.

The other colored cards were of identical nature, giving Charles Simmons utter and complete power of attorney, over the accounts of this same Seymour Rance in, respectively, the firms of Satterslee, Gowd & Co., Ealing & Co., and Ince & Ince. All four firms mentioned were first-class New York Stock Exchange stockbrokers.

Drago restored them carefully, pocketed the wallet, looked round him. There was a blank brown metal door facing him, obviously leading to the lobby floor. He pressed against it—it had no door handle. It was locked from outside. Hotel fire-doors were usually built this way—simple of opening from the hotel corridors but impossible to open from inside the shaft. He looked upward.

It was more than probable that the door on the fourth floor would be broken open, but he saw no point in climbing the stairs to find out. He walked out the back door into the alley, skirted the hotel and walked into the revolving door in front.

The lobby was small, cozy, overheated, done in bright red leather and black oak, to achieve the English air. The one bellboy that dozed on the tiny bench beside the desk, as Drago came in, wore a red mess-jacket, pill-box cap and blue trousers. He did not stir. No one stirred. Apparently, the wind had blanketed the flurry of shots behind the place, sufficiently so that they had not been heard here, at any rate. There was no desk clerk in sight.

The elevator boy, also dozing, also in red mess-jacket, jerked awake when Drago walked into the car and slammed the door shut. He grabbed for the lever.

The corridors on the fourth floor were also done in bright red carpet and dark wood. Suite 4-A seemed to be on the corner of the building.

It was. It was the suite Drago had been watching from below. Light was coming over its transom, but there was not a breath of sound within. After two minutes of holding his breath, Drago knocked gently, and the hot gun was in his hand when he did. When three knockings got him nowhere, he tried the knob soundlessly. It was open.

With one hand he knocked, while he kept the knob turned, then, in the middle of the knock kicked the door flying open and went in, crouched over.

HE STRAIGHTENED up and was in a small living-room which continued the English motif. Here the furniture was green leather and oak. There were two English hunting-prints on the walls, hanging drunkenly. Otherwise, the room was neat and orderly. He was alone in it. A door in the right-hand wall stood open, but the room beyond was darkened. He shot a flash beam into the room with caution, then with less caution. He stepped in and switched the room's overhead lights on and was in a man's maroon-and-cream bedroom.

At a cream desk that stood midway the room's inside wall—the corridor wall—a slight, sandy-haired man in coat sleeves sat with his head on his crossed arms. His hands were wax white, as was the scalp that showed through his thin hair.

"We've had quite a time getting to you, boy," Drago said.

He walked straight across the room and turned on a light in the small, green-tiled bathroom. Beside the bathroom door was a clothes' closet. He took no chances when opening it, but there was only a meager supply of worn, inexpensive clothing and shoes inside.

He looked under the maroon-spread bed, glanced at the shabby dark overcoat and gray hat, shiny blue serge suitcoat that were thrown across it. He went over and put his hands at the sides of the dead man's head and lifted it to look into the face. Glassy, sightless gray eyes stared at him from the cool flesh. On the table beside the crossed arms was a small bottle whose stained, gummed label bore spidery handwriting—*Butyl-Chloral-Hydrate*. There were two inches of smoky white liquid in the bottle and a small whisky glass was overturned beside it, having spilled a little liquid on the maroon blotter.

In between the crossed arms, he saw a segment of note-paper, bearing handwriting, which he picked out, laid aside. The rank, heavy odor of sweat came up. He let the head down and touched the green-striped madras shirt sleeves. They were drenched, still wet.

He looked down. There was a fountain-pen by the man's foot—presumably the one the note had been written with. Drago stooped down, freeing a hand from a glove and ran his palm under the dead man's shoe sole. It came away wet. He pulled the glove back on before reading the note.

It read—

Naomi, dear:

I know I am taking the coward's way out, but your going has removed the only thing that made life worth while. All my efforts to get the thing you wanted have ended in disastrous, miserable failure. There is no light ahead, and they are closing in on me.

The writer had neglected to sign it. Drago laid it on the man's crossed arms and reached for the telephone that stood by the desk, on the floor. He gave the number of the hospital where McTigue was laid up, and got the grizzled old inspector on the wire.

HE CHECKED the old man's feverish, vicious flow of questions. "I'm getting under way now. I've found the thing that young Birn got in the way of, I think—though it's all dark yet. I'm at Suite Four-A in the Graff Arms hotel. Craven is trying to muscle me and I daren't take a chance on calling in officially, but I need a doctor. A smart doctor, from the M.E.s' office, and I need him fast."

"What for?"

"To tell me some things about the dead man I'm looking at."

"What! A homicide?"

"Well, he's rigged out as a suicide, complete with note. But a lot of funny things have happened. I'll tell you about it later. Now, please get me that doc."

"You'll tell me now," McTigue stormed. "What the— Hold the wire." His voice came faintly through the transmitter, yelling, "Hey," to someone at his end.

A full minute later, he came back on the wire. "Your doctor's coming. Now, spill."

"I tell you, it's all dark. Young Birn got shot because he picked up some keys and tried to return them to three men. I figure the men must have thought he was pointing a gun at them, or something. I found the keys and came here— they belonged to this Charles Simmons.

"From outside, I saw two men—well, maybe three men—chasing each other around the room. Then one of them tossed a wallet out. A minute later, they came downstairs and tried to kill me—very carefully and deliberately. I suppose it was to get the wallet, but they weren't fooling. I got away and so did they. I found the wallet and here I am. And here Charles Simmons is, with a bottle of poison. That's all so far, Mac. Thanks for the doc. I'll call you again, the minute I get this thing open a little."

"This Simmons is one of the three killers?"

"One of three, I think. But not a killer. He's a little rabbit of a guy, though I'll admit I don't know how he comes to be living in a fifteen-dollar-a-day suite. What I saw of the other two doesn't make me think they were partners of his. What the doctor says may change the whole picture."

"How?"

"About when he died."

"My God, you think the other two were dragging him through the streets dead?"

"I wouldn't know, Mac. Let me go to work now, and I'll find out."

HE TURNED to the bed. He patted the breast of the shabby blue suitcoat, felt no bulk in any pockets, but there was a queer, gritty substance scattered over the shiny lapel and the front of the coat. He turned on a reading-lamp at the head of the bed and the tiny particles shone, becoming, on closer inspection, little grains of something hard and white.

Carefully, he smoothed them from the coat onto the bed-cover. He could make nothing of them. He got an envelope from the desk and brushed them in, sealed it and put it in his own pocket.

The shabby coat gave up nothing else but a handkerchief; the frayed, dark-blue overcoat some small change. The dead man's trousers and waistcoat yielded a dollar watch, three pencils, a book of stamps—trifles. No papers, no writing, no information.

The bureau drawers were no better. He stared into three compartments and saw a spare, worn assortment of inexpensive body linen, and that was all.

He looked round the room, went over and stared down at the bedside table, on which he had placed all the articles. He took out the wallet and spread its contents out separately, thumbed back the brown hat on his shining, rippled black hair and sat with gloved hands in his lap, studying.

Someone knocked at the corridor door of the other room—the living-room.

He walked silently out into the green-and-oak living-room and to the door. He put the gun in his pocket with his finger on the trigger and the safety catch carefully off, and opened the door quickly.

It was a long-legged, intensely pretty girl with blue-black hair and white skin, in a nightgown and black velvet wrapper.

CHAPTER FOUR
LADY BABE

THE GIRL'S pebbly-blue eyes went wide, startled, when she saw Drago, and she looked quickly up at the numerals on the door. "I—I guess I have the wrong room," she said faintly. "Excuse me."

"You're a friend of Mr. Simmons?"

"I—yes, but please don't bother." She started backing down the hall.

Drago palmed his shield and showed it to her. "Please, come in. Mr. Simmons will be here any minute. Maybe you could answer a question for us."

She stood still, her eyes frightened, starting to shake her head.

"Without the whole corridor hearing us," Drago added.

Her face was pale, but she came hesitantly in. Drago closed the door behind her.

Her voice was a scared whisper. "I—I really don't know Mr. Simmons very well," she said. "He hasn't done anything, has he—anything that—"

Drago gave her a smile. "Nothing like that." He looked her over covertly. She was neither short nor tall. Her long, graceful legs were beautifully tapered to light-blue slippers. Her blue-black hair was in braids wound round her head, above her perfect ears. Her neck was not plumb, but the blue nightgown that showed in the V of her black negligee was stretched tight over full-molded breasts. The hand that held her gown together was shaking slightly. "There's nothing to be worried about, Miss—"

"Crain," she said almost inaudibly.

"Oh, yes. Miss Namoi Crain?"

Her eyes were puzzled. "No. My—my name is April."

"You live in the hotel, and you dropped down to pay a friendly call."

She blushed. "Oh, no. I—I had a dreadful headache. Mr. Simmons was good enough to—to give me some headache medicine a week ago. I heard him moving around down here—my room is right above. I came down to beg some more from him."

"Do you remember the name of the medicine?"

"I— No, I'm afraid I don't."

Drago's brown eyes were thoughtful on the point of her shoulder. "I think he has some butyl in there. Would that be it?"

"It—it might be. Yes, I think—" Her pebbly-blue eyes were wide, ingenuous. The name of the poison had not disturbed her.

Drago stood aside, nodded at the open door of the bedroom. "It's on the desk in there. Just help yourself, Miss Crain."

Confused, hesitant, she took a step, looked anxiously at Drago and went in quickly.

Drago was at the door behind her when she saw the dead man. She was three steps in. She did not scream. She gasped and the back of her free hand went to her red mouth.

"He's—he's white. He's—dead."

"Wasn't he when you were in this room a few minutes ago?"

"Oh, my God. I swear I haven't."

"You're overacting. A person'd think you'd never seen a dead man before."

"I haven't. Oh, I haven't!"

Drago was at the bedside table. He picked up the black wallet. "You ever see this before?"

"No, no. Oh, you've made some terrible mistake. I—"

"You ever see me before?"

"Oh God, no." She suddenly buried her face in her slim hands, burst into racking sobbing.

"I guess you didn't, at that. I was behind floodlights, and you were up on a platform. Are you a member of the English nobility?"

The sobbing ceased. Pebbly-blue eyes peered through her parted fingers, fastened on the gun that Drago now held in plain sight. "No."

DRAGO SAID: "Last time I saw you, you were trying to convince the Chicago dicks that you had a title, Lady Babe. Seems to me you're still wanted on manslaughter, no? Some rich old man you had got frightened to death when you and your man put the pay-off on, or something like that. Or maybe you killed him yourself."

Her hands jerked down. "I didn't."

"But you did kill this one," Drago's finger jabbed at Simmons. "Why? What's behind this racket? What's worth all this killing? Talk up—and fast. It's your last chance of a break, of any kind."

"Wait, copper." Her blue eyes had retreated into her head, and her voice was husky, but the hysterics were gone. She was really frightened now. "It's—murder?"

"You know what it is."

"Copper, honest to God—I know nothing about—"

Drago's forehead was flushed. "My patience is right at its end, Babe. The persons that did this to Simmons also killed a cop—and came a hair from killing me. I'm not letting them get away. I have no way of reaching them— no way of knowing who they are. I can only see one way to play it—to find out what this scheme is that's got them on fire and try to get aboard myself, for the pay-off. So far, I've only got one sure lead—one sure way to find out what I want to know."

"What—what is it?"

"You."

"I swear it's a wrong steer—"

For the second time within minutes, there was knocking on the corridor door of the living-room.

They both fell silent.

Drago hefted the gun in his gloved hand and said quietly: "Walk ahead of me. If you don't think I'd put a couple of bullets in those pretty legs of yours at this point, just make one wrong move."

The gun muzzle followed her as she crossed the room. Drago looked at the articles on the bed-table beside him, hastily picked the colored cards as being the only items of importance, and dropped them in his pocket, just in case. He followed on behind her, out into the living-room.

He motioned her to a corner where he could hold her under his eye as he covered the door with his gun. On inspiration, he pantomimed to the girl that she was to invite the person to enter.

"Come in," she said huskily.

The door banged inward and a big-boned, red-faced man, in clothes too small, stood in the doorway, a big revolver in his red hand. His straw-colored blond hair was thick under a hard hat, his pale-blue eyes a queer mixture of anger, surprise, anxiety. He had ears like handlebars.

"Chester Ford McSpadden," Drago said. "What next?"

"D-Drago."

"What brings the Wall Street Squad into this?"

"I—I ain't on the Wall Street Squad—not for two months. I'm with World-Over Indemnity. What do you mean 'into this?' Hey, what's happened? Hey—nothing's happened to Simmons?"

"I ask mine first. What's World-Over's interest in Simmons? What brought you up here?"

"World-Over's got a bond on him for twenty thousand. He's been seen in brokerage houses. On forty a week, they don't see it, so they put me behind him to—to read his damned mind. That's about the size of it. I been living with him six weeks. For nights, I got myself a plant in a dough-nut shop across the road where I can watch the windows.

"Tonight, he come in at ten, like he usually does, and I—I kind of dozed off. First thing I know, I wake up and see two guys—not Simmons—one of them had black thick hair and the other kind of pink—up here. Then the light goes out in the bedrooms, somebody starts shooting down the street, a prowl-car comes shooting around and some-body—you, I guess—beat it out and sent them on, and then come in the hotel, and a minute later the light goes on here. I don't know what to do, see, because I got no orders to do nothing definite, but when the black-haired guy and the pink guy come coasting around the corner and get out, almost right in front of where I'm sittin', then duck into an area over there, I get worried."

"What! Those two are across the street now?"

"Yeah—in an areaway, right next that doughnut—"

"Listen, hold this girl here. Keep your gun on her. I want those guys. God, what a merry-go-round!" He ran out the door, as the big scarecrow's gun jerked over to cover the girl.

HE STARTED for the elevators, changed his mind and threaded corridors at a run till he found the fire stairs. As he had expected, the lock at this level was broken. The door could be opened from either side. He ran down the four flights, stopped at the bottom to change the clip in his pistol and switched out the lights, went out into the roaring night. He hugged the wall of the hotel, half ran, half trotted, toward the corner.

Standing against the corner, not daring to swing round it, he could just see the doughnut shop, and the areaway of a milliner's shop, opposite the front of the hotel. He could make out no sign of the men he wanted.

Two blocks behind him, just emerging from Central Park, he heard the low, vicious snarl of a siren. He spun back and saw a prowl-car winding out of the parkway, heading down toward where he stood. He uttered a silent prayer that it might be the one that had given fruitless chase to the killers.

It was. The car drifted down to the call-box opposite where Drago stood and stopped. One man got out. Drago stepped away from the wall, whistled. They saw him, backed and came to get to the curb beside him.

He showed his shield, pointed to the areaway as they started to make excuses for not catching the high-powered car. "Never mind. The men you were chasing doubled back on you. They were in that areaway, minutes ago. I think they're still there. Drive up the street and back, and throw your searchlight into that hole. Be ready to shoot first, because if anyone was ever on fire, these two are."

The car swung round, drove up the street. It drove back, came abreast of the areaway and its thousand-watt search-light blazed into the areaway. The car stopped, and the two uniformed men jumped out, guns in hand, ran over to peer into the hole.

Drago was halfway across the street, when they turned back and looked at him questioningly.

The areaway was empty.

They ran the searchlight over the fronts of half a dozen buildings, but there was no sign of the fugitives.

Drago's eyes suddenly went back up to the window of Simmons' suite. He told the prowl-car men: "Phone these descriptions in and get them on the short wave for me wanted for killing young Birn." He gave swift descriptions of the big man with the black thatch of hair, and the stringy one with the pinkish look.

"Before you do that, go over and see if either of those men entered the lobby of the Graff Arms over there, in the last ten minutes. Don't let them confuse you about a big scarecrow of a man with a hard hat and blond hair. But find out about the other two. Then sit here, till I get up to those lighted windows. I'll look out, and, if you wave, I'll know you haven't got any trace of my friends."

"How are you going to get up there?"

"By the killers' entrance. It's in the rear," he explained grimly. "The latest thing in hotel construction."

He left them, made his way cautiously back the way he had come, flashing his beam carefully into the little alley before venturing into it.

In the fire-well, he switched the lights back on again. He heard no sound in the flights of stairs above him, climbed back up, seeing and hearing no one. He stepped out into the red-carpeted corridor and hurried back to Suite 4-A.

The door's being ajar stopped him for a second. Then a cheerful man's voice inside the room ahead of him said: "Hell, you're all right."

Drago burst in, his heart in his boots.

Chester Ford McSpadden was on hands and knees, like a huge St. Bernard in the middle of the living-room floor. His hat lay in the bedroom entrance. Blood was running down his cheek from a cut in his forehead. A bronze candlestick lay in one corner of the room.

A bright-looking young man was swabbing the wound with cotton, a square black bag open on the floor beside him.

Drago said savagely, "You lunkhead," and jumped around them, into the bedroom. His eyes whipped the room. Everything seemed as it had been. Then his eyes came to a halt on the bedside table. Everything was as it had been—except that the black wallet was gone, and, of course, the girl.

CHAPTER FIVE
WHEN SUICIDE IS MURDER

MCSPADDEN'S WAILING voice was complaining: "You didn't tell me there was no dead man in there. You didn't say nothing about no dead man. When I see it, I'm all off center. Then, when I see it's Simmons, and see that note, I grab for it and she— Damn you, Drago—it's all your fault! If you'd of told me there was a dead—"

"Shut it off," Drago snapped and was at the telephone. He asked the switchboard girl: "Have you an April Crain registered in the room above here?"

He was told the room was vacant.

"This is police," Drago told her. "Send a bellboy on the run out to the front of the hotel. There's a prowl-car waiting there. Have one of the men in it get to this phone fast."

When he got the prowl-car's sergeant, he said, "There's an alley at the back of this hotel. Go back and cover it. Let no one out—least of all a girl."

He wiggled the hook, demanded the manager and, when a hoarse, resonant voice came on the wire told him: "Police. There's a dangerous criminal in this hotel—a woman." He described her swiftly. "Have your lobby locked so she can't get out—or, at least, you're responsible to see that she doesn't come out that way. I've covered the rear. Better get up here yourself as soon as you can."

He depressed the hook again, said, "Police Headquarters," and got the radio-room. "A girl that was mixed up with Chicago killers a few years ago. She was known as 'Lady Babe,' among other things. I can't remember her real name. Get her description from her record, and she's badly wanted—this cop killing."

He hung up, having done everything in his power to repair McSpadden's blunder, but sickly aware that the girl had had at least five minutes in which to make her escape. Lady Babe would ask no more.

He walked out and stared dully down at the wabbly McSpadden, as the big man climbed slowly to his feet. His pale-blue eyes were still a little glassy. He started whining, "If you'd of told me," and wabbled over, flopped in a chair, his hands holding his head.

Drago asked the bright-looking young man: "McTigue sent you? There's a body in the next room for you to see."

"So I gathered," the youngster grinned.

"Tell me how he was killed, and when, if you can."

The youngster sauntered in to the bedroom with his bag. "McSpadden!"

The big man jumped in his chair.

Drago put pressure in his words: "Who is this Simmons? Why does he live in a fifteen-dollar-a-day suite if he's a forty-a-week man?"

"What? Hell, he's the accountant here in the hotel. They give him this. The joint's half empty and they let him take his pick."

Drago took out a handkerchief and mopped his forehead. "Now, we're getting somewhere. He's the accountant in the hotel. He makes forty a week. He's been playing the market—"

"I don't know that," McSpadden said petulantly. "All I know is he's been around brokerage offices."

Drago jerked the colored cards from his pocket. "What are these?"

The glassy pale eyes fell on the cards. The glassiness went away, and fright came in. The big man jumped to his feet. "My God," he said huskily. "That proves it. That's what they all do—take a phony name when they're embezzling, and—"

"Your company thinks he was embezzling—all right, that he might be embezzling—and they put you behind him to watch him—to try and get something on him that would justify their canceling their twenty-thousand-dollar bond on him. Right?"

"Yes, yes—"

"You've followed him around six weeks and all you got was that he frequented brokerage offices. You didn't ever see this girl that I left with you, with Simmons?"

"Eh? No, no."

"Has he got a lady friend named Naomi?"

"N-no, I don't think so." Full sense returned suddenly to the pale-blue eyes. McSpadden started. He cried hoarsely: "Hey, I got to look at the hotel's books!"

There was a knock at the door. Drago jerked it open and faced a tall, distinguished man of fifty. The man stammered: "I—I'm Charles Ambers, the manager and owner—"

"Come on in."

AMBERS WAS a fine-looking, spare man, with wavy, crisp gray hair and a distinguished face. The distinguished look persisted in spite of bloodshot eyes, and a short gray stubble of whiskers. His finely drawn face was white with anxiety. He was clad impeccably in morning clothes, with one or two exceptions. First, he had forgotten collar and tie, and his gold stud gleamed in his stiff neckband. Secondly, he wore red-leather Turkish slippers over bare feet.

The minute the door closed behind him, he burst out anxiously: "What—what has happened? Why are the police in my hotel?"

"Did you block off that lobby?"

"Yes, yes! My house officer is at the door. Please—"

Drago put his hand in his pocket. "They give us this shield so people will answer our questions first," he told Ambers. "Simmons is your accountant?"

"Eh? Yes."

"Could he have stolen money from you—embezzled?"

The manager-owner's face dropped. "Why—why, of course, he could. He has full control over the books and the bank accounts, but such a thing is ridiculous. He has been with me for years—"

"Embezzlers always are. Otherwise, they wouldn't be given chances to get their hands in the till. How much would Simmons be able to get away with?"

"Why—why, our bank balances run from forty to seventy-five thousand dollars. I don't know exactly how much he—well, that much, anyway."

Drago said: "The place must be prosperous."

Ambers smile was thin and ghastly. "Just this prosperous. If he has—if he had taken that money, or even most of it, we would be bankrupt. We have to have a good-sized revolving fund, but the banks own me. They own every hotel in town, nearly." Sudden, desperate hope sprang into

Ambers' distinguished gray eyes. "But he's bonded!" he said. "Even if he had—"

McSpadden blurted defensively: "Only for twenty thousand! If he's taken more than that, we're not responsible!"

Drago said, "Wait a minute." To Ambers, he made a little bow. "Excuse us a minute." To McSpadden, "Come here."

He stepped inside the bedroom, and McSpadden followed, his splotched red face dully, pathetically hopeful. He gulped: "God, this means my job, Drago, if he—"

"We'll think about that, later. Play with me and maybe you can get back on the Wall Street Squad."

The big man gasped. "Honest? If I do what you tell me, you'll get McTigue to—"

"You fool, shut up. Craven, of homicide, is in charge of this job. I've stretched my time out to the last second. It's a miracle he hasn't pounced down on me before this. It's a matter of minutes now. Make up your mind whether you're going to take my orders or his."

"Yours. Yours—absolutely."

Drago sliced with a gloved hand. "Then, listen. Go down with the manager and find what you can in the books. But don't come back up here. Meet me down there, in the lobby. Keep yourself out of sight. Craven, as I say, will be here any minute, and, if he sees you, you can't get away from him. What you'd better do is try and keep the manager in his office till I get there. We'll hope the time element works out. Got that?"

"Yes."

THEY WENT back out to the living-room. Ambers was standing, first on one foot then the other. His gray eyes clung to Drago's smooth, brown face pleadingly, as the latter made the brief introduction.

"This is Mr. McSpadden," Drago said. "He was formerly on the Wall Street Squad and is an expert on books and figures." He hesitated and added, "Whether he looks it or not.

"We have every reason to think Mr. Simmons has been embezzling. I'd suggest that you and Mr. Ambers hurry down and look your accounts over. The sooner we know where we stand, the sooner we can go to work on the remedy."

Ambers' long hand had discovered the absence of his collar and tie and he was fumbling about his throat in a half effort to conceal the gap. "May I—may I ask exactly where Mr. Simmons is?" he said anxiously.

"Sorry to be abrupt," Drago said, "but he's in that room—dead."

"Dead!" Ambers gasped.

"He's committed suicide," McSpadden added bitterly.

"That's the surface indication," Drago said. "I believe that he was murdered."

A cheerful young voice in the bedroom doorway behind them said: "If you're talking about that gent in there, he's dead from natural causes. I'll give a certificate of heart disease, any time. You sleuths!"

Drago spun on him, his dark face lead-colored. "What! With that poison sitting there, you mean to say—"

The cheerful young doctor lit a cigarette. "It's a screwy set-up. Whoever planted that poison must have been in a big hurry. They didn't even put any in his mouth, much less his stomach."

Ambers, mopping his fine face, blurted: "Thank God for that, anyway. If it had been murder—the hotel would have been sunk. God knows, we don't need much of a black eye to push us over."

Drago clipped at McSpadden: "Go on—get moving. This doesn't change anything."

When they had gone, he turned back to the doctor. "Listen, that doesn't make sense. Not only was this man murdered, but in the doing of it, they shot down a cop. They tried to shoot me. My God, Doc—it can't be natural death!"

The doctor shrugged good-naturedly. "You can get another doctor to say different, maybe. I say he had a bum ticker and it stopped about three hours ago."

"Three hours!" Drago swung out his wrist. "Then he must have died just a half hour or so before young Birn—" He clamped his lips suddenly, dug in his inside pocket. He brought out the envelope with the white gritty particles he had scratched from the dead man's coat front. "Can you tell what these are?" he asked the doctor.

The youngster jiggled the envelope, stooped and picked up his bag, set it on the couch. He got out a powerful magnifying-glass and turned on the table-lamp. Under its strong light, he studied the particles.

Drago took two bottles of reagent from his bag, dropped a little from each on specks of the shiny white particles.

"Sure," he said finally. "It's enamel—white enamel."

"Enamel!" Drago burst out. "Hell—of course!"

He turned back into the bedroom, strode to the side of the dead accountant. The man's head was back now, hanging over the back of the chair where the young doctor had left it.

DRAGO TOOK the man's lips in his gloved fingers, folded them open, put one probing forefinger along the side of the man's upper gum, forced the dead cheek up so the teeth could be seen. "There's a flashlight in my pocket. Turn it in here," he told the doctor.

The flashlight's strong beam showed Simmons white, healthy teeth. Three of the teeth had small holes, no larger than a BB shot, drilled in them, up close to the gum. Drago let the man's mouth close and stepped away. He mopped his forehead with a handkerchief.

"All right, Doc," he said. "Thank you very much. So his heart stopped?"

"Uh-huh."

"It's still murder."

The doctor shrugged again. "You through with me?"

"I am—and I'd appreciate it if you'd be on your way as soon as possible. I don't want a certain person to find you here. Don't think I don't appreciate what you've done."

He made one more painstaking search, after the doctor had gone, spending every minute he dared, trying to think through the tangled, murderous puzzle.

Then from down the street came the crescendo of police sirens—half a dozen of them. It was not a paean of urgency, but had rather a comfortable sound. This was Craven, arriving in pomp.

Drago ran to the side window of the living-room, threw it up and leaned out.

Below, he saw the dark bulk of the prowl-car he had stationed at the hotel's rear entrance. He waved an arm. Metal glinted in the dark as a uniformed man looked up, his face now an oval in the first faint indication of dawn.

"That's all," Drago bawled down. "Go back to your precinct."

He closed the window, as the prowl-car moved away—fortunately not in the direction from which the other cars were coming. He looked swiftly once more through the apartment, replaced the bronze candlestick with which the girl had felled McSpadden, and went out into the scarlet corridor.

The elevator let him out on the lobby floor, and he walked rapidly toward the front door. Halfway to it, the revolving door began to move. Sirens were still wailing outside. Drago turned right about without stopping, hurried back toward the elevator.

Craven, coming in the door, bawled: "Drago!"

Drago stopped, turned back, trying to make his dark face mirror confusion. He stood still, his eyes dull, as Craven plowed up the corridor.

"So, sticking your nose in again!"

"Listen, Craven," Drago said rapidly. "I've got a good lead here. Those keys belonged to a man named Martin Simmons, who lives in Suite Four-A."

"We know all about that," Craven snarled. "Just get out of the—"

"Look, we'll go up together, eh? Work it out together—"

"Sure we will—in a pig's eye! Out of my way, and stay out. Hey, Hazlitt! Stay by the elevator here and watch the stairs. Don't let this jobbie go up either of them."

Drago stood stony-faced, as the four detectives with Craven piled into the elevator, left Drago alone in the lobby, save for a cherub-faced, forty-year old detective who fidgeted by the elevator.

Hazlitt said uncomfortably: "Hey, I hope you don't take this as personal, Drago. Myself, I'd be glad—"

"Oh, sure," Drago said, and turned disconsolate, wandered around the desk.

When he was out of sight of the elevator, he quickened his pace, made for the manager's office.

CHAPTER SIX
GRIEF FOR A GIRL

AS DRAGO went through the swinging door, he saw, just inside it, a pretty, pansy-eyed girl, with brown hair, at the switchboard. She directed him to a door across her cubicle, and he went in without knocking.

Ambers was standing in the middle of the floor, hands on his wavy gray hair, eyes stunned. "I wouldn't have believed it. I can't believe it. Simmons an embezzler. My God!"

Drago let the door close behind him, looked at McSpadden in quick question.

The big insurance detective was sitting at the desk, two open ledgers before him, a slip of paper in one hand, resting the side of his face in the other hand. His pale eyes were gloomily fastened upon the slip of paper. He swiveled them miserably to Drago without moving any other part of him.

"Thirty-eight thousand, nine hundred dollars," he said. "The poor chump didn't even try to conceal it. If anybody else had even taken a look at these books, it could have been stopped, three months ago."

"He started embezzling three months ago?"

McSpadden's big blond head nodded. "He took it out in twos and fives—thousands, I mean. The last one was two weeks ago—twenty-nine hundred. He couldn't take any more, or the banks would've jumped down on the—on

Mr. Ambers here for an explanation. He was at the end of his rope."

There was a second's silence. The phone rang.

Drago put up a checking hand as Ambers moved for it. He answered it, himself. "Yes?"

Craven's bull tones came over the wire.

"Gimme the management."

Drago made his voice issue from flattened lips. "This is he."

"Well, this is the cops. We're in Suite Four-A. Get to hell up here as fast as you know how. You've got a murder."

"Y-yes, sir."

He hung up. Ambers looked dully, hopelessly at him with faint curiosity. Drago's dark face was somber, preoccupied.

McSpadden said bitterly: "Thirty-nine thousand fish. And World-Over is stuck for twenty of it."

Drago felt the four colored cards in his pocket, took them out and looked at them. "I guess this is where it went."

McSpadden nodded dully.

Ambers said in a hopeless voice, after a minute: "If you don't mind, I guess I'll finish dressing. I dread what I have to tell the bank."

Drago nodded. "Go ahead. Take your time. Whenever you get round to it, come back up to Simmons' suite. No hurry."

Ambers went out. Drago looked down at the red face of the ex-Wall Street copper. "What's the next move?"

McSpadden made a harsh throat sound. "Me getting my pants kicked into the street."

"Apart from that—we'll have to make a check of these brokers. From my experience, we'll have to get court orders, or they'll tell us nothing."

"Not quite that bad," McSpadden said listlessly. "When I was following Simmons around, I grabbed onto some friends in those houses, naturally. Besides, World-Over bonds most of them. As long as it's not for court use, I think they'll be reasonable."

"How early can we catch them?"

McSpadden looked up at the wall-clock. "Not for two or three hours yet. Not before ten."

"Then you clear out of here—fast. There'll be a hornet's nest around your ears—mine, too—when Craven wakes up to the fact that we've covered the ground we have. That can't be helped. You need my help—to get back on the force, you say. All right—I need yours with these brokers, and with technical items, if any. If Craven catches us, neither of us'll be able to help the other.

"Go out here and turn right. Don't go around the other side of the desk. Craven's got a watchdog on the elevators, and he might spot you. You can find your way through the kitchens and duck out the back door."

"What—what'll I do, then?"

"I don't care what you do. Meet me at"— he pulled a colored card from his pocket—"at Enderby, Throttle and Company's uptown branch, at ten o'clock sharp. Don't get picked up by any other cop. If you do, call Inspector McTigue at Mercy Hospital and he'll get you out. Now, dust."

DRAGO WAITED behind, troubled eyes on the books. A hunch was rising in him that made him uneasy, worried. He reached across the desk for the phone, to warn

McTigue to protect the insurance operative, in case Craven had him picked up.

He got no answer on the phone. Outside, he heard the switchboard buzzer droning monotonously, but he got no answer.

He replaced the receiver, pushed the door open, and a line cut the middle of his brown forehead. The girl was still sitting at the switchboard, her back to him, her slim back curved in a tight arc, sitting motionless. He ran around her, quick concern in his brown eyes.

"Excuse me, Miss," Drago said.

Her eyes seemed to jump and sense came back to them. Every drop of color left her face, save the lipstick on her lips. She stood up with a jump, one hand crawling to her throat. She was trembling violently now.

"What's the matter?" Drago asked.

"They've killed Martin," he could hardly hear the husked whisper. "They're going to kill me."

Drago's eyes were bewildered. "Martin? Martin who?"

"Martin—that I was going to marry." She was not seeing Drago. Her eyes were terrified on a point in space beyond him. Even the whisper seemed a fearful effort to get out. "They want his books and papers and they're going to kill me if I don't give them up."

Drago's mouth was open. "Wait—brace yourself, girlie. Come in here."

He took her arm, piloted her into the manager's office. Before he followed, he whistled the bellboy who was visible through a network of partitions. "Hey, come here and work this thing."

He went in the office. The girl was at the desk, her face on her sprawled arms, weeping violently.

"Don't do that," he said sharply. "Tell me what happened—who threatened to kill you. It's all right," he added swiftly and showed her his shield.

She was on her feet in a minute, white rings showing around her eyes. "They—they told me not to go to the police."

"They always do. It means nothing. I swear I'll protect you. We'll catch the ones that killed this Martin, if you'll help me. Who is he?"

"Martin Simmons. He was the accountant here."

"He was your fiancé?"

"Yes!" Her voice was rising and she was grinding her clenched hands together. "It was Mr. Ambers! I know it was!"

"Wait a minute. Ambers killed Simmons?"

"Yes. He—he—I heard him just now. He pretended to be shocked when you told him Martin had—had embezzled from him, didn't he?"

"Yes."

She was a small, wild fury, her childish face pinched and dingy. "Well, he knew before. He knew because Martin told him last night—told him in this very office. I overheard Martin say, when he went in at ten o'clock last night, that he'd come to confess he'd embezzled thirty-nine thousand dollars from the hotel!"

"He told Ambers that at ten o'clock last night?"

"Yes."

DRAGO BLINKED, chased that surprising information around his head anxiously. Then a lot of questions began to group themselves in his brain. If what the girl said was true, then—

"Is that what makes you think Ambers killed young Simmons?" he began.

"Dear Heaven! Can't you see? That money that Martin took was enough to ruin the hotel. It means Mr. Ambers is penniless. He killed Martin in revenge."

"Did you see your fiancé last night—after he talked to Ambers?"

"No. He wouldn't see me—I couldn't get to him."

"What's your name? It isn't Naomi?"

"No. Mary Murdock. Who is Naomi?"

"A child of someone's imagination, I guess. Never mind it. Listen, Miss Murdock—if Ambers wanted to be revenged on Martin Simmons, he could have sent him to jail for ten years—maybe more. The way your fiancé was killed indicates that at least three people are implicated. Under the circumstances, would Mr. Ambers hire gunmen, take the chance of killing a policeman in the process—for that is what these people did—just to revenge himself on Simmons for defaulting?"

She stood rigid, fists clenched, but her deep eyes were suddenly uncertain. "Then—then who did kill Martin?"

"That—and why he was killed—are the things I'm looking for. Who threatened you on the phone just now?"

"I—I don't know. I don't care. Don't you understand? I don't care what they do to me, now."

"Then they will kill you," Drago said sharply. "Listen to me, Miss Murdock. At the present moment, you're the only thread we have that leads straight to the people who killed your fiancé. You want them caught and punished, don't you?"

"Yes! Yes! They ought to be—"

"Have no fear. They will be, if we can get our hands on them. But you've got to help us. First, by helping me stop you from being killed. Second, by—well, I'm not to that, yet. You must get hold of yourself. Exactly what did the person say to you on the phone—the one that threatened you? Think carefully. Give it to me as close to verbatim as you can."

"It was a man's voice—hoarse, as if he were out of breath. He said, 'Lady, we've just found out that Martin Simmons give you some books and papers. We want them. Don't give me any argument. We've killed—and we'll kill again. There isn't anything that can stop us. I'm telling the God's truth—nothing can stop us. We're in too deep and there's too much at stake. We've only got twenty-four hours left. If you cross us, we'll butcher you as sure as hell'."

Drago's face was grim. "Did he tell you how to deliver these papers?"

"Yes. I told him they were in the bank's safe-deposit box—that I couldn't get them before ten. He told me to get them, and to be near Times Square by twelve noon. He said that if I were a second late, they wouldn't give me another chance. They'd put killers on my—my trail at once."

"What papers have you got of Simmons'?"

"None. I—I have his family Bible, and his mother's jewelry and a few letters he wrote me. I told the man that. He snarled, 'Bring every damned last scrap of them', and hung up."

"When did he tell you he'd killed your fiancé?"

"He didn't. I—I listened in when that policeman called from upstairs. I heard him say there was a murder. What—what can I do to help you catch the beasts? I'll do anything."

"Where's your hat and coat?"

She nodded at the door. "Out there, by my switch—"

"Is there any place in the hotel where you're positive you can hide for five minutes?"

"Y-yes, but why?"

"Go there and hide. No matter what happens, don't disclose yourself. That applies to every moment from now on. I wouldn't tell you this if I didn't believe it, but I'm afraid you're in real danger. It won't be momentary danger till twelve o'clock. You hide for five minutes. Then meet me at the back door—the fire-door. You and I are going to stay together till ten o'clock. Then you can get your things from the safe-deposit."

Her eyes were aghast. "I won't give them Martin's things!"

"No, of course not. But you've got to seem as though you were going to. They may be watching the bank to see if you do come. At least it will keep them back till noon—keep them from taking action. Now, go to that hiding-place. You're positive it's secure?"

"Yes. Where are you going?"

"What's Ambers' room number? I want to have a word or two with that gentleman, if I'm not too late."

She told him. He ushered her out of the office and told the scarlet-coated, weedy bellboy: "Stay there for five minutes and operate the board. If Miss Murdock and I are not back by then, call the manager for instructions."

CHAPTER SEVEN
TICKER TRAIL

HE LED her out of the cubicle into the lobby, now clad for the street. She went on, hesitantly, toward the back of the lobby. Drago turned and walked out the door of the lobby, into the night. He had his hand warm on his gun, as he circled the hotel to the fire-door in the alley. The streets were beginning to get light now, and the wind was dying down.

He had to go up the fire-stairs to the fourth floor, in order to get out of the shaft into the lobbies, but the stairs were accessible from where he found himself and he had no trouble getting to Ambers' room. It did him no good. The door was locked and dark and he got no answer to his knocking.

He hesitated only a minute. In a left-handed way, it was conceivable that there might be justification for Ambers not telling the whole truth. At any rate, he did not feel that chasing the hotel man now, probably into Craven's presence, to question him on the point, was vital. He went down the fire-stairs.

The girl was waiting. They stole out the back door and slipped up the street, flagged a taxi on the street behind the hotel.

In the cab, the girl asked breathlessly: "What are you going to do? Have me go to Times Square with policemen around me?"

"Lady, in the crowd that infests Times Square at noon time, it would be impossible to plant enough cops to be certain of capturing the person we want. If we had as many as half enough, the rats would be sure to spot some of them and they'd never come up to collect."

"Then what are you going to do?"

"It depends on what I can learn between now and noon. Maybe nothing, up till that time. I want to see the items of Simmons' that you have. It may give me a clue as to what this nightmare is all about. If I find nothing there, I've got to see the brokers with whom your fiancé was trading. We'll have some breakfast first."

Over breakfast, she cried a little, told him about her Connecticut younger years, and about Martin Simmons, who seemed to have been a timid, kind little man. Drago read into what she told him that the dead man had made his first speculation in order to provide funds for marriage with the pansy-eyed, brown-haired little switchboard operator. After that, the usual story—attempts to recoup, pay back.

THEY WERE at the bank at quarter to ten. Because her business was in the vaults, she was able to enter the bank a little early. Drago covered her as closely as he dared, during the trip into the building, and out again, but he saw no signs of undue interest on the part of anyone. He could not go into the building with safety. It was more than a ten-to-one shot that the murderers involved in this holocaust by now all knew him by sight.

His heart started beating again normally, only when she was in the cab with him, and they were driving up Fifth. Drago's gloved fingers ran over the old-fashioned Bible, the box of out-of-date jewelry—none of which had more than sentimental value—and he leafed through the few letters.

There was absolutely nothing that his burning mind could twist into value.

"It looks as if they've made a mistake," he told her. I can't see anything here that they would want. The thing they seek—whatever it is—is somewhere else. I'm afraid you're in a bad spot, Miss Murdock."

"Bad? Why? If—if you really think I should, I can meet them and give them this, show them that it is all I have."

Drago said uncomfortably, his brown eyes on the floor of the cab: "I'm afraid that wouldn't work."

She suddenly clapped her tiny hands to her cheeks. "Oh, you don't think they would believe me? Is that it? You think they would suspect me of holding back the thing they want?"

"Well, something like that," Drago said.

"Then"— her face went white— "then—no matter what I do, now, they are going to come after me? They're going to kill me, anyway?"

"No," Drago said. "But they might try."

"What—what should I do?"

Drago leaned back in the cab, his gloved hands in the tight pockets of his coat, his smooth, brown face turned away from the girl, looking out at the morning street. "You should get on a train and run," he said. "I'm hoping you want your fiancé's killers bad enough to risk the danger you'll be in."

Her chin came up. "I do."

"Then I'm going to take you to a small hotel where everyone is a friend of mine. You're going to hide in an unregistered room till I get in touch with you. I don't know how long it will be, but when I do call you, it may be that I'll ask you to take your life in your hands."

"I'll do anything. I've said that."

Drago leaned forward and gave the driver an address. When he shut the sliding window, the girl's voice, a little stiff, asked: "What—what are you going to do now?"

"Try to find something that will give me a gambit to play—some light on this puzzle, so that I can at least risk your life intelligently."

HE THOUGHT he had it, in the first brokerage office that they visited—Enderby, Throttle & Co. The efforts of the big, scarecrowish McSpadden finally induced the dignified, elderly manager to tell them in confidence: "Yes, we handled an account for Mr. Rance, but it was closed out three months ago. It is too bad that the young man had such limited capital. He made only one transaction with us—a purchase of Gulf Railway Common. A very volatile stock. It—er—wiped him out in three days. Had he been able to advance more margin—" He shrugged regretfully. "The stock has made a really surprising comeback since."

Drago groped. "Did Simmons—that was his real name—seem to have any special information or anything of that sort?"

The manager smiled thinly. "I have never had a customer yet who didn't."

"Why was the account closed out?"

The manager looked at pale, perfectly manicured hands. "To be perfectly frank, this firm does not care for—er—

distress trading. The young man was unable to furnish margin within the time limit we imposed, and we had to close out his account. He did come to the office a few days later with further funds, but we—er—as I say, we prefer not to deal with clients whose resources are as limited as Mr. Rance—er, Simmons'—obviously were."

IN THE offices of Ince & Ince, they received almost identically the same information, from the roly-poly, brisk manager. "Yes, remember the fellow perfectly. Too bad he couldn't have held on. When Gulf Rail moves, it certainly moves—up or down. Took ten thousand dollars of the chap's money like that! Less than two weeks."

"That was over two months ago?"

"Yes."

"Did he give any reason for discontinuing the account?"

The roly-poly manager coughed behind his hand, eyed the center button of Drago's brown coat. "The fact is, to be frank, the firm rather frowns on shoestring accounts. When we had to close him out once, we—well, rarely reopen accounts to which that happens."

AS THEY rode in the elevator that housed the uptown office of Ealing & Co., McSpadden burst out bitterly: "All those crooks of brokers knew he was embezzling. Anybody who has been in the business as long as they have, can smell it the minute a man starts trading. But they wouldn't give their own bonding company a break—oh, no! Not ethics. Damn them!"

"I'm out of my depth here," Drago confessed. "Do you think Simmons might have had some real, valuable information that could be the heart of this mess of murder?"

McSpadden's big, reddish face screwed up into a thoughtful scowl. "Oh, it's possible. But it looks to me as though someone simply gave him a good tip for the stock is back up, 'way over where he bought it, this morning. Like most stock-market amateurs, he didn't know that the president and majority stockholder of a company can be wrong—*temporarily*—on their own stock. I'd say that Simmons simply went overboard too soon—bought every share that he could margin. Then, when the dip came, he was squeezed out. Although we haven't got the whole picture yet. We've accounted for seventeen thousand of thirty-nine thousand—leaving twenty-two."

Ealing & Co. accounted for only two thousand of that. Judging by dates, this had been the first brokerage firm to which Simmons had gone. He had bought fifty shares of Gulf Rail, outright, for cash.

The manager of Ealing—a perfect figure of an undertaker if ever there was one—toupée parted in the center above a pinched face and funeral manner in much better keeping with that profession than with finance, said: "The stock, as you know, dropped sharply. I, I am sorry to say, became impressed with Mr. Simmons' claim to absolute certainty that the stock would go up. I, as it were, introduced him to margin trading.

"When his stock had shrunk to two-thirds its original worth, I suggested that he leave it with me as collateral and buy a few more shares. Thus, when the anticipated rise took place, his profits would be doubled. Unfortunately, as you know, the stock dropped even further, and he failed to respond to a margin call. We had to close out the account."

McSpadden said grimly, as they reached the street: "Twenty-five thousand to go."

"One broker to go," Drago said.

SATTERSLEE, GOWD & CO. ended their search. Here, to Drago's surprise, he found as manager an old acquaintance, "Sport" Hambly, a three-hundred-pound swarthy ex-fight-manager. The branch office was established near the Garden, the assumption being, evidently, that Hambly would draw trade from among the sporting fraternity. Hence, the policy of the office was less strict.

There was a queer, ghoul-like feeling in tracing Simmons' education in stock-trading procedure.

The mammoth Hambly had heavy black brows which he moved up and down continuously while he talked with a slight lisp: "A thucker, if you athk me, and thrictly among friends."

He cheerfully sent the bookkeeper for a detailed account of the Simmons—Rance account. He looked it over himself before passing it over.

"At that, I wonder where he got hith hot tip on Gulf. If hith money had only lathted another three weekth—"

The statement was composed almost solely of purchases—and sales at lower figures—of Gulf Rail. Early in the statement was notation of purchase of a 'call'. Drago asked what a call was.

"The thuckerth delight," Hambly explained. "You pay a hundred and thirty-theven dollarth and fifty thents. That giveth you an option on a hundred thare of thtock, which you can pick up any time within thirty dayth. The joker ith that you have to pick it up a cetain number of pointh above where the market wath at the time you bought it. Like thith trade, for inthtanth.

"Your pal bought a call on a hundred shares of Gulf at fifty. It was thelling then at forty-four. If it went up thix pointh in a month—he exerthised the option and could thell the stock for a profit. Only, as you thee, it didn't go up thix pointh, and the option jutht died quietly at the end of thirty dayth. Matter of fact, we don't trade in one put or call in a year. When I thaw that on the bookth, I called Ranth—Thimmonth, you thay his name ith?—in here and told him what a thucker bet it wath. The only real function of a call ith to hedge a short thale, but that hath nothing to do with thith, and you guyth have got enough education for nothing as it ith."

Drago handed back the statement. It showed a total cash loss of twenty-four thousand, one hundred and nine dollars. The account had lasted from two months ago, till two weeks ago when, like all the others, it had been closed out for lack of margin.

WHEN THEY arrived at the ground floor and were out in the cold, overcast street again, Drago's watch showed ten minutes after two. For one second, a cold hand seemed to squeeze on his heart, as he realized that the deadline the murderers had set for Mary Murdock, Simmons fiancé, had passed.

He tried to think quickly of some excuse to rid himself of McSpadden, but none came to mind. He went in and telephoned the hotel where he had left the girl, and found that she was still safe. Having no answers to give the questions he knew she would ask, he did not talk to her directly, but to the manager of the hotel.

He put in a call for the Graff Arms, and tried to reach Ambers, the manager of that establishment. There was still the matter of the manager's concealing his previous knowledge of Simmon's defalcation to be explained. He was told that Ambers was not in, and then asked to hold the wire.

He said disgustedly, "Don't be silly," and hung up.

He decided to put no more tax on his already spinning brain, to devise an excuse to shake McSpadden. There was a shooting gallery, less than two blocks away, in which there was a bolt-hole unknown to the public and which he had used before.

He rejoined McSpadden, and they headed for it. He was a little startled when the big, plodding insurance dick spoke thoughtfully.

"You know—I just thought of something. That guy Simmons used to be kind of intimate with the switchboard girl in that Graff hotel. I wonder if he ever gave her any jewelry or money or like that?"

"You wouldn't have some ghoul in you, would you?" Drago asked. "My God, we've checked out all but a few hundred dollars of the shortage. If he spent that little bit on her, you aren't seriously intending to try and recover that speck for your company?"

"Well, no, now you remind me. But she might know something."

Drago stopped dead in the street. "Say, that's not a bad lead. I don't dare go near that hotel, but I tell you what you do. Call her up and get her to meet you outside. There's a phone in that drugstore."

CHAPTER EIGHT
TWIN OF THE DEAD

H E SAT on a chair beside McTigue's bed in the white hospital room, dangling his hat between his knees, his eyes strained. "Simmons was taken out of his hotel room by two men. He was taken to a dentist's—the dentist above that butcher store—and tortured. Why he was tortured, I don't know. He had a bad heart. The torture was too much for him—they drilled into the nerve in three teeth. His heart stopped. The thugs took him out. When Charlie Birn tried to stop them, they could hardly be found with a dead man between them, so they killed Birn.

"There's something they're after—more than one thing maybe. I can't get my fingers on what it is.

"When I got to the hotel, they seemed to be after the wallet. There's a girl in with the killers—a girl with a pretty grim record—Lady Babe." He checked himself, frowned. "Or maybe she isn't in with them, at that. When I first saw her she was struggling with the two men, and she threw a wallet out the window. I got the wallet—and I guess they spotted me, though how, I don't know. Anyway, she wanted the wallet, too. She wanted it badly enough to hang around and make a try to get it from me. She got it, too—through this mutton-headed McSpadden.

The two thugs—all the description I can give of them is that one is a big, burly gent with a big black thatch of hair, and the other a skinny one with pinkish blond hair—tried to kill me to get the wallet.

"Now, for some reason, they've turned their attention to this Mary Murdock, the switchboard girl in the hotel and Simmons' ex-fiancé. They seem to think she's got what they want. They've threatened her—nearly frightened her to death. Not that I blame her. These people are ruthless, if nothing else. They gave her a deadline, but it's gone now. They'll be hunting her. I've got her put away in a place that will be safe for a few more hours, anyway.

"I'm running around in figure-eights, trying to catch hold of this racket, and getting absolutely nowhere. And I've got to get somewhere, now, Mac—fast. I've put that girl's life into the pot. They'll kill her, I feel sure, if they can find her before I find them. And she's nice—a damn sweet little kid. I promise you this. They'll have to get me, if they get her.

"On top of everything, there seems to be a gigantic amount of money involved somewhere. Logic says there has to be—to cause all this. The thug that threatened Miss Murdock on the phone said as much, too."

The grizzled inspector's china-blue eyes bored down at Drago. "You're sure Simmons lost all the money he stole?"

"Positive." He took the colored cards from his pocket, tossed them on the bed. "We've been to his brokers. He was a babe in the woods in the stock market. Although, at that, he seems to have had a good tip to begin with. The stock he bought"—Drago consulted a slip in his pocket—"from forty-eight down. That is, he started buying it at forty-eight. He got sold out on that, bought more at forty-two, got sold out, more at thirty-five, got sold out, and so forth, till he bought the last lot at twenty-six, and that went. The stock's back up now, they tell me, to above where he started buying it, and, if he had been able to hold on, he would have cleaned up. I'm a little hazy about details, but according to McSpadden, Simmons let go his money on sucker plays too soon. We've accounted for practically all of what he embezzled."

"Did McSpadden dope that out, too?"

"No. I saw the statements."

"That guy has no brains."

"I wouldn't argue with you, but he knows his Wall Street—and his books and figures, which is all I want him for."

"If all that money's definitely gone, where is this fortune that you think is in the background of this thing, coming from?" McTigue frowned.

"I don't know. Maybe it's not cash money. The only thing I've been able to imagine is that it's information—in document form. They seem to have killed Simmons to find where it was. It seems to have been in that black wallet of his, at one time. And yet, they seem to think now that the switchboard girl—Mary Murdock—has it."

MCTIGUE RUBBED his bald head. "How about this? The girl—Lady Babe—sneaked into Simmons' room, after the killers had redeposited the body there, and some-how found the wallet. The killers, for some reason, came back and caught her there. She managed to throw it out the window to stop their getting it. They ran downstairs to get it away from you. She saw you stand them off and pocket the wallet. When you came upstairs she went to work on you and, as you say, got it.

"The thugs may not know that. They may think you still have it."

"So they jump on Mary Murdock, Simmons' ex-fiancé. What sort of sense is that?"

"Well, maybe there's two separate things they want. One that was in that wallet and one that the Mary Murdock girl has."

Drago shrugged.

"Well, if you want my advice, you'll get over and stick with that switchboard girl," McTigue growled. "You say the blow-off's got to come tonight—in the next few hours?"

"Sometime during the night. They told her that."

"Then you'd damned well better sit beside her for the next twenty-four hours. If they find her—God knows what'll happen to you when the inspector finds it out."

"Why? What should I do?"

"Do? The girl ought to be in the Tombs, where she's safe."

"Sure. And the minute she lands there—or under any police protection in the city—Craven hears of it. He outranks me and he'll just take her over."

"Well, the least you can do is guard her, yourself."

"Sure. While these rats hammer their scheme home to completion! Then they're gone—with their loot, whatever it is, and for all we know, the girl may in danger the rest of her life. That's not the method for this, and you know it. We know they're still working it out—still trying to get to the pay-off. I've just got tonight to find what the devil it is they're doing—and smash it up. And you think I should sit and hold the girl's hand. Damn it, Mac, I'm not made of stone. I want those pups.

"I knew young Charlie Birn, and he was a fine kid. If we had twenty thousand like him, this city would be some-place to live in. What happens? These rats, trying to steal a fortune, have one man die in them. Because Charlie Birn merely looks as if he might be going to interfere with them, they shoot him down like that! Damn it, who do they think they are? And me—they tried to do the same to me, in the matter of that wallet.

"They could have tried to frighten me away from the thing—let off a volley of shots and grabbed it in the rush, but no. They call out to me, try to get me to stand still so they can pour their damned lead into me and be sure they kill me. A mere cop, standing in the way of their filthy, thieving strutting! Well, I want them, Mac, for all those reasons—for the kid, for myself, for young Simmons—even though he was an embezzler—and, maybe most of all, because I want this Mary Murdock's life cleared up as much as it can be. And that'll be only when I've got those killers—all of them—sitting in the death cells at Sing Sing.

"I've got just these few hours to do it in. I can't sit still in a hotel room, even with that girl, while the blow-off runs to its finale. I've got her in the safest place I know and the rest I've got to risk."

THE PHONE by McTigue's bed rang. He twisted his big body on the pillows and growled an answer: "Yeah…. Yeah, this is me…. Well, I dunno. What it's about?… A message from who?… *Who?*" His red, Irish face screwed up in effort at concentration. Presently, he said, "Wait a minute," and covered the mouthpiece. To Drago he said, "It's Mike at headquarters. He says a guy just called there, trying to locate you. The guy lisps. He said he was manager of something called Whatterby, Gowd."

"Satterslee, Gowd. That's Sport Hambly, used to manage prize-fighters—"

"What? That crook? Say, he wouldn't be above a share in this thing, himself! He—"

"You have to be honest in that business, till you get farther up the ladder than Sport is. Did he leave a message? Get it, if he did. I don't want to show."

McTigue growled into the transmitter: "I don't know where Mr. Drago is. He might call here, though. If there's any message, you can leave it with me.... Eh?" He reached out a big, seamed hand for the pad of paper and pencil on his bedside table and said: "Go ahead." He nearly covered two sheets of the paper with illegible scrawl.

When he hung up he told Drago:

"Hambly called and asked for you. After you left his office this afternoon, seems he was gossiping about Simmons and all, to a couple of his other customers. One of them was very much surprised and got Hambly alone. This guy's name is Fennal. Fennal told Hambly that he'd met Simmons around the office and they'd gone to lunch a couple times together and got friendly. Fennal told Hambly that he knew something that the police ought to know, so Hambly called for you. When you weren't in, he got Fennal to leave his phone number for you to call when you came in. Here it is."

Drago's eyes were startled. "Dear God—am I going to get a break! Call him, Mac, will you?"

When he finally took the phone himself, a petulant, thin tenor voice said: "Yes, yes! Mr. Simmons confided something to me that I feel I ought to tell you, in view—in view of what Mr. Hambly tells me has happened. Of course, you may know it already. Are you aware that Mr. Simmons has a twin brother?"

"What! No! Go on."

The other hesitated. "Really, Mr. Drago, it isn't—the rest of it isn't something that I could speak of over the telephone. Could I come and see you in the morning?"

"No! I mean—where are you now, Mr. Fennal?"

"At my office, of course."

"I'll run over and see you." Drago said. "Where is your office?"

"It's on Sixth—in Greenwich Village"—he gave the number—"but I'm afraid it isn't convenient today. As a matter of fact, I was on my way out when you—"

"When will you be back?"

"Not more than fifteen or twenty minutes, on this call, but I have to—"

"I'll be there when you get back, waiting," Drago urged. "You have no idea how important time is, as it happens."

After a minute, the tenor voice said: "Very well. My office is on the third floor. I'll leave the door open so you won't have to wait in the hall."

Drago hung up and said in a bleak voice: "My God. Simmons has a twin brother. This gent implies there's more to it than that. What a madhouse."

He got up clapped the brown hat on his shining black hair.

"What about the girl?" McTigue said.

"Stop worrying about her, Mac, I'm doing enough for us both. I'll see this gent and then move her. I've got to take advantage of all the time that reason allows. I've only got a limited number of places I can move her to. And every time I move her, there's the risk of being seen—either by the rats we're fighting, or by someone who will tell Craven."

The phone rang again.

McTigue answered and immediately turned his head away from the phone and whispered, "McSpadden."

"You don't know where I am," Drago said, "but I left word for him to meet me at—well, at that Sixth Avenue address, in half an hour."

CHAPTER NINE
"PUT YOUR HANDS UP!"

IT WAS not many blocks from the bottom of Sixth Avenue—an ancient, street-line, sagging gray-stone building. It occupied the frontage of a small block and its ground floor was occupied by a line of stores. It was a chore to locate the narrow little entrance in the middle of the block that led to the building proper.

He went two long flights up wooden, creaking, dusty stairs, before he found a musty door whose glass panel read *R. Fennal, Importer*, knocked, got no answer and went in.

Drago stood impatiently waiting, his gloved hands in the pockets of his coat, presently decided on one of the wingchairs and reached for it.

The closed door of the cupboard that was momentarily at his back, burst open and a voice said: "Don't move, Mr. Drago. Put your hands up!" It was a woman's voice.

Drago's hands went slowly up. His brown face was now ashen. He turned his head over his shoulder and looked dull-eyed at the girl who, in the Graff Arms hotel, had given her name as April Crain, but who, in Chicago, had been known as Lady Babe.

"You can turn around," she told him.

"A very nice little plant," Drago said. "Now, all we need is the tenor voice that—"

The second cupboard opened and Charles Amber, manager of the Graff Arms hotel, stepped out, white-faced, his gray eyes strained, but there was a revolver in his gloved hand, also. Somehow, even his conservative Chesterfield coat and muffler, the conservative hard hat on his distinguished silvered hair, did not seem unsuited to his present grim position.

It was a jolt to Drago. That the hotel owner had come out into the open, had let Drago see his face without hesitation, could only mean one thing. They did not plan to let him leave this room alive.

The girl said sharply: "All right, Drago. You know what we want."

"Of course," Drago said. "But it would avoid confusion, if you'd tell me."

"You know, all right. I'll tell you what we're going to do. We're going to give you a little whiff of chloroform, and tie you up a bit, to give us the time we need. After, of course, you hand us certain little items."

Her pebbly-blue eyes were intent upon his face, as if in question. Drago's vermillion lips showed white teeth for a second. "You're a little late," he told her. "A smarter girl than you managed to get them—er, it—from me, and lit out."

"Mary Murdock!" Ambers exclaimed.

"A good guess."

The girl's eyes narrowed. She snapped: "Search him, Charles. Take everything out of his pockets."

DRAGO HOPED for a chance, but there was none, as the hotel owner advanced. The girl ran around and stood with her gun at Drago's back, as the man cleaned out his effects. When every article lay on the desk, she moved back and examined them, keeping the desk between herself and Drago. Her lips tightened and she looked grimly at Drago.

"Where is the girl?" she wanted to know.

Drago's eyes blinked slowly. "If I knew, do you think I'd be likely to tell you?"

"Then you do know. Yes, you'll tell us—or you'll wish you'd never been born."

"For how much, Lady Babe?" His brain was searching feverishly for a formula to get him out of this. "Don't talk torture to me. I won't let you get near enough to me to try it. You're not anxious to shoot. Maybe I do know where she is. Maybe I can find out. But by Judas, I'm going to declare myself in. What's it worth to you? I can't handle the girl myself, but I can put her where you can get her."

The girl's pebbly eyes were like ice. "I think this is a stall, but if it's on the level, ten thousand dollars."

Drago grunted. "Stage money. Where are you going to get ten thousand dollars?"

"That needn't worry you."

"The hell it needn't. I can't see enough in this job to let you toss that much around as if it were nothing."

"It isn't nothing. It's a lot of cash."

"All right. I'm not going to try and beat you out of more. But this isn't such a healthy spot for me. If I'm going to stick my neck out by helping you, I want to know that the money's safe. Have you got it on you?"

"No, naturally not. We'll pay off tomorrow morning."

"How do I know that? I'll take my chances on your skipping. I can always catch up with you and take it out of your hide. But I won't take any chances on the offer not being backed up by the real green, right now. I'm serious. It happens that I need money right now—badly enough to go through with this. But not blind. Show me where the pay-off comes from, and that you can collect if you get the girl—and I'll turn her up."

Ambers said eagerly, "We—" and put his hand in his pocket.

"Tie him up, first, you nitwit!" the girl said. "Drago, if you're on the level, we can fix up this thing. If you're not—you're not going to get very far."

"I'm waiting to hear what's what," Drago said patiently.

Ambers was at the desk, jerked out a drawer. He set a can on its top, drew out four rolls of adhesive tape.

"I still think this a little phony, Drago," the girl said. "At least, I think so enough to plug you if make one false move."

Drago shrugged, to conceal the inner consternation that was pulsing up inside him. "I'm not going to give you a fight."

They trussed him at hands, ankles, knees and elbows, till he looked like a mummy.

"Hop over to that cupboard," the girl said.

"This doesn't make sense," Drago complained. "What—"

"Hop over there."

Her finger was white on the trigger. Drago hopped. When he was beside the cupboard, she said: "Give him a push, Charles."

As he flopped painfully onto the floor of the musty, bare cupboard that had contained the girl, Drago understood. He cursed desperately, inwardly. He had said the wrong thing.

The girl kept over him, every second, the gun centered on his face. "Get the chloroform, Charles. All right, Drago—where is the girl?"

"Don't be silly. I'm not giving anything out, until—"

"All right. Maybe we can find her without you. Soak that handkerchief and put it over his nose and mouth," she told Ambers. "Drago, if you let out one sound, so help me God, I'll kill you. I'm giving you a chance to live, by keeping quiet."

DRAGO KNEW what was coming now. A gun was noisy, embarrassing. The girl was shrewd enough to talk him to death. He began to take furtive, deep breaths, to prepare his heart. He knew there was only one chance in a thousand of his surviving what was about to be done to him, and the desperate part of it was that he was utterly powerless. He had no doubts whatever that the girl would shoot.

Then the white, dripping cloth was slapped across his face. He had barely time to take a quick gulp of breath.

He told himself that he would have to hold his breath for five minutes. By thinking toward five minutes, he might possibly hold out for a little less. His only hope was to make them think he had taken more than he had.

His head began to swell, his lungs to burn with sucking. He fought desperately to keep from gulping in the chloroform fumes. It seemed to him that time must have forgotten about him—that the two standing over him must be planning to spend hours, forever—

He slept.

CHAPTER TEN
HUMAN BAIT

HE STUMBLED out of the closet into the office, sick, dizzy, half blind, lay on the floor, nauseated beyond movement. He fought for minutes and minutes—for hours, it seemed—to get his head above the dancing, torturing inertia. His head cleared slowly. He was weak. He felt himself on the verge of tears and laughter—weak, silly laughter. He lay still, forcing his eyes to stay open, fighting for strength, panting.

He finally got to his feet, sick at his stomach, his head pounding, held himself erect by the desk, till he was sane again. He pressed his head—and suddenly his mind was clear again. He looked round at the window behind him, and his heart turned over as he saw that it was almost dark—twilight. He threw himself toward the door of the office, stumbled back and snatched up his belongings from the desktop. Even his gun was there.

He flung out the door, and a rush of icy air came up at him from the stair-well. It got icier, as he went headlong down the steps. He emerged onto Sixth Avenue, and was in a cab at the curb, in one long dive. He checked the address at the girl's hiding-place on the tip of his tongue, substituted directions, and urged speed.

HIS MOUTH was drier than a blotter when he finally reached the hotel and sailed into the lobby, certain that he had not been followed. An elevator took him to the girl's room and when, in answer to his knock, she said instantly, "Who's there?" he sweated with relief.

She pulled open the door without waiting for his answer. She was tense, white-faced, but her eyes were feverish. She said: "Thank God! You got them?"

Drago came in and dropped his hat on the table, sat down in an armchair. "No. They got me."

"What do you mean?"

"Just that," he said wearily. "They laid a trap for me and tried to kill me."

Her gasp was sharp. "Oh! Your face is all red and splotched! Did—did they do that?"

"Uh-huh." He roused himself with an effort. "Come on, we're getting out of here."

"Where to?"

"Another hotel I have in mind. It's a miracle they haven't traced you here by now."

She ran and stood stiffly in front of him, nursing one wrist. Her face was desperate.

"I won't go! I've gone nearly mad here, all day long, all by myself. A dozen times I nearly ran out into the street. The only reason I didn't was because I'd promised you. And I thought you were out getting them. My God, can't you understand? I've got to do something or go crazy. They've killed the sweetest thing in my life. I want to claw and tear and torture them!"

Drago's burning eyes were searching, hot, on her face for a good minute. "You don't know what you're saying," he told her. "Everyone concerned in this terrible business is looking for you. I can't see why. It may be that they are under some crazy misapprehension. But the danger you would be in, the minute you stepped onto the street—any street—is very great. At least four desperate people are rushing around, trying to find you. Their plans, at the very climax, seem to be at a complete standstill, till they get you. God knows it's a terrible temptation to use you for bait, but I—Judas, what am I saying? This is the sort of thing Craven would do."

"Stop talking!" she almost screamed. "It's the only thing left—the last chance we have. You said so, yourself. I'm going through with it. I won't let you stop me because of your prissy fussiness. I want you to be with me—but I'm going to do it whether you are or not! I swear if you won't use me, I'll go to this Craven. I don't care if I'm killed."

Drago's brown face was livid. "If my nerves weren't crawling to get my hands on these killers—if there weren't a certain fine boy that these rats killed and that I'll see the rest of my life if I don't square up for him—in other words, if I weren't a little unbalanced myself, I wouldn't listen to you. Now, I don't know what to—"

Her palms flew to her hot temples and she ground them in. "Oh, God, stop," she cried crazily. "What are we going to do?"

Drago's teeth showed between his vermilion lips. There were tiny beads on his smooth, brown face. "All right. I'll be a rat. We'll do as you say. We'll expose you so that they can see you. We'll pray that they try to capture—not kill you—on sight. Where—where do you live?"

Her eyes were suddenly shining, savage. "About twenty minutes out in Royal Oak, on Long Island."

"A house?"

"Yes. We have a little house—my mother and I. But my mother went away to see my aunt last night—to Jersey. I was going to stay in town till she got back."

"Tell me about the house. I've got to know the exact situation."

"Royal Oak is a little suburb of Garden City. It's away off at the outskirts—a subdivision, you could still call it. There's the beach, and then a sort of long, narrow woods, and behind the woods is our place."

"You mean all by itself?"

"No. Not exactly. Though there are two or three vacant lots on either side of us. There are other houses dotted up and down the street."

"Tell me the arrangement of your house. What I'm driving at, is that, when you show yourself, you will probably—I'll say certainly—be seen by one of four people who are looking for you, or maybe by someone working for them. I'm praying, as I said, that they will try to follow you—get hold of you somewhere in a secluded place. I want that place to be as nearly as possible under my control as can be. It's in my mind that you'll lead them to your house, and I want to know how I can be in position to cover you every minute."

"That—that's easy. Our house is just a little one, and the middle of it is all the dining-room. It runs the whole width of the cottage—not that there's much width. Do you see what I mean? There are windows on both sides of the room. You can be on either side and look right into the room. Only, the north side, there's a little tool shed, only a few feet away from the windows. If you wanted to, you could lie on top of the tool shed, and—"

"All right," Drago said without pleasure. "That'll do. Where were you going to stay in town?"

"At a girl's—a friend's."

"Would people know that at the hotel? I mean, would they be able to furnish the address of that place to anyone who asked?"

"Yes."

"Where else would it be reasonable to think these rats were watching for you?"

"Maybe at my aunt's, in the Bronx."

"Anywhere else?"

After a minute she said: "I don't think so."

"Then, wait a minute."

HE PICKED the phone from the bed-table and phoned McTigue. The grizzled old inspector bellowed: "Where in God's name have you been? Damn you, you've had me going through hell and high water. I'm about ready to—"

"I know, Mac. I'm sorry. Listen, the girl—Mary Murdock—never mind why—is definitely going to bat. I've got to have at least two more detectives. Get them for me."

"To guard her? You fool, Craven's got every man on the force looking for you! If they see you and don't report to him, he's promised to have them—"

"I know all about that. But I hope this is the last play. I've got to take the chance. I'm going to give the detectives so dizzy a ride around town that they won't be able to tell Craven where we're heading for. He'll probably catch up to me sometime, but I'm gambling I'll either have this thing smashed, or be in such trouble that I won't care about Craven, or what he does. Do I get the detectives?"

"Yes, but what's it all about?"

"I'll be in and tell you all about it, a little later. I can't talk now. Have those detectives meet me at—" He turned and asked the girl the address of the Bronx aunt, and estimated the cross street. "Have them meet me a block from there—on the corner. Don't tell them who they're meeting. That way, they'll have to be in the car with me before they know, and they don't have much chance to phone Craven. Right?"

"I hope to God you know what you're doing."

Drago hung up and turned to the girl. "All right. Ready?"

She flew into hat and coat. "What—what are we going to do?"

"First, I'm going to pick up two more men. Then you're going to show yourself in all those places, ending up with the Graff Arms. That's one place that they'll almost positively be waiting for you. Now, you've got to remember that there'll be police around these places, too—at least, around the hotel. They won't be keeping very close watch, but you mustn't blunder into their hands, or we're done for. Understand?"

"Yes."

"These killers that we're after are almighty clever. If they pick up your trail, you'll not see them. It's even probable that we won't see them. Maybe you'll feel them. That ain't as funny as it sounds. I want you to do something, if you get a sort of hunch that they've frozen on behind you. Take off your hat and run a hand through your hair. That'll keep us doubly on guard."

He hesitated, and the vein was showing on his dark forehead. "You understand that you'll have to go in a car by yourself. We'll follow as closely as we dare, but we can't exactly be with you. For God's sake, if you see anything that frightens you—anything that even faintly looks as if someone were going to attack you—call out my name.

For, if they attack you openly, it means they want you out of the way, and our plan goes into the discard. You've got to promise to obey orders."

"I promise. You haven't told me all of it yet. What do I—"

"We'll make the round of these places. You've got to show your face openly, but you've got to make up little things to do so they won't suspect that you're doing—what you're doing."

"That's easy."

"Then, after you've covered the places, you'll go to the Long Island Railroad and take a train home. I think you'll be safe on the train, and we'll be waiting for you at Royal Oak. You needn't look for us. Don't look for anybody, as a matter of fact, any time. Just go there as if you were going home naturally."

"But won't the police be there, too?"

"No. It's outside our jurisdiction. They'll have looked there, but it's very improbable that they're keeping strict watch. Go into the house and turn on the lights. Be sure the window that faces that tool shed is open, and down from the top, a foot or so, so I can hear what's said in the dining-room. You'll put all these things"—he waved at the package that she had brought from the safe-deposit box that morning—"on the dining-room table, to make sure that whatever takes place in the house, does so in that room."

"Then what?"

"God knows," Drago said. "God only knows. But I'll be there, covering you. If there's a chance to get any information from anybody, which there probably won't be—remember that I'm watching and listening."

"What if no one follows me home?"

Drago winced. "Don't think of that. We'll have to start all over again, if that happens. But it won't. I know it won't. If there's one thing I'm sure of in this crazy-quilt, it's that someone will follow you home."

Someone did.

CHAPTER ELEVEN
HORROR HOUSE

THE THREE hours that they spent in New York were unbreathing torture for Drago. With the two detectives, he followed the girl's cab around, racked between the urge to get closer to her and the tantalizing danger of being seen by those they were seeking.

They drove through the night—the Bronx, Greenwich Village, the Graff Arms—and the girl got out each place. She was playing her part perfectly, giving the impression of furtiveness, yet managing to be perfectly recognizable by any one within fifty yards of her.

The last stop—the hotel—was the most racking of all, but nothing happened. The hotel's lighted canopy blazed out over the sidewalk in silent dignity. Nowhere was there any hint of the tragedy that had stalked the hotel the night before. People were passing on the sidewalks of Fifty-seventh. It was an alive, light thoroughfare at ten o'clock.

The girl did not touch her hat—made no effort to flash the signal that she thought she had been spotted. She climbed into her cab, in front of the hotel, without giving the slightest sign. Drago cursed under his breath, but he was not deceived. That the girl's tense nerves had not picked up any indication of pursuit only spoke well of her courage.

The girl's cab turned down toward the Pennsylvania Station.

Drago felt a hollow feeling in his stomach as they followed that hack to the terminal. He waited till the last minute before he told one of the two detectives: "Holdrahan—you get out and follow her. She's taking a train. Don't let yourself be spotted, and, for God's sake, don't let anyone lay a hand on her."

The other detective spoke casually in the darkness of the jolting touring-car: "Where's she going?"

"What do you care?" Drago asked. "Just buy a ticket to the end of the North Shore line and get off when she does. We'll be waiting."

THE UNMARKED, black touring-car that Drago had secured, flew through the night, ate up the few miles between New York and Royal Oak in minutes. They slid into the deserted, lonely little board shack of a station, ten minutes before the train was due, and found a place in the wide acre of gravel that surrounded the station where they could park and be reasonably free from observation.

The train roared in. The girl got off one end of it. Holdrahan got off the other. The girl stood on the platform a moment, *took off her hat, shook her brown hair, ran a hand through it and put it back on.*

No one else got off the train.

For a moment, Drago was startled, afraid that the girl had mistaken Holdrahan for a follower—even though she had seen him a few hours earlier. Then he realized that the killers he was pursuing would be too cagy to disembark at a lonely station like this. Especially when, as is the case with the Long Island North Shore line, the next stop was only a mile or two away.

A battered, dilapidated, green-painted old Model-T rattled up—evidently the town's only taxi. The girl got in and drove off without a backward glance.

"All right," Drago said. "Pick up Holdrahan," and the dark car swung out to take the detective aboard. Drago told the driver: "Step on it—not along the street she's taking but the one that ends in the beach. Get there fast."

"I don't see no one following her, but the train was full," Holdrahan reported. "Geez, you should of told me where we were headed for. I near didn't get off."

"So you could have passed the information along to Craven, eh?" Drago said.

There was no answer.

The car ran to the end of the road, and the cold bite of the wind, the restless surging of Long Island Sound, was in front of them. Drago sprang out on the sand, looked down the black shore. The line of heavy woods came down to within eighty yards of the water, paralleled it as far as the eye could see in this blackness.

He told the two in the car: "All right. I know you're both waiting for a chance to phone Craven. This is it. You can phone him, if you want to take the chance, but get this. I'm telling you to go and cover the front of the house the girl went to. If you're not there, somebody may be murdered. If they're murdered because you're not there, I'm going to personally kill you both with my hands. Now, get."

He ran on down the sand, trying to estimate the distance he was covering starting at the row of closed summer cottages along the beach-front, staring at the thick belt of woods behind them. The girl had told him the approximate distance that would bring him up behind her house. He tried to pace it off, carefully. There was supposed to be a break in the row of cottages, almost exactly behind—

He came to the break, turned and plowed into the woods. It was only twenty yards through, and he emerged into what seemed like a mammoth, black field, dotted here and there with trees, sparsely, and with not more than half a dozen houses scattered over a mile frontage. One or two of them showed light—the nearest at least a quarter mile away.

There was, here and there, a little frozen snow on the ground. Had it not been for that, even the faint breath of light that enabled Drago to pierce the darkness slightly, would not have existed. The girl had neglected to tell him that there were no lights on the street.

HE HEARD the green station taxi chug up to the door. It stopped, a hundred yards straight ahead of him, so that he knew he was in direct line with the back of the girl's house. He went quickly across the stubbly field, making as little noise as possible, crouched over, a gun in his hand. By all reason, it ought to be a few minutes before whoever had been following the girl reached the next station, got off and came back. Nevertheless, Drago moved with the caution of an Indian.

There was a low stone wall across the back of the girl's property, she had told him, with a few feet of that wall running up the two sides of the lot. The rest had not been built.

He came up against it suddenly in the darkness—just as the lights flashed on in the house.

The stone wall was about the height of Drago's waist. The lights, flashing on, put a little radiance over the whole piece of ground.

Directly across the stone fence, looking squarely into Drago's face, stood a man holding a gun.

The man snapped, "Don't—don't move!" and a light beam flashed on Drago's face.

"You fool, douse that light," Drago whipped. "Where the devil did you come from, McSpadden?"

The big man's jaw dropped open. "Drago!" The light went off. "How did—hey," he suddenly complained, "what kind of run-around are you giving me? This is a fine way to treat a pal. I waited down there on Sixth Avenue a whole hour. I thought we were—"

"Shut up, you jackass. Talk lower."

"Aw right, talk lower then," he whined in a whisper. "If I hadn't happened to think about that switchboard girl, you wouldn't of even thought of coming here. Hell, if you—"

"Can it, now," Drago whispered. "The girl's in the house—"

"Don't I know it? Ain't I figured that's where she'd eventually—"

"For God's sake, shut up," Drago exploded. "We're sitting on a keg of dynamite. The killers are on this girl's trail. They'll be here before long. Look—do you see that little sort of box, just beside the window there?"

"Huh? Oh, yeah."

"We can lie on top of that. It's a tool shed. We can look right down into the room. Get up there—and get up without sound." Drago vaulted the stone wall.

They lay on top of the tool shed. McSpadden wanted to continue complaining, but Drago snapped him into silence.

THROUGH THE window, opened a foot from the top, they commanded a view of the entire little snug dining-room. The girl was there now, hat and coat off, pretty, child-like face flushed, eyes strained. She was laying the family Bible and the box of jewelry, the packet of letters, on the oak sideboard. She did not look up. Then she did—but not at Drago. She looked out the window on the opposite side of the room. Drago heard it, too—the noise that had evidently penetrated the thin walls of the cottage. It was the sound of an automobile, coming into the street, a full two blocks distant.

The car was coming down the street now, slowly. Its headlamps danced on the mud road in front of the girl's house.

It stopped in front of the house. The headlamps were dimmed, but there was still radiance from them.

In the radiance, Drago saw a crouched figure come running along the side of the house, toward where they lay atop their perch. Fire came into Drago's brown eyes. The figure was a woman, and the Cossack hat atop her head was terribly familiar. Lady Babe had arrived.

For a minute, he did not understand her actions. She paused a moment, directly under them. If the shed had been a foot lower, Drago could have reached down and grabbed her hat. She peered in at the room.

Mary Murdock, inside, was going about, straightening things, for all the world as if she had heard nothing. The door-bell rang. The girl could not repress a start, but she smoothed her dress, walked out of the room toward the front.

Drago understood then, as Lady Babe slipped swiftly to the back door of the house. There was a slightly metallic fumbling. Then the back door opened for an instant, closed again.

Lady Babe was inside the kitchen.

Drago's face was strained, moist, as he eased his gun hand into more comfortable position.

Mary Murdock suddenly backed into the dining-room. She had the gun that Drago had given her, pressed tight into the stomach of the distinguished-looking hotel manager, Charles Ambers, who followed her, a foot away, his hands in the air.

"But, my dear Miss Murdock," he was expostulating.

Lady Babe's voice spoke from the door between dining-room and kitchen. "All right, girlie. Drop the gun if you don't want a bullet in the back."

THE BROWN-HAIRED girl's gasp was perfect. She dropped the gun, swung around to confront the black-seal-coated Lady Babe, her deep, pansy eyes registering shock, awe, desperate fright.

"Just stand still," Lady Babe made a slight gesture with the gun in her hand. "Charles, there's the stuff on the table. Look through it and see if what we want is there. Otherwise, we'll have to persuade little Miss Muffet here to tell us where it is." Her voice was bitter and sharp now, tense.

The gray-haired Amber jumped quickly to the sideboard, picked up the Bible. He held it, leaf edge down and shook it, riffled it thoroughly, fingered through the jewelry and examined the letters.

Drago's eyes were glued on the man's distinguished face, reading his expression.

"It isn't here," Ambers told Lady Babe. "Dash it, it isn't here!"

The tall girl's pebbly-blue eyes swung back to the girl's frightened pansy ones. Her lips were like steel edges as she told Mary Murdock: "All right, sweetie-pie. Where is it?"

Drago half eased himself up on his free hand. He did not know what might be coming now, and he was ready to shoot—more than ready. At what happened, it is a miracle that he didn't shoot. If his nerves had been less strong, he would have. It was totally, stunningly unexpected.

Suddenly, in the flash of an eye, the window at the other side of the dining-room shot up. For a split-second, the face of a vulture-like, tall man, with a head drawn almost to a point, and with pinkish-blond hair, was framed behind a gun in the window. The man said: "Drop it, baby."

He did not know with whom he was dealing.

Lady Babe spun, in the minute that the window crashed open. By the time the man's speech was out, her gun had exploded. The lead smacked squarely into the pink-haired man's nose, and he was blasted away from the window.

As if that were not enough of the unexpected, so fast—almost in the same instant that the other window had gone up—a dark form sprang, seemingly from the ground underneath Drago, flung the window on this side open and fired. Lady Babe was almost knocked from her feet by the slug.

The movements were so synchronous that the two shots—Lady Babe's, and that of the huge, bareheaded man who was shoving his thick black thatch of hair through the window on this side, behind his gun—sounded like the twin impact of a one-two punch.

The burly, black-haired man growled "Don't move! None of you!" and blocked the window with his body, as he climbed in.

McSpadden could contain himself no longer. He eased over and almost whined in Drago's ear: "They're all here. The whole mob."

Drago jabbed the end of his gun into McSpadden's lips, almost wrung a cry from the big man.

CHAPTER TWELVE
A FORTUNE TO FIND

INSIDE THE dining-room, the big black-haired
gunman stood bull-like, staring at the others, his
back to Drago. Ambers, his face putty-colored, was in one
corner. Lady Babe was flat against the wall by the sideboard, one hand pressed to her other shoulder. Red was
dripping from between her white fingers. Her gun was
yards away, on the floor, where it had skidded when the
black-haired man shot her shoulder numb. Her pebbly-
blue eyes were on fire.

The switchboard girl, Mary Murdock, stood against
the wall, also, her two hands outspread, palms against the
wall-paper behind her. Her face was transfigured, her eyes
shining with the light of an insane person, as if she were
about to laugh.

"All right," the big man said. "I guess nobody here needs
to be told what I want."

"Aren't you going to look at your friend?" Lady Babe
said quickly.

The big man turned his head a little. He had a big stupid
face, brutal and cruel, and shining, darting black eyes. He
wore an ill-fitting black-bottle coat, buttoned to the neck,
and black cotton gloves. "I don't have to, lady," he said with
heavy ominousness. "I seen what you done to him."

Lady Babe's eyes seemed to recede a little, but her quick tongue did not desert her. "Tell us exactly what you want. We'll help you get it."

The big gunman considered this a minute, heavy black brows drawing low over his shining black eyes.

"Aw right. I want a green slip o' paper, about the size of the page of a book. It says across the top of it 'Thirty day option.' And in one corner, in heavy black letters, it says 'Call.' This thing is a call, see? Underneath, it says that a guy—I forget his name—hereby guarantees to deliver to Obermeter and Company—that's a stockbroker, see?—one thousand shares of Gulf Railway, at twenty-eight dollars a share, any time within thirty days from date. Then, all over it, is stamped the date—which is just twenty-nine days ago. Tomorrow is thirty days from date, see?"

"All right," Lady Babe said quickly. "Then you know that that call means that the one who can exercise it—"

"Wait a minute. I ain't through. On the back of the green slip, it says 'Obermeter and Company hereby assign this option to Seymour Rance.' That means that it belong to Seymour Rance and, up till tomorrow, he can claim the thousand shares of that stock, at twenty-eight."

"You know what Gulf closed at today?"

"Huh?" The big man said stupidly. "Hey, lady—I don't know what all that means. I just was told and had to memorize it."

Lady Babe bit her lip. "Well, see if this gets through your thick head. That slip, along with twenty-eight thousand dollars, can be presented at a broker's office, and, by telling the broker to sell the stock and take up the option, it can be turned into just about seventy-five thousand dollars, at today's market prices. About fifty thousand profit, right now. Tomorrow, during the day, that profit can be doubled and tripled—depending on whether the stock continues to go up, which it's almost sure to do. Follow that?"

"Sure, lady, even my thick head can follow that. That's why I was sent for that green slip. On account," he explained elaborately, "we want all that cush you was talking about."

LADY BABE made a sound of exasperation. "All right. You think that slip is floating around loose. You think one of us have it. Well, you're wrong. You're absolutely wet. Get that."

"Am I? Well, I'll—"

"Get this. This is what I'm leading up to: That green slip is where nobody can get it. And you, blundering around looking for it, are going to pass up the biggest piece of money you ever saw. I know—we know—exactly what we have to do. You don't. I tell you, you don't. You can kill us all, and on my dying breath I swear that you—or your boss, whoever he is—has made a blunder and you'll never see a red cent. Now I'll make you a proposition. Join with us, and we'll all go in together. This I'll promise you—that you'll make more money even with all of us in it than you expected to split among you and your friend Pinkie and your boss. I guarantee it."

The big man's eyes were curious. "Lady, don't make no mistake. I ain't double-dossing my boss, see? But, apart from that, go on talkin'."

Lady Babe went on vehemently, rapidly: "Simmons lost all his money, excepting just enough to buy that option, understand? It was his last despairing gesture. He threw every cent on this million-to-one shot. He hadn't any hopes himself, really, of cashing in, but he piled everything on that one chance, because he was at the end of his rope."

"I already know that."

"Yes, you maniac, but what you don't know is that Simmons really made a good job of it. He not only had the option on a lot of stock at twenty-eight, but he left that option with his brokers, Obermeter and Company. He left it with them, with orders to pyramid on it, if the stock went up. And, when the stock went up, his orders were carried out. Today, at the current market, his account could be sold out for half a million, cold cash."

The big man's eyes were stunned. "Wait," he mumbled hoarsely. "Wait, say that again."

Lady Babe explained it with desperate patience.

"Simmons left the option to buy a thousand shares at twenty-eight, with Obermeter. He also told them that, if the stock went up to thirty-three—that's five points, understand? Five dollars each share. If it went up there, they were to call the stock in from the man who had sold the option, and pay twenty-eight for it. Then they had stock worth thirty-three dollars a share. In other words, there was five thousand dollars profit, right there.

"That is only the beginning of it. With that five thousand, they were to buy more stock in the open market. If that went up five points, then he would have more profit. You can see that, can't you?"

"God, yes."

"That process was repeated, every five points up. The brokers kept buying more and more stock. The stock, as soon as they bought it, jumped up more and more. In the last three days, that stock has run up from twenty-two to seventy-eight—and it'll go even higher tomorrow. Right now, there are thousands and thousands of shares—God knows exactly how much—lying in Simmons' account. On every share of it, he has a tremendous profit. But unless it's sold—unless somebody gives the broker orders to sell it, and collects the cash before the cops catch up with that account—nobody can get a cent of it."

THERE WAS a stunned silence. The full, incredible situation seemed to have finally been instilled in the big man's head. Sudden wonder, even admiration, came into his eyes. He turned to the wounded Lady Babe. "How—how did you get to know all this?"

"That doesn't matter. As it happens, young Simmons, last night, when the stock was up a good deal—enough so that he could sell out first thing this morning and be clear—came to my husband here and confessed. He confessed that he had embezzled the money, but also told him that he would put it back this morning. He told my husband the whole story. I saw the possibilities, and I went up to the boy's room. I thought I could—" She broke off and looked contemptuously at the flattened-out Mary Murdock. "It seems the poor sucker was going to marry this little mouse. He knew she had heard him say he was an embezzler, and he was feeling pretty good because she evidently still loved him, anyway. He wasn't going to tell her different, till he'd cleaned everything up. I worked on him, but he didn't even know I was doing it, damn his little soul! I couldn't get anywhere. He was nice and polite but he practically turned me out of his room."

"Wait a minute," the big man said. "What were you working on him for—if that green slip was in the brokerage office like you say, and not in his pants."

"My God, can't you understand it yet? That account in the brokerage office can't be touched by anybody but Seymour Rance or Rance's authorized agent. Do you know what that means?"

"Yeah."

"You don't. I'll tell you. Somewhere, there's a green shiny card, made out by Obermeter and Company. That card, plus a little simple forgery, entitles anybody who has it to walk into Obermeter and do what they please with that account—and no questions asked. Simmons doped out the system while he was embezzling. So that his name wouldn't appear on the books of the brokers. He pretended there was such a man as Rance, and that he, Simmons, was his agent. That's what we've got to get—that green card. That's what I was trying to get from Simmons. Once we had that, we could kill him and collect.

"When I couldn't get anywhere with him, I had to get out. I doped out a different approach and went back an hour later. He was gone. That was when you had him out killing him. Then, when he did come in, and I found him dead, I was looking for that card when you jumped me, and"—she glossed over hastily— "there was all that confusion about the wallet and the cops and everything.

"I tried working on the dick, Drago. I got away with the wallet but the card wasn't in it. We got hold of the dick again and he gave us the idea that little brown-eyes here had it. That's why we're here. Not so much because we believe what dicks tell us, but because she's the only one left that *can* have it."

The big man grinned. "No, lady. You forgot about us. We got that card!"

THERE WAS a stunned silence in the room. Drago, almost numb from the incredible, fantastic picture that had been unfolded, lay with his mouth open. McSpadden beside him, was almost crying. He whispered crazily: "You hear? World-Over won't lose a dime. The dough ain't lost. Imagine it coming through! God, if we'd only thought—

Only nobody'd ever think of an embezzler winning. Who ever heard—"

Drago's elbow dug into him. "You fool, that girl is in worse danger of her life now than ever. Get ready."

In the room, Lady Babe finally found her voice. "*You* have that card! Where did you get it?"

"Well, like you say, this fat boss of mine had it wrong."

Irrepressible, McSpadden gasped in Drago's ear: "Sport Ham—" and got Drago's frantic elbow in the ribs.

The big, black-thatched man continued on, in the room: "He knew that Simmons had this option, see—this green slip? He didn't know that he'd left it in the broker's office, like you say. He knew it was worth a pile and going to be worth more, but—well, anyhow, he wanted it. He got in touch with us and made up a proposition. We grabbed Simmons and took him where we could work on him. He wouldn't hardly say nothin' and all of sudden—bingo! He passed out on us. So we had to lug him back and dump him in his room. We had to iron out a cop that was in our way, doing it.

"We beat it back to our boss and showed him the green card, thinkin' he'd maybe said 'slip' when he meant 'card'. It wasn't what he wanted. We had to go back and try to find the slip. That's when we caught up with you, and we naturally thought it was in the wallet you chucked out the window.

"Then we got all tangled up, and only for seein' the little twist here up at a certain place in the Bronx which we was told to watch, we'd of lost out."

"You'd of lost out, anyway, if we hadn't seen her at a place we were watching in the Village," Lady Babe said. "Without us, you'd have been holding your hand on your neck."

"I guess that's right," the big thug conceded. "Well, what do we do now?"

There was a sudden silence again. Every eye in the room was turned on the brown-haired, pansy-eyed Mary Murdock.

"Well, I guess there's not much more use for angel-face there—now, that her man's dead," Lady Babe said. "I wonder what he saw in her, anyway?"

The big man asked, "You mean we better give—" and fell silent.

Then, so suddenly that Drago went drenched in cold sweat, the big thug's gun whipped over toward the girl.

Fire and flame vomited from Drago's hand.

The big man cried, "Ah-h-h!" and sagged, his gun falling, unfired from his hand. Drago leaped from the roof of the shed. Above him, McSpadden's gun exploded.

As in a red mist, Drago saw the girl, Mary Murdock, collapse, and, for one mad moment, he thought she had been shot. She fell to the floor.

The big thug recovered, dived for his fallen gun. Drago's pistol cracked twice, and the big man's legs folded up under him. He sprawled on his face.

Somewhere, the hotel owner, Ambers, found the urge to dive for the gun that Lady Babe had had shot from her hand. He was on his knees, snatching it up, when Drago nailed him through the shoulder. Lady Babe made one quick, cat-like snatch at the gun that had fallen from the big man's hand—and Drago's bullet hit the gun on the floor itself, sent it spinning away.

Then, suddenly, from four directions, rose the scream of police whistles. McSpadden's gun banged—again and again, furiously. At what, Drago did not understand. Then he saw the puffs of dust flying from the back of the big thug's coat. He roared, "Stop it, he's dead!"

He plunged in the open window. There was a scrambling and a crash behind him, as McSpadden fell off the roof of the shed. The police whistles were being augmented by sirens now, drawing closer.

DRAGO RAN for the girl, Mary Murdock—and his heart started beating again as she sat up from her faint. She clutched her head in her hands as she saw the dreadful carnage strewn about in the room.

Drago jerked her to her feet, put a gun in her hand, said rapidly: "Keep this on Lady Babe. Shoot if she moves. Go in the other room. Wait for the police. Craven is on his way—hear? Tell him you'll talk to him, *in my presence only* and stick to that. Say nothing. They can only take you to the Tombs—and I'll be there before you. Have you that clear?"

"Yes, yes. Where are you going?"

"To get the man behind all this—the boss."

He swung for the big thug, ran and dropped to one knee beside him, tugged him over on his stomach. He tried his inner coat and vest pockets. He found the green slip in his trouser hip. He jumped up, as McSpadden tried to crowd his ludicrous big bulk in through the window, his red face scarlet with excitement.

Drago jumped and straight-armed him. The big man went out backward with a yelp, crashed on the ground outside. Drago lit almost on top of him.

"Come on, you nit-wit. We've got to get out from under this police net. Craven will round up this garbage. We've got to get to the head rat."

"My gun," McSpadden wailed. "Hey, I've lost—"

Drago saw a glint on the ground, swooped and picked up the big man's revolver, sprinted for the stone wall. "Come on, I've got it."

The big man lumbered after him. They made a spot in the center of the rubble-filled field before the police net squeezed in on the house, screaming, wailing, men running.

Running cops passed right over the two detectives in the field. Drago husked, "Come on," and they were up and sprinting for the trees at the water's edge. As they ran, Drago said, "We'll have to steal a car. They'll have someone watching trains."

"Where—we—going—to—take him?" McSpadden panted. "I mean Sport—Hambly."

"I know where he is, but we'll have to make a quick stop at the hospital. I've got to see McTigue, for just a second."

CHAPTER THIRTEEN
THE BIG RAT

THEIR STOLEN car squealed into the curb in front of Mercy Hospital, just thirty-five minutes later. Drago sprang out, yelling, "Come on," at the breathless insurance detective. He pounded up the steps and into the antiseptic corridor, made his way on silent, swift feet, to McTigue's room, had to wait for the panting McSpadden, before he closed the door.

As McSpadden came in, Drago was saying into the phone: "Send me a couple detectives here—a prowl-car. Inspector McTigue's room. Have them wait outside the door."

He told McSpadden, as the big man closed the door, "This is the only place that's safe to phone from right now."

McTigue yelled, "Hey, what in God's name is this? My God, rushing into a man's room in the middle of—"

"The case is cracked," Drago said. "We've got a few minutes while we're waiting for those dicks. Here's the layout." He whipped quick, concise sentences at the red-faced, stunned old inspector.

At the end, McTigue gasped: "But—but this boss? Is it Sport Hambly? I warned you, remember, about him? By damn, that scaly fat crook."

Drago was suddenly dull-eyed. He stood with hands in gloved pockets, calm.

"Be yourself, Mac. I knew from the first that it had to be somebody who knew all the ins and outs of stock-trading. I knew there was some angle like that in it. You told me! Hell, it had to be not only a market expert, but someone who knew Simmons' moves intimately. The two thugs were obviously hired men. There had to be a heavy thinker behind them. Unfortunately, we may have some trouble in convicting the boss, because the only one of his hired men that could actually put a finger on him, was shot dead by stupid here."

"By me!" McSpadden wailed. "There were more of your bullets in him than mine."

"Well, it doesn't matter much. When we take this head man, I doubt very much if he'll live to see trial. After all, he's a cop-killer. But there was one thing just happened in that fight that was funny. Did you notice it, Chester Ford?"

McSpadden blinked. "Uh—no."

"There was a hired killer—a regular hood, undoubtedly with a record—stood there and turned down a chance to double-cross his boss. It would have meant a lot of money to him to do so. He actually stood there and warned them that he wouldn't cross his head man."

There was silence. McTigue said: "That sure is funny."

Drago stood up and put his hands in his pockets. "Not so funny. Not when you consider that the rat knew that his boss was standing just behind him—just outside that window, with a gun in his hand. *McSpadden—you filthy rat—did you think you could get away with it?*"

THE BIG man's pose of stupidity, dropped with the words. His hand flashed to his pocket and his gun gleamed steadily on Drago's heart. He was breathing hard. He said nothing for a second. "Stand back, Drago," he finally got out in a dry voice. "I'll give it to you if you try to stop me."

"I wouldn't doubt it. Four men are dead now—and you're guilty of them all, through your hired thugs. One of them, a poor little devil of a clerk that had a dream of wealth, and one—one, McSpadden—a cop. I wouldn't like to be in your shoes."

The fear that had been bottled in the big scarecrowish man came out now, in huge drops on his forehead. He gritted: "They'll never take me."

"You're wrong," Drago said. "I'm going to take you. I don't like to see what happens to cop-killers when they get them in the station house, McSpadden. But I want one crack—just one—at you, for myself. Then I'll never see you again. I'll never have to testify at your trial. In five minutes, you'll have seen the very last glimpse you'll ever catch of me. So good-by, rat."

McSpadden's mouth was shaking.

Drago took one step, slowly, unhurriedly, without taking his hands from his pockets. McTigue cried frantically: "Drago—look out."

"Back!" McSpadden's finger tightened on the trigger. Drago was six feet from him now. Drago took another step. McSpadden's teeth showed.

The gun clicked—empty.

Drago's left hand whipped out of his pocket and his brass knuckles drove into the murderer's face. Teeth crunched under the frightful impact. McSpadden's head was knocked almost backward from his shoulders. He slammed, turning to the ground and lay still.

Drago walked to the door. Three uniformed men were running up the hall when he opened the door. They piled in.

Drago indicated the unconscious man. "There's your cop-killer," he said. "The inspector will explain."

"Where are you going?" McTigue shouted.

"The Tombs," Drago said. "I have a date."

www.ingramcontent.com/pod-product-compliance
Lightning Source LLC
Chambersburg PA
CBHW051101030726
47504CB00006B/1734